"A taut mixture of action and suspense."
—Smexy Books Romance Reviews

Dying Wish

"A superb paranormal suspense."
—Genre Go Round Reviews

"Butcher's rise to the top of the paranormal and romantic suspense genres has been swift. . . . Her hallmark is consistent, superior storytelling that combines emotional punch with high-adrenaline danger—a recipe that can't miss!"
—*Romantic Times*

Living Nightmare

"There's only one way to describe this book to me: fabulous!"
—Night Owl Reviews

"[An] action-packed story of the brooding and angry warrior Madoc and his journey to the future. This series rocks!"
—Fresh Fiction

"Utilizing her ability to combine excellent characterization with riveting danger, rising star Butcher adds another fascinating tier to her expanding world. You are always guaranteed generous portions of pulse-pounding action and romance in a Butcher tale!"
—*Romantic Times*

"Ms. Butcher's written word began to grab hold of my imagination and lead me on a ride unlike anything I have read before."
—Coffee Time Romance & More

continued . . .

Running Scared

"What an entertaining and thrilling series! The characters are forever evolving, secrets are revealed, powers are found, new details come to life, and love is the cause of it all. I love it!"   —Fresh Fiction

"Superb storytelling. . . . I am amazed how Ms. Butcher's intricacies and subplots continue to expand the story without bogging down the overall plot."   —Romance Junkies

"This book jumps right in the fray and keeps you hooked till the end, and I was unable to put it down. Emotionally dark, this is a wonderful blending of paranormal romance and urban fantasy [with] many twists and turns."
—Smexy Books Romance Reviews

Finding the Lost

"Exerts much the same appeal as Christine Feehan's Carpathian series, what with tortured heroes, the necessity of finding love or facing a fate worse than death, hot lovemaking, and danger-filled adventure."   —Booklist

"A terrific grim thriller with the romantic subplot playing a strong supporting role. The cast is powerful, as the audience will feel every emotion that Andra feels, from fear for her sister to fear for her falling in love. Finding the Lost is a dark tale, as Shannon K. Butcher paints a forbidding, gloomy landscape in which an ancient war between humanity's guardians and their nasty adversaries heats up in Nebraska."   —Alternative Worlds

"A very entertaining read. . . . The ending was a great cliffhanger and I can't wait to read the next book in this series. . . . A fast-paced story with great action scenes and lots of hot romance."   —The Book Lush

"Butcher's paranormal reality is dark and gritty in this second Sentinel Wars installment. What makes this story so gripping is the seamlessly delivered hard-hitting action and wrenching emotions. Butcher is a major talent in the making."   —Romantic Times

Burning Alive

"A wonderful paranormal debut. . . . Shannon K. Butcher's talent shines."
—*New York Times* bestselling author Nalini Singh

"Starts off with nonstop action. Readers will race through the pages, only to reread the entire novel to capture every little detail . . . a promising start for a new voice in urban fantasy/paranormal romance. I look forward to the next installment." —A Romance Review (5 roses)

"This first book of the Sentinel Wars whets your appetite for the rest of the books in the series. Ms. Butcher is carving her way onto the bestseller lists with this phenomenal nonstop ride that will have you preordering the second book the minute you put this one down." —*Affaire de Coeur* (5 stars)

"Absorbing. . . . Butcher skillfully balances erotic, tender interactions with Helen's worries, and intriguing secondary characters further enhance the unusual premise. Fans of Butcher's romantic suspense novels will enjoy her turn toward the paranormal." —*Publishers Weekly*

"Ms. Butcher offers fresh and delightfully creative elements in this paranormal romance, keeping readers engaged as the story unfolds. *Burning Alive* is a well-crafted beginning to this exciting new series, and will have fans of the genre coming back for the next adventure in the Sentinel Wars." —Darque Reviews

"An exciting romantic urban fantasy. . . . Shannon K. Butcher adds her trademark suspense with plenty of tension and danger to the mix of a terrific paranormal thriller." —*Midwest Book Review*

"*Burning Alive* is Shannon K. Butcher's first foray into paranormal romance and what a doozy it is! Filled with sizzling love scenes, great storytelling, and action galore; fans of paranormal romance will rejoice to have Ms. Butcher finally join the genre!" —ParaNormal Romance

"A different twist on the paranormal genre. . . . Shannon K. Butcher has done a good job with *Burning Alive*, and I will definitely be reading the next in the series." —Fallen Angel Reviews

WILLING SACRIFICE

THE SENTINEL WARS

SHANNON K. BUTCHER

A SIGNET BOOK

SIGNET
Published by the Penguin Group
Penguin Group (USA) LLC, 375 Hudson Street,
New York, New York 10014

USA | Canada | UK | Ireland | Australia | New Zealand | India | South Africa | China
penguin.com
A Penguin Random House Company

First published by Signet, an imprint of New American Library,
a division of Penguin Group (USA) LLC

First Printing, March 2014

 REGISTERED TRADEMARK—MARCA REGISTRADA

ISBN 978-0-451-24111-5

Printed in the United States of America
10   9   8   7   6   5   4   3   2   1

For Terri L. Austin,
a fabulous writer and even better friend

Character List

Drake Asher: Theronai warrior, bonded to Helen Day

Briant Athar: Sanguinar

Connal Athar: Sanguinar

Logan Athar: Sanguinar, blood hunter, Hope Serrien's mate

Aurora: Athanasian servant

Cain Aylward: Theronai warrior, Sibyl's protector

Angus Brinn: Theronai warrior, bonded to Gilda

Gilda Brinn: the Gray Lady, Theronai, bonded to Angus

Maura Brinn: Theronai, Sibyl's twin sister

Sibyl Brinn: Theronai, Maura's twin sister

Canaranth: Synestryn, Zillah's second-in-command

Meghan Clark: blooded human

Helen Day: the Scarlet Lady, Theronai, bonded to Drake Asher

Eron: Athanasian prince

Neal Etan: Theronai warrior

Madoc Gage: Theronai warrior

John Hawthorne: blooded human

Mabel Hennesy: blooded human

Dakota Kacey: Theronai, bonded to Liam Lann

Lexi Johns: the Jade Lady, Theronai, bonded to Zach Talon

Nicholas Laith: Theronai warrior

Liam Lann: Theronai warrior, bonded to Dakota Kacey

Samuel Larsten: Theronai warrior

Thea Lewis: human woman living at Dabyr

Tynan Leygh: Sanguinar

Lucien: Athanasian prince

Andra Madison: the Sapphire Lady, Theronai, bonded to Paul Sloane

Nika Madison: Theronai, Andra's sister

Victoria (Tori) Madison: Theronai, sister to Andra and Nika

Torr Maston: Theronai warrior

Beth Mays: blooded human, Ella's sister

Ella Mays: blooded human, Beth's sister

Jake Morrow: human, member of the Defenders of Humanity

Blake Norman: human, Grace Norman's stepbrother

Grace Norman: blooded human, Gerai

Jackie Patton: Theronai, daughter of Lucien, bonded to Iain Terra

Andreas Phelan: Slayer, leader of the Slayers

Lyka Phelan: Slayer, Andreas's half sister

Joseph Rayd: Theronai warrior, leader of the Sentinels

Viviana Rowan: the Bronze Lady, Theronai, bonded to Neal Etan

Hope Serrien: Logan Athar's mate

Cole Shepherd: blooded human

Alexander Siah: Sanguinar

Paul Sloane: Theronai warrior, bonded to Andra Madison

Carmen Taite: blooded human, Gerai, cousin to Vance and Slade Taite

Slade Taite: blooded human, Gerai, cousin to Carmen, brother to Vance

Vance Taite: blooded human, Gerai, cousin to Carmen, brother to Slade

Zach Talon: Theronai warrior, bonded to Lexi Johns

Iain Terra: Theronai warrior, bonded to Jackie Patton

Morgan Valens: Theronai warrior

Zillah: Synestryn lord

Chapter 1

Torr Maston would rather have fought a hundred poisonous demons bare-handed than face the man lounging on his motel room bed.

Nicholas Laith pointed the remote at the crappy TV, not even glancing away from it as Torr stepped out of the cramped bathroom. If Nicholas had found him, then more of his brothers would be close behind. They'd all gang up on him, try to convince him that he should return home. And when that failed, words would turn to force.

Torr really didn't want to hurt any of his brothers.

"Nice shower?" asked Nicholas. His face was heavily scarred, the crisscrossing marks making it hard to read the man's expression.

"How did you get in?"

"Electronic key card lock. Easy to open."

Torr silently cursed Nicholas's techie skills as he forced his words out slow and even. "Why are you here?"

"You asked me to come."

"No, I didn't." Company was the last thing Torr wanted. Isolation was better. Easier.

"Not directly, maybe, but you definitely issued a challenge by disappearing like you did. You knew I'd have to come looking for you just to see if I could find you." A grin creased his scar lines. "Surprise. I win."

Torr instinctively moved toward his sword, only to find that it had been relocated. His sword belt was on the nightstand across the room rather than propped just outside the bathroom door, where he'd left it. "How'd you find me?"

The man who'd been his friend a lifetime ago—before Torr's world had been shattered—shrugged and switched to the next TV station. "You didn't make it easy. Ditched your cell phone. Ripped out the truck's tracking devices. Never used any plastic. You really shouldn't have challenged me like that if you didn't want me to come find you."

Torr's hand tightened into a fist on the damp terry cloth around his hips. "Do you think, maybe, that I disappeared because I *didn't* want you to find me?"

Nicholas shrugged again and paused for a commercial selling videos of drunken young women lifting their shirts for the camera. "Don't care what you want. It's time to come home."

"No."

"*No?* That's it? I track you down after you being AWOL for seven months, and you just refuse to come back? I found you fair and square. That means I win and you have to come home."

"Since you're apparently no good at taking the not-so-subtle hints I left behind that I want to be alone, I thought I should make it easy for you to understand. I don't know how to be any clearer than a single word with only two letters."

"You've pouted long enough. Time to move on. Get back to work."

"Pouting? You think that's what I've been doing?"

"I know you loved the woman, but she's gone now." Nicholas's voice dipped low, to that gray area between sympathy and pity.

A flash of rage ignited just beneath Torr's skin. One second he was standing several feet away from Nicholas. The next, he had his brother-in-arms pinned against the wall with a forearm digging into his throat.

The skin between the scars on Nicholas's face darkened from the lack of air, but the man didn't fight back. He just stared at Torr, his bright blue gaze calm. Accepting.

Torr wished Nicholas would fight back. Smashing heads would have gone a long way toward distracting him from his misery.

But Nicholas didn't fight. He didn't even blink. No way could Torr hit a man who wasn't fighting back.

With a feral growl, Torr shoved away from his brother and stalked across the room.

Nicholas rubbed at the bruise already forming on his neck. "I'll let Joseph know you're not fit for duty."

For some reason that pissed Torr off even more than if Nicholas had tried to drag him back. "I fight fine. I just need you all to leave me alone."

"So you can get yourself killed?" Nicholas shook his head and started texting. "I don't think so. You need to stay out of the field until your head's screwed on straight."

"I don't take orders from you."

"Are you still taking them from Joseph? Or have you stopped giving a shit about everything you used to hold dear?"

"I vowed to fight, to protect humans, to kill Synestryn. And that's what I've been doing. It's what I'll continue to do whether you, Joseph or anyone else likes it or not."

"Until one of the Synestryn brings you down. Which will be soon if your state of distraction is any clue."

"I'm not distracted."

"No? Then how did I find you? I've been on your trail for a couple of days now, keeping my distance. You never noticed me once."

"Maybe you're just that good."

He snorted. "Or maybe I'm not and you're in no condition to fight alone. I know losing Grace has upset you, but—"

"Upset me?" Torr stripped off the towel and started dressing so that he wouldn't attack his friend again. "I'm so far past upset I can't even find a word to fit where I am."

Nicholas's tone turned gentle. "You will get over her. You've been alive long enough to know it's true. It sucks, but it's true."

"I don't want to get over her. I want to be with her."

"It's not possible. Even if she survived, she's on another world."

"I know that," growled Torr as he fastened his jeans and belted his sword around his hips.

"You have to let her go."

"Don't tell me what I have to do. I know all the platitudes, all the hollow advice. Move on, stay strong, life goes on." He couldn't bring himself to look at his brother as he confessed, "I love her. She's still out there. She may even need me. And there's not a damn thing I can do to change any of that."

The metal disk attached to his back pressed against his spine as he bent over to lace up his boots.

Grace had put the disk on him—embedded it in his flesh in an effort to save his life and reverse his paralysis. The magical device had worked, leaving him whole and strong. His wounds, his pain, his weakness—they were all hers now, slowly killing her human body and stealing from him the fragile spirit it housed. He would have done anything to take back those wounds and spare her, but the device worked in only one direction.

She could heal him, but he couldn't do a thing to help her.

His sweet, selfless Grace had sacrificed herself for him, leaving him both grateful and furious.

"There are a lot of things we can't change," said Nicholas, his voice ringing with absolute certainty— the kind that comes only from hard lessons learned. "And we've all lost people we love."

"Knowing other people suffer doesn't make me suffer less. I just need to be alone. Why can't you get that?"

"Because it's likely to get you killed, and we need you too much to let it happen. You're one of the most deadly warriors we have."

"I used to be."

"You still are. I saw you fight last night. Whatever rust might have grown on you during your paralysis, you've knocked it all off. You fight like the warrior I remember. Maybe even deadlier."

"Then there's no problem. You can report back to Joseph that I'm fine. I'll come home when and if I'm ready."

"I said you were deadly. Not careful. You took too many risks. And you weren't watching your back."

"I'm not suicidal, if that's your worry. There's no way to know what might happen to Grace if I die wearing this disk. We're still connected, and as long as that's the case, I'll be careful."

"If you call that careful, then you're worse off than I thought."

"Calculated risks, Nicholas. I've been fighting for a lot longer than you have. I know what I'm doing."

"So do I, which is why you and I are going to be partners for a while."

"I don't want a partner."

"I think I already mentioned that I don't care what you want."

"Don't push me, Nicholas."

He smiled, making his scars pull tight. "You think I'm afraid of you?"

"I think you should be."

"Aww. You *do* care. How sweet. No wonder Grace was crushing on you."

"Stop talking about her."

"Nope. This is a deal-or-die kind of situation, and it's my job to make sure you deal."

"It's none of your business."

"Let's pretend it is, just for giggles."

"I'm serious, Nicholas."

"And that's part of your problem. You need to lighten up."

"The woman I love may be dying, and you want me to lighten up?"

"She might be dying. She might not be. But even if that freakishly powerful Brenya chick is able to heal her, she's still human. She's still going to die in the blink of an eye. That's a fact, and you have to find a way to move on. I figure now is as good a time as any— before we lose you, too."

"I don't know how you can be so casual, talking about her death like it's of no more importance than what you had for breakfast. I thought you were a better man than that."

"Just because I accept reality doesn't mean I don't care. I risk my life for humans every day. But they're different from us. We were never meant to be with them—not in the way you want to be with Grace. Letting her in was a mistake, and if you don't believe me, then all you have to do is look to that ache in your chest for proof that I'm right."

"So . . . what? I just stop caring?"

"No, you face reality. It doesn't matter if she lives or dies today. She's human. A few decades from now—a mere blink of time for a man like you—she will be gone. The leaves on your lifemark will have fallen. Your soul will die, and there's not a damn thing that either one of you can do to change that." Nicholas stepped closer, his voice dipping back to the land of pity. "She can't save you, Torr. She can't be what you need her to be for you to survive. All she can do is stand in the way of you finding the woman who *can* save your life and be your true partner. And if she really loves you—which her actions shout that she does—that's not the kind of life she'd want for you. If she were here, she'd tell you to move on, too."

"You can't be that cold."

"You can't be that blind."

"I don't care if she can't save my soul. I want to be with her anyway."

"Well, you can't. She's worlds away, and not even your determination is strong enough to activate a Sentinel Stone and open a doorway to her. The only way she's coming back is if Brenya allows it."

In that moment, Torr realized the truth. Nicholas was right. Brenya was in complete control. She was the one who would decide if Grace lived or died. She was the one who would decide whether to let Grace come home. Brenya was powerful in a way Torr could barely comprehend. She knew the score. She knew that the Sentinels—men like Torr and Nicholas—were losing the war against the Synestryn, and that if they lost, Brenya's home would be flooded by demonic beasts who fed on the blood and magic of her kind.

She wasn't going to let that happen, even if it meant keeping Grace out of his reach forever.

Brenya needed Torr to fight to defend her home world, and the way he would do that best was if he sought out a woman like him—a Theronai who was compatible with his power and could take her place at his side in battle.

That had been Brenya's endgame all along. He'd thought she offered to help Grace because he'd sworn to fight for Brenya in battle if she ever needed it. But he was already fighting for her. He'd been doing so for four centuries—since he'd been old enough to swing a blade. His vow to protect humans ensured that he also protected *her*.

The crescent-shaped mark she'd left on his shoulder—the one that allowed her to summon him at any time—

burned with betrayal. She'd tricked him. Offered him hope. Kept him fighting rather than wallowing in grief.

She'd told him that so long as the disk on his back stayed in place, Grace was alive. Now he questioned even that comfort. What if Brenya had lied just to get him to do what she wanted?

Nicholas let out a long, sad sigh. "You finally figured it out, didn't you?"

Torr nodded. "Brenya is devious. I bought her lie. For all I know, Grace is already dead." Even saying the words ripped something vital from his chest.

Not even the scars on Nicholas's face could hide his sympathetic frown. "Which is why you have to let go. Grace gave up her life so that you could have one. Don't belittle her gift by squandering it."

"I didn't ask for this. I didn't want Grace to sacrifice herself for me."

"But she did. Of her own free will. The only way to honor her memory is to make sure the life she gave you counts. You owe it to her to live as long as you can and find some way to be happy. Fulfill your purpose. Find your mate and kill as many fucking demons as possible."

"It's not enough," said Torr. "It will never be enough."

"Maybe. Maybe not. But it is your duty to try."

"You clearly already have opinions on where I should start, don't you?"

"I do. Rory and Cain located a system of caves down south in desperate need of a good cleaning. Thought you could join us."

Torr opened his mouth to respond, but before he could pull in a breath, the air around him shifted. The flickering fluorescent glow of his hotel room morphed into a brilliant, fiery swath of light. The drops of shower water drying on his bare back heated, adding to the thick humidity creeping across his skin. The floor beneath his boots disappeared, leaving him feeling weightless for a split second before he once again felt substantial.

A giant wave of dizziness slammed into him. High-pitched female screams of fear and the pounding of rushed footsteps echoed in his ears. The smell of dirt and smoke choked him.

Torr blinked to clear his swimming vision, but all he could see was color and light. Metallic blue streaked with brilliant orange.

His hand curled around the hilt of his sword, its cool, rigid contours a welcome familiarity. He didn't dare draw the blade for fear that some innocent might be close. Instead, he planted his feet and shut his eyes in an effort to locate the cries for help.

A warm hand settled on his shoulder. He tried to shrug it away and face the potential threat, but the grip was too tight.

"Settle, young Theronai," ordered a familiar feminine voice.

Instantly, the world stopped its whirl and he was once again able to focus.

The sky was orange. The trees were covered in shiny

bluish leaves that looked more like metal than plant matter. One sun burned high in the sky, and below it, smaller and more distant, a second one cast its light low over the ground.

Wherever Torr was, he wasn't in Kansas anymore.

Chapter 2

Torr spun to face the woman who'd touched him.

Brenya's long silver hair whipped around her shoulders as she grabbed his arm and started to run, forcing him to follow where she led. A layered mess of fur, coarse fabric and leather covered her body, frothing around her calves with each hurried step.

They ducked into a rough hut made from inky black sticks and thick, stiff grass the color of gunmetal.

"Where am I?" he asked.

"Temprocia, the world I now call home."

"Where's Grace?" demanded Torr.

"No time for that. We are under attack."

No way. Torr might get only one chance to find the woman he loved, and he was not going to waste it. "Your attack can wait. Where is Grace?"

Brenya pulled aside a leather hide covering a window and pointed across the clearing. Several huts dotted the area. One large fire burned in the center of the clearing, ringed by pink stones. Just on the other side of the fire crawled a reptilian animal twice Torr's size. It had six legs that sent it slinking across the ground like a centipede, but faster. Its long tail was forked, and each prong moved independently of the other. Both were thick and covered in bonelike spikes. Its elongated head was filled with rows of conical teeth meant for ripping apart meat and crushing bone.

"Your Grace is dead if you don't help. Now go forth and slay the beast before it reaches my baby girls."

A small child with white-blond hair raced toward a hut, but her chubby little legs weren't fast enough to carry her out of harm's way. The beast saw her and charged.

Torr drew his sword as he bolted out of the hut. A bellow burst from his lungs, drawing the creature's attention away from the child.

It hissed, tensed its body and a second later used that massive forked tail to fling itself toward him.

Torr leapt out of the way, rolling as he hit the ground. Rocks and sticks dug into his bare back, grinding the disk against his spine. The pain of it was a distant, inconsequential thing that he gave no attention to.

He came out of his roll, landing on his feet, his sword level and ready to swing.

The creature was only a few feet away. He could see now that it had massive eyes the color of swamp water. Its skin seemed to shift on its frame, creating a dizzying pattern of movement that drew his attention.

Nicholas was right. Torr was way too easily distracted.

From the corner of his eye he saw movement. A

woman sprinted across the ground to scoop up the little blond girl and carry her to safety. For a second, Torr thought he recognized the woman. She almost looked like Andra, but younger.

Tori? It was possible, but the woman he saw was too old to be the same one who'd left Dabyr with Grace only a few months ago.

Now wasn't the time to worry about who she was, not when the beast was preparing to charge.

Torr shifted to his left, using the fire to protect his back. There was no way to know if this creature was alone, and the last thing he needed was a nasty surprise.

Another hiss erupted from the reptile, and its tail curled up under it, preparing to launch it into the air again.

Torr held his ground. The thing charged through the air. He stepped cleanly out of the way, letting it jump headfirst into the roaring fire.

No! called Brenya, her voice a resounding boom inside his skull. *Not the fire!*

Torr had no idea what she meant until he saw that the creature wasn't screaming in pain. It wasn't even moving fast to escape the blaze. All it was doing was burning as it turned around for another attack.

That's when Torr realized what Brenya meant. Fire wasn't hurting the creature; it was simply giving it another advantage. Because now, he wasn't just fighting a giant flying lizard—he was fighting a giant *flaming* flying lizard.

And he wasn't fireproof.

The creature launched itself toward Torr again. He spun out of the way, but the beast came so close that it left a singed patch across his bare ribs.

Blade in hand, he turned to face it, angling away from the fire and the surrounding huts. The lizard followed him, one huge eye focused on him and the other moving, scanning for more danger. Or prey.

Torr growled and thrust his sword at the creature, making sure he was the most dangerous target around. The little blond girl was safely hidden inside one of the rough buildings, and Brenya had the good sense to stay out of sight. A couple of flimsy doors were cracked open enough for Torr to make out people watching. The woman who'd rescued the little girl was struggling against the hold of two other women, who barely managed to restrain her from combat. Her short sword gleamed under the orange sky, but she was unable to break free without using it on them—something she was apparently reluctant to do.

Good. The last thing he needed was another distraction, and an unknown partner in combat was definitely that. The odd patterns on the lizard's skin were more than enough to absorb his attention, especially now that they seemed to be moving faster under the flames coating its hide.

He kept backing up, drawing the beast away from the women.

The ground beneath his feet became softer. The humidity hugging his skin grew thicker. Shadows enveloped him, and heavy drops of warm water hit his bare shoulders.

He'd entered the edge of the surrounding forest. As thick as the trees were here, the lizard was going to slam its head into a trunk if it tried to come flying at him again.

The creature's skin hissed as water dripped onto it, but the flames remained steady. There was too much humidity here for the brush to ignite. At least Torr hoped that was the case.

A thick black tree trunk loomed on his left. A low branch ran nearly parallel to the ground, supporting a rustic swing made from rough rope and a warped plank of wood. The tree's metallic leaves reflected the firelight in a dazzling display of indigo and gold. If not for the hissing creature and its flaming skin and bone-shattering teeth, Torr would have found this place strangely beautiful.

He slowed to a stop, choosing a location just inside the tree line. The dense tree growth was going to impede his blade, but not nearly as much as it would the beast's flying trick.

Torr charged, keeping his sword angled to fit between the surrounding branches. He went airborne at the last moment, avoiding the lizard's open jaws as he leapt over its head. A razor-sharp tongue flicked out, slicing cleanly through the fabric of his jeans. He landed on the creature's back, ignoring the searing lick of flame singeing his skin. All he needed was one clean blow—one single jab into the lizard's brain and then he'd deal with his burns.

Staying atop its thrashing back, he gouged the tip of his sword right between the swamp water eyes. Rather than sinking cleanly through meat and bone, his blade merely skittered off the thing's tough scales with a shower of greenish sparks.

No way was he going to be able to bash through that hide without a sledgehammer. He needed a soft spot.

The searing heat drove him off the beast's back. He jumped up onto a low branch, out of the lizard's reach. The tree swayed with his weight, raining fat drops of water that had pooled on leaves above him.

He swiped the water from his eyes and watched for an opening below.

The lizard reared up on its forked tail, obviously preparing to launch itself into the tree after Torr. He stood still, flexing his fist around his sword in anticipation.

As soon as the beast became airborne, Torr spun himself around the trunk with one arm, putting the solid girth of the tree between him and the lizard.

It slammed into the wood with a hard *thunk*, followed by a screaming hiss of pain. By the time Torr eased himself to the ground, the lizard was on its back, thrashing in the matted, metallic leaf litter that covered the ground.

He didn't hesitate to take his shot, keeping out of range of that sharp tongue. He slammed the tip of his sword into the thing's chest, feeling his blade shift as it slid between two ribs. With a savage burst of strength, he changed the angle of the sword and shoved it deeper into the lizard's rib cage.

Thick orange blood poured from the wound. Its body convulsed, and the heavy forked tail hit Torr like a battering ram.

He flew through the woods a few feet before coming to a painful, abrupt stop against a tree trunk. His head rattled with shock so fresh that there was no pain yet. But it was coming. The wind was knocked from his body, and it was all he could do to still the panic of suffocation. Only the need to be sure the lizard was dead gave him the will to regain his feet.

The pain arrived like a speeding freight train— massive and completely unstoppable. A wave of dizziness caught him off guard. His eyes refused to focus enough for him to tell if the animal was moving or if it was just a trick of the eyes.

He stumbled forward, sword ready. His chest burned with the need for air. Pain radiated out from his spine and skull. His legs were strangely weak, reminding him of the time he'd been paralyzed and helpless.

Torr had promised himself he'd never be helpless again, yet here he was, falling to the ground, and there wasn't a thing he could do to stop it.

Chapter 3

Torr woke up inside a dimly lit hut with Brenya's face hovering only inches above his. Even this close he couldn't tell her age, but she looked older than when he'd last seen her, and more tired.

Movement within her eyes caught his attention, reminding him that this woman was neither Sentinel nor human. She was Athanasian—an ancient race of beings who'd birthed his kind as well as the Sanguinar and Slayers.

She didn't blink, and he swore her irises looked exactly like leaden waves kicked up by a storm.

Like all the Athanasians he'd met, there was an unearthly quality to her—a kind of power that radiated out of her that he could only imagine possessing.

The disorientation cleared, and the spinning in his head slowed until he remembered where he was. "Did I kill the lizard?"

"Yes. We will eat well tonight," she said, easing back out of his personal space. Bits of fur and feathers were laced through her long silver hair. It swept over his bare chest as she moved, and the branches of his lifemark—the image of a tree embedded in his skin—trembled in response to her power.

Torr's stomach heaved, and he wasn't sure if it was the thought of eating the giant lizard, the concussion or Brenya's nearness that caused it. He swallowed down his nausea. "Is everyone okay?"

"Yes."

"Even Grace? Is she alive?"

Brenya paused, frowning as if searching for the right words. "Parts of her are."

He was stunned silent for a moment, trying to figure out if he was hearing her correctly or if his concussion was playing tricks on him. "Parts?"

"It is too complicated for someone of your limited abilities to understand."

His mind went to a dark place where Grace's body had been ripped apart, the pieces harvested for organs. While he knew that someone as selfless as Grace would have wanted no less than to save others in her death, the idea infuriated him.

His voice came out cold and edged with steel. "Then use small words."

The older woman pressed her lips together in irritation, as if dealing with a whiny child. "I tried to restore her. Make her whole. But she had given too much of herself to heal you, and there was nothing more I could do."

Nothing more . . . The words were a bleak echo in his head.

"Is she . . . dead?"

"In part."

This was not the time to be fucking with him. Frustration, grief and fear prowled under his skin, too close to the surface to hide. His voice was a cold whip that lashed out at her. "You'd better start making sense. Fast."

Irritation tightened Brenya's mouth until tiny lines formed. She was silent just long enough to remind Torr that he held no control here.

"Some of the woman you knew lives on. Some of her did not survive my efforts to heal her and are lost forever. And some of her lingers between life and death, struggling for survival even now."

What the fuck did that mean? "I want to see her." Maybe if he did, he could make sense of what Brenya was telling him.

"No."

He tried to sit up, but the spinning in his head had him thinking twice about the move. The last thing he needed was to show weakness and convince Brenya that he couldn't handle the truth of what had happened to his Grace.

Brenya pushed him back down, and the instant she touched his skin, the crescent-shaped mark she'd left on him a few months ago burned.

"Why the hell not?" he demanded.

"You will want to be her heart, but the parts of her that loved you are gone from her. She will not know you."

"Not know me? Of course she'll know me. She nearly died to save me."

"Memories of you are one of the many things lost to her."

"You don't know that. Not for sure. She hasn't even seen me yet."

"I do know. The healing I did bound us inextricably. I'm part of her now, as she is of me. I know her mind. And you, young warrior, are no one to her now."

Those words, delivered without warmth or pity, hit him harder than any wound he'd ever suffered. His voice cracked with pain. "You're wrong. Let me see her and I'll show you how wrong you are."

"What will you do if you see her? Confess your love? Demand that she remember a man who is no longer a part of her mind? Grace is still weak. All your words can do now is damage her more."

"I'd die before I'd hurt her."

"Then give me your words. Pretend you do not know her. Speak nothing of her past. Stay silent until you see that what I say is true."

"Whatever you want. Just let me see her." He had to see her with his own eyes, to know she was safe. And no matter what Brenya thought, the bond that he and Grace had went deep. She'd been willing to die for him. She nearly had. No matter how much she'd changed, she couldn't have forgotten him.

"Vow it," demanded Brenya, the stormy waves in her eyes rising.

"I swear. I won't say a word to her until you allow it."

As soon as the words left his mouth, the weight of the vow he'd given bore down on him, making it hard to pull in his next breath. Even if he wanted to speak to Grace, the magic binding him to his word would make it impossible.

"Lie still," ordered Brenya. "I will bring Grace to tend your wounds so she will not question why she is here. If you do anything to upset her, I will fling you back to your world and never call on you again. Grace will live out the rest of her years here, never to see you again. Do you understand?"

"I do. I promise I'll be good."

Sadness made Brenya's strange eyes tilt downward. "I wish that goodness could be repaid by something other than disappointment."

"Grace has never once let me down. She'll remember me."

"That Grace—the one you think you know—is gone. The sooner you accept that, the less pain you will suffer."

He didn't care how much pain he had to endure. Grace was worth whatever price he had to pay to have her back again. And this time he wouldn't squander the gift she was. Nicholas was right that her human life would be only a brief moment of time to Torr, but he would relish every second and spend what time there was making her the happiest human who'd ever drawn breath.

Brenya let out a long, sad sigh. "I had hoped you would have chosen the easier path. I see the folly in that now." She stepped across the room and sat on a stone stool. "Brace yourself, young warrior."

Anxiety and excitement buzzed along Torr's veins. The pain of his wounds was still there, but none of that mattered. Grace was alive. Nothing could diminish the relief that gave him. Even if she was weak from risking her life for his, even if she was no longer quite herself, he didn't care. She was still his Grace, and the side effects of her sacrifice for him could not possibly make him love her less.

Torr found the strength to push himself upright just as the door opened, letting in dusty shafts of sunlight. He refused to squint at the sudden brightness. He didn't want to wait even one more second to see her again.

"You summoned me, Brenya?" Grace asked in a quiet, sweet voice he would have recognized anywhere.

He still couldn't see her from this angle. She was standing outside of the doorway, blocked from view. Still, his entire body became alert, every cell standing at attention in response to her nearness.

The need to see her—to see proof with his own eyes that she was alive—nearly drove him to his feet. Only his worry that he might topple over and embarrass himself kept him pinned in place.

Brenya waved toward him. "This man was injured slaying the beast. Tend him."

"Yes, of course."

Grace stepped into the hut. The door shut. His eyes adjusted to the dimness almost immediately, revealing a slight glimpse of the side of her face.

Her hair was longer now. Much, much longer. Soft black curls fell nearly to her waist.

There hadn't been time for her hair to grow that long, had there? She'd only been gone for seven months.

Some bit of stored knowledge tickled the back of his mind, but his head was throbbing too much for him to grasp the thought.

Her arms and legs were bare beneath a short leather tunic, showing off muscles he was certain hadn't been there before. His Grace had always been softly rounded, with curves that made him pant with need. The leaner, harder body he saw now was proof that she *had* changed.

Maybe food was scarce here. Maybe that was why Brenya had seemed so pleased about a giant pile of lizard meat.

Just the thought of Grace going without the basic necessities was enough to make a sudden wave of anger swell in his gut.

Never again. So long as he lived, Grace would never go hungry again. And even though his vow was silent, its weight was as solid and real as if he'd spoken the words aloud.

She turned to face him then, and he was struck breathless. Her beauty was so brilliant and glowing it made him feel the need to shield his eyes. Those sweet brown eyes of hers, always so filled with sincere concern, were just as he remembered. Her skin was a bit darker from sun exposure, but still as flawless and smooth as in his dreams. Her hands were adorned with intricately knotted fiber rings and bracelets, but her slender, gentle fingers had touched him too many times for him not to know them instantly.

Had he not given Brenya his vow of silence, he would have still been struck speechless. Endless days of wondering if she was safe—if she was in pain—were finally at an end.

His Grace was alive, and everything inside of him wanted to rejoice.

He gripped the side of the cot he sat on, hoping to prevent himself from sweeping her up in his arms. He'd told Brenya that he would never do anything to hurt Grace, and he meant every word. No matter how hard it was for him to restrain himself, he would find the strength to pretend he didn't know her.

She offered him a tentative smile that showed no hint of recognition. "The village hero. I'll have you patched up in no time. Where do you hurt?"

Torr remained silent and glanced at Brenya.

"He can't speak, child. His throat was injured. I'll see to that later. You tend the wounds you can see."

Grace's gaze swept over him, taking in his cuts, burns and bruises. Her visual journey slowed as she saw his lifemark, then again as she noticed the crescent-shaped mark Brenya had burned into his skin. She studied his face, brushing his hair away from a shallow wound across his forehead.

Sympathy warmed her brown eyes, and her touch was so gentle it nearly brought tears to his eyes.

He hadn't been able to feel all those times she'd

touched him before, seeing to his care as he lay trapped inside his paralysis. He'd lived for the times she'd shaved his face or trimmed his hair, reveling in even the slightest contact he could actually feel.

Now he was whole, feeling everything, because she had saved him. Surely that had left some kind of mark on her—some connection that even Brenya couldn't predict.

Torr kept waiting for her to show some sign that she knew who he was—some tiny spark to light her eyes the way it used to whenever she'd come into his suite back at Dabyr—but that sign never came.

Brenya was right. Grace didn't know him anymore. She'd sacrificed herself to save him, and yet he was no more to her now than a stranger.

She crossed to the far side of the hut and began opening wooden boxes, taking out strips of cloth and other supplies.

Something hot and vital shriveled in Torr's chest. He tried to fight back the swell of grief and rage that rose up within him, but it was a lost cause.

He'd gone through every scenario he could conceive, imagining her whole and healthy, running into his arms, unconscious as he'd last seen her, paralyzed as he'd been. He'd even pictured her dead when he could no longer control himself enough to keep that image away. He'd suffered through countless strings of chaotic emotions that each daydream and nightmare had caused. But never once had he thought that she wouldn't know him, that he would mean nothing to the woman he loved.

A low, animalistic moan of pain escaped before he could stop it.

Grace dropped what she was doing and rushed to his side. Her warm fingers settled on his bare shoulder, and every fiber of his being rose up in welcome.

He would have known her anywhere. By her touch, by her scent, by the sound of her voice and even by the taste of her lips. She was a part of him that went deeper than anyone else he'd ever known, which made her stranger's gaze feel like a betrayal.

Torr covered her hand, pinning it in place so she couldn't move away. He stared into her eyes, silently willing her to see his soul. To see his love for her.

All he got in return was more of her tender concern—the kind she would have given to anyone she met. "You're in pain, aren't you?" she asked. "Let me go and I'll get you something that will help."

Nothing could help him now. The Grace who'd loved him was gone, just as Brenya had said, and no painkillers were ever going to make that okay.

Chapter 4

Grace had to work hard to keep from staring at the stranger. He was beautifully built, completely intriguing and equally unsettling.

Brenya was hiding something about this man. Grace was used to the older woman's cryptic ways, but there was something more to it this time. Something important. Something she felt like she should know.

Not only was this the first man Brenya had ever allowed in their little village—which was enough to make Grace suspicious—but he kept looking at her expectantly, like he thought she'd say something important.

She was only four years old, thanks to years of lost memories. What could she possibly have to say?

"His name is Torr," said Brenya, speaking for the man who couldn't.

Grace lifted her gaze to greet him properly and was struck mute by his bright, amber-colored eyes. She'd seen that exact shade somewhere before, but like most of her memories, it slipped away before she could grab hold. But this time a small, fleeting remnant of emotion lingered behind.

His eyes made her sad and joyful all at the same time, and she had no clue why.

She had to clear her throat before she could speak past the rush of emotion. "My name is Grace."

He nodded once. A muscle along his jaw clenched with frustration.

Instincts made Grace take a long step back, out of striking range. She didn't know why certain things set her off, making her insides light up with fear, but it wasn't the first time it had happened. Sometimes she just freaked out for no good reason, and there was no predicting what would cause it. A look someone gave her, a loud noise, a sharp smell—they all had the power to terrify her.

Brenya knew why, but she refused to tell. She said that some things were best left forgotten.

Grace forced herself to move close to Torr again— close enough to feel the heat his body was giving off. Dirt and dried blood marred his skin but did nothing to take away from his animalistic beauty. Like a sleek predator's body, his was made up of muscular contours meant for speed and power. Every breath lifted his chest, creating the illusion that the tree image on his skin was swaying.

The green leaves were strange, but somehow oddly familiar.

A flicker of an image formed in her mind. A bright

golden light shone down on her, shielded by a canopy of green leaves. She could feel cool grass tickling the backs of her bare knees, hot tears sliding over her temples and a deep, throbbing ache pounding in her cheekbone. Sadness and shame filled her soul, along with a burning need for escape—escape that she knew would never come.

Torr's hot hand settled on her bare arm, making her flinch and step back out of his reach.

"Settle, child," came Brenya's calm voice from the corner of the room. "All is well here and now. You are safe."

His palm was still outstretched. A look of concern drew his dark eyebrows together, but she saw beyond that to the hurt that her insult had caused him. He looked . . . betrayed.

"I'm sorry," she said, unable to look at him. There was too much shame riding her, reminding her of just how weak she was. "I'm a little jumpy sometimes. Just ignore me."

But he didn't ignore her. Instead, he stood up from the bed and took both her hands in his.

His touch was gentle, but there was no mistaking his strength. His fingers surrounded hers, both rough and supple. Restraint vibrated through his touch, and it took everything she had not to jerk away. His thumb glided over the back of her hand, sending a familiar shiver racing along her arm.

Shock made her look up at him. Way up.

A little spurt of dizziness hit her, and even that felt

familiar. There was something about this man that un-settled her and left her reeling.

She started to pull away, but his grip tightened just enough to tell her wordlessly that he wasn't ready to let her go.

He cradled her hands against his chest and stared into her eyes. His heart picked up speed, pounding hard and steady against her palms. Vital heat poured into her, forcing her to stifle another shiver. As close as he was, she could smell his skin—a rich mingling of scents she couldn't name but knew as well as the feel of her own skin.

His scent made a blizzard of feelings erupt in her brain, so thick she couldn't possibly tell one from another. Pain, sorrow, joy, love, hope—too many emotions for her to do more than groan against the weight of them all.

She swayed on her feet. Torr grabbed her bare shoulders to hold her steady, and the strength of his grip was strangely comforting.

She didn't like anyone touching her, and yet for some reason this man's firm grasp didn't terrify her.

Grace stared up at him, trying to figure out what it was about him that left her so unsettled. She stepped away, rubbing the skin where his fingers had just been. "Do I know you?"

Brenya spoke before he could shake or nod his head. "Torr has never been to Temprocia before."

She'd saved Grace's life. She'd nursed her back from the brink of death at great personal cost to herself. Never once had the older woman lied to her. She'd kept

plenty of secrets, but had never lied. At least not that
Grace knew.

Still, something was going on here—something strange.

"Is that true?" she asked Torr.

He gave Brenya a long, cold stare before finally nodding.

Brenya pushed to her feet, her movements slower
than usual. "I must go now. You will be safe with this
man. He will not hurt you."

Grace wasn't so sure, but she wasn't about to stop
Brenya from getting the rest she needed. Come nightfall, the whole village relied on her to be strong so her
magic could keep the Hunters at bay. "I'm fine, Brenya.
Go rest. I'll come check on you when I'm done here."

As she passed, she spread her fingers at the base of
Torr's thick throat. It looked more like a threat to stran-
gle him than an effort to heal, but Brenya's ways were
often as odd as they were effective.

Her tone was a cold, hard warning. "Injure her in
any way—*any* way—and I will end your world. Do
you understand completely?"

Torr nodded again, the simple motion somehow
laced with cold fury.

"Good. Then speak again, and choose your words
carefully, as if each one were a poisoned blade aimed at
your heart."

"I gave you my word," he said.

Brenya nodded, as if that was all she needed to hear.
Then she shuffled out of the hut, her steps slower than
they'd been this morning.

"She's weak," said Torr, his deep voice an alien sound to Grace.

There were no men here, and she literally could not remember the last time she'd heard a man speak. She knew she had, just as she knew she'd eaten strange foods that she couldn't name and had seen objects that didn't exist here in her new life.

"She nearly killed herself bringing me back from the dead," said Grace. "She's been weak ever since."

Torr stilled to the point that she couldn't even see his chest move with his breath. His voice was quiet, as if he didn't want to say the words aloud. "You were dead?"

"I must have been. It's the only thing that explains why so many of my memories are gone."

"Is that what Brenya said? That she brought you back from the dead?"

"No, she said she *remade* me, but I think that's just her way of saying the same thing. She talks funny sometimes. Not that it really matters exactly what she did to me. I'm alive, and it nearly killed her getting or keeping me that way. I've been here four years and she still suffers from what she did for me."

"Four years? How is that possible?"

"One day after another. Isn't that the way it works where you're from?" she asked, teasing in an effort to lighten his mood.

"Of course. That's it," he said, as if figuring out a great mystery. "Time moves slower where I'm from. What seems like months to me is years to you."

"You're from Athanasia, too?"

He blinked as if surprised that she knew about the other worlds connected to this place. "No. I'm from Earth."

"That's where Tori is from."

Instant recognition lit his face. "Is Tori okay?"

Grace nodded. "She keeps to herself. Hunts a lot. But she seems healthy, if that's what you mean."

"Has she hurt anyone?"

Loyalty forced Grace to evade his question. The people Tori had injured had forgiven her, so it was Grace's job to do the same. Besides, Tori hadn't willfully injured anyone in a long time, even though it was obvious from the look in her eyes that she'd wanted to.

"Do you know her?"

"A little. Enough to know she's dangerous."

"She's the best hunter we have—brings in more food than all the other women combined. I'd never want to be the one to make her mad, but she protects us. On the way here, I heard the women talking about how she saved one of our children from the creature you killed."

"The little blond girl," he said, as if answering his own question. "Maybe you can take me to see Tori. I'd like to say hello."

"Maybe. Like I said, she's out hunting a lot. She may not still be around. How long will you be here?"

"A while, I hope. I'd like to spend time with some people here." There was an odd quality to his voice, like he was somehow aiming that remark at her.

"Can you open portals like Brenya?"

"No. She was the one who brought me here."

"Then I guess it's up to her how long you stay. But if you ever want to go home, I suggest you be nice to her."

"That was my plan, but for the sake of curiosity, what makes you say that?"

"I don't remember much about my life before, but I'm certain I've never seen anyone who can do the things she does. She knows everything I do, everything I say. I swear, sometimes it feels like she's inside my head." Grace sprinkled some powder into a bowl. "Have you ever heard of anything like that before?"

"I know a few people who are connected like that— powerful couples who are united in a way I can only dream about. They're the lucky ones."

She waved him back to the bed, urging him to sit. "Then I guess it's not as strange as I thought. I haven't exactly been allowed to get out and see much of the world."

"Grace, are you a prisoner here?"

She poured clean water over the powder and set the bowl of disinfectant next to the bed. "No more than anyone else. We don't roam far except to collect what we need. It's too dangerous."

"Because of creatures like the one I killed?"

"They're dangerous, yes, but not nearly as scary as the new things that have started lurking around at night."

"What kind of things?"

She used a cloth to clean blood and dirt from the wound on his head. His skin had already healed shut, leaving behind more mess than damage. She tried not to get distracted by his vivid eyes and the way they never left her, but that was easier said than done.

His whole body was a distraction, from the beautiful curve of muscle and bone to the intriguing images he wore. She'd seen the crescent shape on his arm before on others, but that tree spanning his chest was new and yet somehow familiar. All she wanted to do was stroke her hands over him until the mystery he presented was solved.

The same was true with the iridescent band that hugged his throat. It was supple enough to cling to the contours of thick muscle and tendon, yet it looked delicate, almost feminine. A mass of color swirled lazily along the silvery surface, drawing her stare.

"Grace?" he said, pulling her attention back to his question, "what kind of things do you see at night?"

She blinked a couple of times to refocus her attention. "I don't know. I've never actually seen all of them, just these strange ridges along their backs. One of the Athanasian women from the village to the south was killed a few days ago. Brenya seems to think it was these creatures who killed her."

"What makes you say that?"

"Brenya says they were sent to find her but couldn't see her in the daylight."

Torr shot up from the bed, easing her away from him so he wouldn't plow into her. "When does the sun go down?"

"Which sun?"

He stared for a second, then nodded, as if making a mental adjustment. "When is it dark?"

"Soon. Why?"

"I need to speak to Brenya."

Grace stepped around him and placed herself in front of the door. His big body towered over her, but she held her ground. Brenya needed to rest, not answer the questions of a stranger. No matter how much Grace wanted to cower or flee, she wasn't budging until he understood that. "She's too tired for visitors, especially ones who look as furious as you do. Besides, I'm not done cleaning your wounds."

"My wounds aren't important. Your safety is."

"Our safety depends on me following orders, and I was told to tend to your wounds. You can't ask me to defy Brenya, not after what she's done for me. Please. Sit back down."

He let out a long breath of frustration but eased back on his heels. He didn't sit down, but at least she wasn't going to need to grab him to keep him here. Though she had to admit that putting her hands on him held massive appeal.

"If you won't let me talk to her, then you tell me," he said. "How do you defend yourselves?"

"Brenya has put up barriers that keep the creatures out at night. So long as we stay inside the village, we're safe."

"The demons can't get in?"

"Demons? Is that what they are?"

"It's likely. Can they get in?"

"No." At least they hadn't yet. Grace still wondered how long Brenya's magic would hold if she became any weaker.

"Then how did that woman get killed?"

"She disobeyed orders and went outside the perimeter after dark. Everyone knows that's against the rules." Speaking of orders, Grace still had hers. Torr wasn't going back to the cot on his own, so it was up to her to get him there.

She gathered her nerve and pressed one hand against his abdomen in a silent order for him to back up. Beneath her fingers, his muscles clenched. His amber eyes darkened, and the strangest look covered his face—something between hunger and need, something she'd never seen before. At least not that she could remember.

Torr backed up until his legs hit the cot. With her hands splayed over his broad, smooth shoulders, she pushed down. He gave in and sat, but grabbed her wrists before she could back away.

His hold was careful but absolute, shackling her wrists in his long fingers. "You need to let me talk to Brenya. A perimeter won't hold them forever."

Delicious heat glided up her arms. She had to try twice to find enough air to speak. "How do you know?"

"Experience. Someone has to go out and kill them."

He meant himself. Grace could see it in the way his eyes narrowed, as if he were already planning an attack.

She didn't want him to risk himself. Of course, she

never wanted any of the women to take risks either, but it was different this time—personal in a way she couldn't explain, even to herself. "You're still injured. If you want to fight the Hunters, you can talk to Brenya about it tomorrow when she's rested. Until then you need to let me do my job."

His jaw was set with determination, and she knew that if she didn't do something soon, he was going to push past her and do whatever he wanted.

"Please," she said, not even caring if she sounded like she was begging. "If you let me finish my job, then when you're feeling better, I'll take you out to find the Hunters. I'll show you the trail I saw and where I think they might be coming from."

He shot to his feet again, a look of fury tightening his mouth. She expected him to yell at her, but his voice was calm enough to chill her bones. "You got close enough to see a trail?"

The urge to turn and flee pounded through her, but she breathed through it, trusting that Brenya would never have left her alone with someone who would hurt her.

"I'm not sure, but I think so. All the leaves and branches were sliced clean, as if something had cut right through them. A Hunter is the only thing I know of that could do that." When she spoke, her voice shook a little. Not that it would have helped if she'd sounded rock steady. She was sure he could feel her frantic pulse pounding where he gripped her wrists.

"Does Brenya know what you saw?"

"Not yet. I just found the trail today and was on my way back when I heard the screams."

"When the lizard attacked," he guessed.

She nodded. "It's too close to dark to go out today, and I won't let Brenya down. You need to stay and let me do my job."

He stared into her eyes for a long minute before he spoke. The whole time his thumbs kept stroking the skin of her inner wrists. "If it were anyone but you I'd already be out that door."

She didn't know what he meant by that, but she wasn't about to question his change of heart.

He let go of her and turned. Right in the center of his bare back was a flat metallic disk just like the one embedded in her skin. In the very same spot.

Surprise and curiosity flooded her, knocking all good sense out of her head. She rushed forward and grabbed his shoulders to hold him still while she studied it.

Intricate markings covered the surface. She wasn't sure if they were merely decorative or if the symbols meant something. As her finger glided over the warm metal, she felt a tingling sensation flicker across her spine. It was gone so fast she questioned if it had ever happened.

"Where did you get this?" she asked.

He was silent for so long she wasn't sure he was going to answer. Then, in a low voice filled with sadness, he said, "It was a gift from a woman I loved."

A tiny spurt of jealousy flashed through her, leaving

behind a greasy film of shame. She had no business feeling envy over women Torr had known. Not only that, but it was clear from his tone that the woman had caused him some kind of pain. Maybe she'd betrayed him, maybe she'd left him. Whatever the case, she'd hurt him, and here Grace was thinking only of herself.

"I have one just like it," she said. "But I've never seen it up close before. It really is pretty."

"Where did you get yours?" he asked. There was something strange about his inflection, but she couldn't figure out what.

"I don't know."

"Really? Seems like the kind of thing you'd remember."

"I don't really remember much of anything before Brenya brought me back to life."

"Have you tried?"

"Of course. I spent months working to regain my memory, but whatever bits are left, they're more like echoes."

"What do you mean?"

"It's hard to explain. It's almost like all those things were scooped out of me and all that's left is a kind of emotional residue that couldn't be completely removed. Sometimes I see tiny glimpses, but there's no context. I feel things, but have no idea why."

"Do you remember any people?"

"No, but I remember loving them, laughing with them." *Hiding from them, cowering in fear.*

She didn't want to think about that, so she turned

her attention from the disk to the surrounding male flesh. Slight bruises lingered along his back, maybe where he'd fallen or been hit. Trails of dried blood and caked dirt led from the lower edge of the disk toward his singed blue pants.

She picked up the cloth and wiped away the mess, revealing puckered scars where the prongs of the disk entered his skin. She traced the marks with her fingertip, and his whole body clenched.

She gave a sympathetic wince. "Sorry. Does it hurt a lot?"

"No. Does yours?"

"Not exactly."

He turned, putting his chest at a level with her gaze. That magnificent tree clung to his skin, tempting her to spread her fingers over the branches.

"What do you mean by that?" he asked.

There was a smudge of dirt along his ribs, and she used the excuse to touch him and wipe it away. He truly was a beautiful creature, and even though the damp cloth muted the feeling of his skin, she could still sense the firm resilience of the flesh below.

His scent surrounded her, and that nagging feeling of familiarity called to her again. She was certain she would have remembered a man like him. Even if she hadn't, surely he would have told her if he'd known her. Still, there was something about him that tugged at her senses.

Then again, she'd heard some of the visitors talk about the men they'd met, how handsome or charming

they were. How they'd been chosen as mates for their
strength or intelligence. Maybe all men had this kind of
effect on women, and she was just experiencing it first-
hand.

"I feel things sometimes," she admitted. "I'm sure
they're coming from the disk."

"What kind of things?"

"It's personal." Sometimes, when she was lonely,
she imagined those feelings coming from a friend—
someone like her, not like everyone else here. She
wasn't beautiful like the Athanasian women and their
children. She didn't have magical powers. She was
physically weak. She wasn't even in training the way
the little girls were. She wasn't strong enough to survive their fierce mock battles.

She was different from everyone here, and while
they all treated her well, she knew she wasn't one of
them. There were no talks of her going on an exciting
trip to fulfill her destiny. As far as she could tell, no one
here even thought she had one.

Maybe that was for the best, because the idea of
walking away from the only world she knew was terrifying. But some days the loneliness was hard to bear,
and the feelings coming from the disk helped remind
her that she wasn't ever really alone.

Torr's voice dipped down until it was a low, quiet
temptation. "Tell me, Grace. I want to know."

"It doesn't matter. I'm sure you have the same feelings, too. Unless I'm imagining the whole thing."
Which she hoped wasn't true.

"Do you feel angry? Sad?" he asked.

He felt the same thing? Relief washed over her, and until this moment, she hadn't realized just how much she worried that she was making it all up. "So I'm not imagining it."

"I'm so sorry," he said, his voice thick with regret. "If I'd known . . ."

"Known what?"

He paused for too long. "If I'd known how much talking about this would upset you, I never would have brought it up. I'll just sit here and be quiet so you can do what Brenya asked."

Thank goodness. The sooner she was done with Torr, the sooner she could find a quiet place and try to figure out what it was about this man that sent her emotions rioting.

Grace pulled in a long breath, forced herself to put on a smile and went to work.

Chapter 5

Torr had been hurting Grace for years.

That was the thought that kept scrolling through his mind, over and over.

That anger and sadness she was feeling? That was all his. The disks they wore connected them. They allowed her to heal his paralysis by taking it upon herself. But her human body had been too weak to fight off the magical poison the demon had used on him. Only Brenya's magic had saved Grace from the fate that had awaited Torr. And now the magic that bound them together—the connection the disks formed—was feeding her all the pain and fury he'd felt since she'd nearly died to save him. Four years ago.

He had to find a way to make it stop.

By the time Grace finished cleaning him up and left, dusk had fallen over the area. He slipped out of the hut while she went to get food for him.

Sneaky, perhaps, but necessary.

He asked a little girl where he could find Brenya.

Her bright eyes were wide with curiosity as she pointed to a larger hut on the far side of the clearing, just past a giant Sentinel Stone. There were fewer runes on it than on the ones he was used to seeing, but the carvings were just as intricate. Like all Sentinel Stones, this one radiated power. As he neared it, he began to recognize that power as the same he felt humming through Brenya.

Torr slipped through the trees, keeping out of sight as he approached the hut from behind. When the coast was clear, he pushed through the rickety door, not giving a shit that he was uninvited.

Brenya sat in a sturdy chair made from smooth black twigs and branches. Her eyes were closed, and she looked older than he'd ever seen her look before. Skin that had been smooth only a little while ago was now drooping and lined with age. Her shoulders were bowed inward, and her whole body rocked like a metronome.

"You should not have come unannounced," she said.

As he watched, her wrinkles smoothed and her body straightened. Whatever magic she used to appear younger drained her visibly, blanching her skin.

"Save your energy. I don't care what you look like," he told her.

She waved toward the door. "They do. They need me to be strong, not old and frail."

"So you waste your power looking younger?"

"Do not judge what you do not understand."

"Fine. Whatever. I came because I need your help."

"I have done for you all I can, young Theronai."

"It's Grace. You said if I hurt her you'd end my world. Well, without even knowing it, I've been hurting her."

"I know. You should have learned to control your emotions better."

"The woman I love was taken from me, possibly dead. That's not the kind of thing a man just shrugs off without feeling something. And for me, it's only been a few months. I hadn't even had time to *think* about getting over losing her, if such a thing is even possible."

She let out a long sigh. "What do you ask of me?"

"How do I take the disk off?"

"You do not."

"She's better now. There shouldn't be any danger."

"She has worn it for too long. Much longer than you."

"I figured that out. She said she's been here four years."

"Not just that. It is part of her. She has never known a life without it. Or without the feelings flowing through it."

"So what do you want me to do? Stop feeling?"

"If you must. You said you would do anything for Grace. This is your chance to prove that was no lie. Find happiness. Give that to her instead."

"Then let me tell her who I am. Who she is. Once she remembers me and the love we shared, we'll both be happy."

"If only you had as much intelligence as you do determination."

"What's that supposed to mean?"

"Some things are best left forgotten. The pieces of Grace that I hid were not ones that served her future happiness. They would have kept her from healing."

"Are you saying you don't think we should be together?"

"She is human. Not your kind."

"So? I'd rather have a short life with her than a long one without her."

"You will live a long life without her no matter what you do. The closer you tie yourself to her, the harder losing her will inevitably be."

"I'm already tied to her as close as a man can get. I love her."

"What about her? You have seen how gentle her heart is. When she realizes that she will die and cause you great sadness, that she will stand in the way of you fulfilling your destiny as a Theronai warrior, do you think that will add to her happiness? Or will she mourn for what she will take from you because you give her no other choice?"

Torr had never considered how it would make Grace feel to know she was going to age and die before him and cause him pain. He'd never even once stopped to consider how it might hurt her to know she kept him from finding the female Theronai who could channel his power and save his life.

He still had several leaves on his lifemark. He still

had time. But it *would* run out, and the years he spent with Grace were ones he would never use to find a mate who could help fight the war against the Synestryn.

Even the idea of looking for another woman to spend his life with—one who wasn't Grace—was enough to make his stomach turn. But it was his duty to live, to fight, and the only way he could stay alive was to find the woman who would stop the decay of his soul.

If Grace ever learned that she was standing in the way of him finding the woman who could save his life, it would kill her.

Brenya closed her eyes in sadness. "So you see now. Being with her own kind is her best chance at happiness. She should grow old with one of her own. Feel that her life is long and full, rather than short and fleeting by comparison."

Finally Torr realized the truth. "You didn't bring me here just to fight that lizard, did you?"

"No. I could have slain the beast with a mere thought. But I needed your presence, and I am tired, even for thought."

"You want me to take her back to Earth, don't you?"

"Among other things. I do have need of you here, but I also knew that if you were the one to escort her home to her own kind, you would see to her safety. Without her memories or knowledge of the danger she would face on Earth, I thought it best if she had a protector. Someone she trusted."

"She doesn't even know me. You saw the way she flinched when I touched her—like I'd hurt her."

"Before you leave, she will know you. Trust you. You will stay here and spend time with her while you drive back the invasion that the Solarc has sent to draw us out."

The Solarc? The instant spurt of fear that shot through Torr was completely involuntary. If the Solarc wanted something from this place, Grace was in horrible danger. So was everyone else here.

It took Torr a minute to wrap his head around just how much trouble he'd stepped in. "Why does the Solarc want to draw you out?"

"I am growing an army."

"Of what?"

"The Sanguinar are dying. Without them, you have no hope of driving the Synestryn back, away from my home world."

"We do what we can, but there's not enough blood for them to survive. If we spent all our time letting the Sanguinar feed on us, we'd be too weak to fight."

"That is why I left Athanasia. Why I convinced my daughters to make the ultimate sacrifice."

Torr had been so wrapped up in seeing Grace again, he hadn't really stopped to think about *why* Brenya was here with all of these women.

"I don't understand. What exactly are you doing here?" he asked.

"You will understand in time. For now it is enough

to know that the women and children here must stay hidden from the Solarc at all costs. If he senses my hand in slaying his minions, then it will be like a beacon showing him the way to me."

"Why are you hiding? I thought the Solarc ruled Athanasia, not this place."

"He does. With terrifying authority. But when I left him, I knew he would not stop searching for me until he found me."

"Why?"

"Because I was the first to leave his domain against his will. I gave his subjects the idea that they did not have to stay under his rule. He seeks to make an example of me."

Torr eased into the nearest chair. The bulk of his weight made the black branches groan, but it held him up.

His mind slowly put together the pieces she laid out. "You were the one who cracked open the Gate. You're the reason the Athanasian men have been able to sneak out and father children with humans. You're responsible for the birth of Helen, Lexi, Andra and the other Theronai women."

"I only opened the door. What my children did with it was their own decision."

Children? "Wait. I thought the men who came to Earth were Athanasian royalty—the sons of the Solarc himself."

"Yes."

"And they were your sons, too?"

"Yes."

"Are you telling me . . . ?"

"I'm the Solarc's wife, Queen of all Athanasia, and he will not rest until I am once again under his control."

Chapter 6

Torr sat there, shocked. The Solarc's wife was not five feet from him. How could he not have known? "No wonder he's looking for you. I can't imagine that he was pleased that you left him."

"He killed thousands of our subjects in his rage. Earthquakes, floods, interrogations. For that, I am truly sorry." Some of her wrinkles deepened for a moment before smoothing once again.

"What will he do if he finds you?"

"He can see through sunlight, peering in on distant worlds. It is why the Sanguinar cannot step foot into the sunlight. He *sees* them and sends his Wardens to slay them. The twin suns here prevent him from seeing me. He must have learned that such a thing blinded him, so he has begun using other means to find me— sending his Wardens to all the worlds where I might hide."

"That doesn't answer my question. What will he do?"

"Bring me home. Strip my mind clean of all I have

done to defy him. All who have ever aided my cause will die a horrible death."

The crescent-shaped mark on his arm burned. "Does anyone else happen to use the same mark as you put on me?"

"No. It is mine alone."

"Then I guess it's in my best interests to make sure he doesn't find you."

"It is. But for more reasons than you may realize. If he finds me, this whole world and every creature on it will be slain. Including your Grace. I have touched her mind in my efforts to heal her. That leaves a kind of mark the Solarc will recognize instantly."

Like hell. "Tell me what to do."

"As long as I am free, he cannot use me to find those I have touched."

"If you're safe, we're safe."

"Yes. You must kill the minions who seek me and destroy their entrance to this world."

"Where is the entrance?"

"When I came here, there were no portals, no Sentinel Stones, no way for any being less powerful than myself to travel here. It was safe. Clean."

"But I saw a Sentinel Stone in the village."

"Then you saw that it only opens to one place: Earth."

"Is that why there were so few runes over the surface?"

"Yes. I needed a way for my daughters to come to me and return home, but I sense every time it opens. Nothing has come through that I did not allow."

"You built it, didn't you?"

"Yes."

She really was powerful. Maybe she was weaker now, but he would be smart to remember that the woman had serious juice. "If you know every time the Stone is used, then how did the Solarc's minions get here?"

"The only way his creatures could be here now is if someone powerful allowed them passage."

"So the Solarc sent them directly," guessed Torr. "The same way you got here."

"Yes, but he would not have sent them after me without some way for them to force my return."

"Are you sure he wouldn't just send his guys here to kill you?"

"He doubtlessly wants me dead, but my death will not be a simple one. Nor will it come quickly. He will make an example of me first."

"And that means bringing you home," he said. "What kind of minions are we talking about?"

"Wardens are likely."

Torr let out a low whistle. "They're hard to kill."

"Extremely. They are designed to withstand the blade of a Theronai, so you will need to find the hammer of a Mason."

"A Mason?"

"They are the Solarc's craftsmen. They built the Sentinel Stones and will likely be here to erect a portal powerful enough to send me home. They work in pairs, so if you see one, know another is nearby."

"Will my sword kill them?"

"For a time."

"What the hell does that mean?"

"They wield the power of creation."

"So . . . what? They rebuild themselves?"

"Yes."

"Then how do I kill them?"

"You do not. You may delay their efforts, but that is all."

"So there's no way to win."

"The Masons are rare, precious creatures. Only the Solarc can create them, and the effort leaves him weakened for a time. The Masons will stay here only until their task is done. Once that happens, they will be sent to the next world to do the Solarc's bidding."

"That means we have to let them do their job, which is probably all kinds of bad news for us."

"Precisely. He will have sent Masons who will carve their own portal. Once that is complete, I will have lost control of this world and what beings come here. That is why I sent for you."

"You want me to find whoever—whatever—the Solarc sent here, keep them away from your people, then destroy their way in before any more bad guys can arrive."

Brenya gave a tired nod. "The Masons have already created beasts to protect them—Hunters that will scour the area in search of me."

"How do you know? Have you seen them?"

"Grace has. I have kept careful watch over her mind

since you arrived, and it was easy to see what she saw earlier today. The Hunters are close. My magic will mask our village, but not for long. You must kill them."

"Won't that give away your location?" he asked.

"Not if it is done by a hand other than mine. There are many worlds like this one—many places the Solarc must search. He will assume my hatred for him will demand I fight back. He will be searching for the essence of my power in every one of his minions' deaths. Nothing I do can give away my presence. If he cannot sense my power trying to keep him from this world, he will keep searching elsewhere."

"You mean you can't kill them yourself or he'll know you did."

"Indeed. He knows the feel of my magic too well for me to mask it. Your strength must be enough to defeat the Solarc's minions. Do this in repayment for me saving the life of your precious Grace."

There wasn't even a question of whether he'd agree.

"I do so swear," he vowed without hesitation, bracing himself for the weight of his word. Not only was the repayment a tiny one for Grace's recovery, but she was still in danger so long as the Solarc touched this world.

With the life of the woman he loved at stake, he would find a way to protect this planet, no matter what it took.

Chapter 7

Torr sat outside all night waiting for the Solarc's Hunters to appear. With Grace's life—as well as those of many other women and children—on the line, he wasn't going to trust the magical defenses of one weakened woman.

The tingling edge of Brenya's protective barrier was at his back. The dark woods surrounding the village spread out in front of him, filled with the sounds of wild, alien creatures.

He saw a few small nocturnal animals scurrying about, but nothing more.

The morning sky was beginning to take on the color of burning embers when he heard someone approach from behind. He turned, sword in hand, to find Grace pushing through the brush at the edge of the village.

As soon as she saw him, relief eased the lines across her brow. "You're safe."

"Did you think I wasn't?"

"Your bed was empty when I came to check on you

in the middle of the night. I've been looking for you ever since."

What he wouldn't have given to have been there in his bed when she'd come. Nighttime had its own sort of magic. Maybe seeing him in the depths of night would remind her of all those times she'd sat with him in his suite back at Dabyr, holding a hand he couldn't feel. He could see her touching him and know that she cared, but her warmth was a distant thing beyond his reach.

But not now. Now if she touched him he'd feel every gentle stroke, every bit of gliding pressure and heat.

It seemed that no matter how close he and Grace were, they were always destined to be separated. He couldn't feel her touch before, and now that he could, she had no reason to touch him. He was no more to her than a stranger.

"I'm sorry if I scared you," he said.

"I'm just glad you're okay." She leaned against the thick black trunk of a nearby tree. The metallic leaves cast shimmering bits of reflected light across her face. "What are you doing out here?"

"Guarding against attack."

"From those creatures? I thought Brenya was doing that with her magic."

"She is. But my way is better."

"What's your way?"

"I won't just keep them out. I'll kill them."

Grace shivered, but he couldn't tell if it was the latent violence of his words or the chill of night that caused it. "You should come back and eat. As soon as it's lighter, I'll show you where I saw the creatures."

He had no trouble seeing in the dim light, which only served to highlight Grace's humanity. She had no magic, no powers she could use to defend herself.

"I'd rather go alone. If you could just point me in the right direction . . ."

"You'll get lost out there. The trees are thick, and it's easy to get turned around."

"I have a good sense of direction."

"Brenya told me it was my duty to guide you to what I saw."

"Aren't you afraid to go with me?" He knew she was. He could see it in her eyes. But she was hiding it well. If he hadn't known her like he did—if he hadn't spent hours talking with her and watching her face and studying her expression—he might not have even seen her fear.

She bit her lip, drawing his attention to the little dent she'd left behind.

Torr wanted to lick away the mark and ease the sting, and make her forget all about her worries.

When she spoke, her voice was steady, without a hint of fear. "After what I saw . . . I wouldn't want anyone going out there alone. If you were to get hurt, you'd never be able to make it back here for help. At least if I'm there, you'll have someone who can keep you safe."

The idea tickled him, forcing a smile to lift one side of his mouth. The move felt so odd after going as long as he had without smiling, he was afraid he might pull a muscle. "You want to protect me?"

She nodded, and curly locks of dark hair slid over her shoulder. "Someone has to."

"Why?"

"Because you're important."

She thought he was important? The idea sent a thrill racing through him until he was puffed up and feeling like a champion. "What makes you think that?"

"Brenya brought you here. She wouldn't have done that unless we needed you for some reason, and that means I should do whatever I can to keep you safe."

Some of his pride deflated a bit, but he tried to hide it. "Do I look like I need a protector?"

Her gaze slid over his body so slowly that he swore he could feel it against his skin. Places that had been chilled by the damp air grew warm, and the disk along his spine tingled.

"You look invincible," she said. "But then, what do I know? You're the only man I remember meeting."

You've met me before. You've felt my lips on yours. Those were the words that bulged behind his teeth, trying to break free. He held them back, but the effort left him shaking with fury that he was required to stay silent when the woman he loved was within reach.

"I'm not invincible," he admitted. "But I'm far more suited to battle than you."

She lifted one shoulder in a shrug, drawing his attention to the slim line of her arms. Goose bumps puckered her skin.

Torr removed the blanket he'd tossed over his shoulders the previous night to cover his bare chest. There were no clothes here that fit him, but he'd been forced to wear worse things than a clean blanket before.

He pulled the fabric around her body, wrapping her in the warmth that clung to it.

The move pulled her close. His fists stayed bunched at the edges of the blanket, unable to let go. Her head tilted back as she looked up at him, and until this moment, he hadn't realized just how perfectly she fit his frame. Since the night he'd met her, after saving her family from attack by Synestryn demons, one or the other of them had been paralyzed. First him, then her. He'd never stood in front of her like this until coming here. It felt incredibly right, which was its own kind of torture.

One hand held the blanket tight. The other slid over her shoulder, across the nape of her neck. His fingers parted as they moved through her hair to cup the back of her head.

Her dark eyes widened, and her mouth opened on a silent, sudden breath.

His hold on her was absolute. She couldn't have broken free if she'd tried. She was trapped, and yet there was no sign of fear this time. Only curiosity and excitement.

"I'm not sure if we should be this close," she whispered.

"Why not?"

"I can hear a voice inside telling me it's wrong. But . . ." She trailed off, frowning.

"But what?"

"If it's wrong, then why does it feel so nice?"

Her innocence hit him like a falling tree. With her memories gone, and no experience with men, she had no way of knowing what a man like him wanted from her.

And he did want from her. So much.

Torr released her and took a step back. It wasn't as far as it should have been, but even moving away that distance was an effort of will.

"Why are there no men here?" he asked.

"Brenya doesn't allow it."

"But she brought me here."

"None of us know why. Unless you're here to give someone a child or meet one of your children."

Shock drifted through him. "What? Why would you think that?"

Grace backed up a couple of steps, gripping the blanket. The flicker of fear that passed through her expression was quick, but he still saw it.

"I didn't mean to offend you," she said. "I'm sorry if that question was out of line."

"It's not that. You can ask me whatever you want. I'm just a little surprised that you'd think that's why I'm here."

"Athanasian women come here sometimes after meeting with special men on Earth. The women stay here and have their children before going back home. I thought maybe you were one of the fathers since you're from Earth."

"I'm not one of the fathers, nor did I come here to become one." It wasn't possible. He'd heard rumors that there was a serum that could restore his fertility and that all the men had been ordered to take it, but in order to get it he would have had to go back to Dabyr. And that wasn't an option. If he had gone back, his brothers might not have let him leave again, and he couldn't have stood being around so many happy couples when he didn't even know if Grace was safe.

Her gaze drifted past him, growing distant. "I've often wondered if I had a child before Brenya saved me. I keep seeing the face of a little boy in my dreams."

Torr guessed it was her stepbrother she saw. Blake. They'd been close, but he couldn't tell her that without revealing that he had known her in her old life. Doing that would come too close to breaking his vow to Brenya. Instead, he settled for, "How old was he?"

"Nine or ten."

"How old are you?"

"I don't know."

Torr did. She was twenty-eight now, after her years here. "You're still young. You would have had to have been pregnant as a child to have a son that old. I'm sure he's just someone you were close to."

"A brother?"

"Possibly," he said, hedging. "If you regain your memories, I'm sure you'll be able to find him."

"Do you think he's looking for me?"

"Anyone who lost you would never stop looking for you, never stop trying to get you back, never stop wondering if you were safe and happy."

A sad smile shaped her mouth. The last time he'd touched it had been the time he'd had to breathe for her. He'd wished his lips had been on hers for any other reason but to force air into her lungs. She'd been so frail then. At death's door. He'd known it might be the last time he would ever see her, and yet here she was, safe and so beautiful it made his chest ache.

"You're sweet," she told him. "If all men are like you, it's no wonder Brenya keeps them away. None of us would ever get any work done."

"Brenya would be smarter to bring more men like me here to keep you all safe."

"If you're going to keep anyone safe, you'll need to eat something. Let's get you some food and I'll see if we have any clothes that might fit."

He fell in line behind her as she started walking toward the cluster of huts around the Sentinel Stone. "Are you saying you don't like me running around half naked?"

"I try not to lie, so I won't say that, but it is distracting. The girls all want to touch you, which I have to admit I *don't* like."

Jealousy? He couldn't be sure. What he was sure of was that he'd wear pink stockings and a clown wig if it made Grace happy. "We can't have that. I bruise easily."

She glanced at him over her shoulder, her eyebrows raised. "I don't believe that, not after seeing how fast you heal. You barely needed more than to have the blood cleaned away."

"Fast healing comes with the job."

"What job is that?"

"Getting beaten to a pulp all the time."

"Well, I hope you're good at it. If we're going after those things in the woods, you're going to need to be an expert."

"*We're* not going after them. *I* am."

"You won't find them without my help. Even Brenya agreed I needed to go along, and she doesn't want me anywhere near danger."

"You can just point the way."

Grace stopped so suddenly he nearly ran into her. Her chin was set in a way he recognized—one that said she was going to get her way.

In that instant, he remembered how she'd gotten him to start eating again after he'd decided to starve to death. None of his brothers would kill him and free him from the prison his body had created. He was paralyzed, and all the Sanguinar around were pouring all of their energy into trying to heal him. Nothing had worked, and he'd become nothing but a drain on the people he loved.

Joseph, his leader, had refused to let him meet an honorable death, so Torr had taken the decision out of his hands. No one could force him to eat. It was the only thing he had left that he controlled.

And then Grace had come to him, so sweetly coaxing, offering to remove one item of clothing for every bite he took. The temptation had been more than he could resist. She'd fed him and made him hunger all at the same time.

He'd found his honor before she'd stripped herself bare, but it had been a close call. Even now he could remember just how she looked with only her bra covering her full breasts. His body had been unable to respond at the time, but it was more than able now. He had to clasp his hands in front of his groin to keep her from seeing what she did to him.

She didn't raise her voice. There was no heat in her tone, but that made it no less final. "I'm going with you. We all follow Brenya's orders here. Even you. And she ordered me to show you where I saw the Hunters."

"And if I refuse?"

"Then I'll just have to find a way to change your mind."

Just as she had with him starving himself.

If she started taking off clothes now, he was sure he wouldn't be enough of a man to stop her. He'd wanted her for too long, and having her close again was almost too good to believe. Touching her—taking her—would definitely go a long way toward convincing him that this was all real and not some beautiful dream.

Torr cleared his throat to keep a squeak from his voice. "Are you saying I should just give in?"

"I'm saying I'll meet you by the well after you're finished eating. Don't leave without me."

Clearly her mind was made up. And he was supposed to earn her trust somehow. He couldn't do that from a distance, so Grace would go with him. But as soon as she showed him where to find the Hunters, he was bringing her right back. No way was he putting his sweet Grace in danger for one second longer than necessary.

Grace led Torr through the woods, relieved that his body was now covered. At least that's what she tried to tell herself.

Not that what she'd been able to find could really count as him being covered. She'd had to cut the sleeves off of a loose shirt that one of the larger women wore. After she sliced open the front to make room for the width of his shoulders and ribs, the shirt was more of a vest. It did nothing to hide his arms and little to hide his chest. Every time he walked, the edges parted, revealing that tantalizing image of the tree and the flashing, iridescent necklace.

"What is that picture you wear?" she finally asked as she led the way to the area where she'd been collecting herbs yesterday.

"It's called a lifemark."

"Why that name?"

"Partly because I was born with it, though it used to look a lot different. It's grown as I've aged."

"It changed by itself?"

"Yes." The way he said it made it sound like he didn't want to explain.

His hesitance only made her more curious. "What's it for?"

"A reminder."

"Of?"

"The passage of time. How precious every day is. My duty to use each one of those days to fulfill my vows."

"What vows?"

"You certainly are full of questions."

"It's going to take us a while to get back to where I saw the trail. We have to pass the time somehow."

"Not a fan of silence?" he asked.

"It has its place. So do questions. What vows do your lifemark remind you to fulfill?"

"To protect humans and guard the Gate to Athanasia."

"That's where Brenya came from. And the women who come here to have their children."

She pushed past a low branch, holding it aside for him to pass. His big hand brushed hers as he took over the job, and she could have sworn she could feel that single accidental touch all the way up her arm.

"Why do they come here to have their children?" he asked.

"They're special babies—ones who would be killed if the women were to have them at home."

"How are they special?" he asked.

"I don't know for sure. I hear things, but Brenya isn't exactly the type of person who explains her actions. All I know is that these women are trying to help fight a war the only way they can. Time goes faster here than on Athanasia, so they're only gone for a few days—a short enough time that the Solarc won't discover them missing."

"Brenya will explain it to me," he said, determination hardening his tone.

Grace stifled a chuckle. "I don't know what makes you think that, but good luck getting her to talk."

"She doesn't get to make unilateral decisions like that. There are lives at stake, both Sentinels and humans."

It was obvious that Torr didn't know Brenya at all, but some people had to learn everything the hard way. "I've never met another human. At least not that I can remember. Are they all as weak as me?"

He took a long step and came up beside her, lifting low-hanging branches out of her way. "What makes you think you're weak?"

"Everything. Even the children here can outrun me, are stronger than me, and can go longer without food or rest. At first I thought it was because I'd been so sick, but Brenya said that's just the way I'm made." It had taken her a long time to get over the sting caused by that unintentional insult. "I'm not allowed to patrol at night. No one wants to spar with me. They're all kind about it, but I know they all think I'm a weakling and that they'll hurt me."

"Humans aren't weak," he said. "Neither are you."

"I have proof to the contrary. And based on your response, I'm guessing that we are weak and you're just being nice, too."

"There are different kinds of strength. You have an adaptable nature that makes you nearly invincible. Your capacity for compassion is its own kind of magic. And you have a quiet force of will that rivals any I've ever seen."

"You say that like you know me."

He looked away and fell back in line behind her. "I know humans. And Brenya wouldn't have brought you here and saved your life if you weren't an exceptional one."

Something about that didn't seem right, but they were nearly at the clearing where she'd spotted the Hunters.

She slowed and lifted her finger to her lips to indicate the need to be quiet. They crept along, skirting the edge of the clearing where herbs grew, until she saw a mark in the dirt.

Grace leaned toward him, going up on tiptoe to get as close to his ear as she could. "A Hunter left this mark." She pointed to the print in the loose soil. The imprint was deep and jagged, showing where the bottom of the creature's foot had sharp protrusions.

A line led through the brush as if it had been cut by a sharp blade. Leaves and branches were severed cleanly, and as she leaned to change her line of sight, she could see exactly the way they'd gone.

"They went that way," she said, pointing.

Torr nodded. He drew a sword that had been invisible only seconds ago. The sudden appearance of the weapon surprised her, forcing her back a few steps.

He noticed her distress and lowered the blade away from her. Orange sky was reflected in the polished surface and winked off of an intricate netting of silver vines that formed the hilt and crossguard.

His knuckles bulged with his tight grip. His skin shifted over bone and muscles along his forearms. The need to feel that masculine power flow through his limbs—to touch it with her fingertips—was almost unbearable.

Grace wasn't like the other girls in the village who chattered and cooed over wanting to stroke him. She had better things to think about than that. Sadly, she couldn't remember a single one of them right now. Instead, all she could focus on was the subtle warming of her skin and the way her clothes suddenly felt too tight for her to breathe.

"I'll take you to the village, then come back and follow the trail," he whispered close to her ear—close enough that she could feel the warmth of his words as they passed.

She stifled a shiver. "No. It will take too much time."

"You can't go back alone. It's not safe."

"Then I guess I'll have to stay with you."

He scowled at that and opened his mouth to argue with her, but a soft rustling came from the south.

Before she could even register that there was danger, Torr shifted his body so that he was between her and the sound. With his free hand, he held her behind him, silently ordering her to stay put.

The rustling grew louder, closer. Grace's heart started pounding hard enough that she was sure it would bruise her ribs.

These Hunters hadn't seen her before. She'd stayed silent and they'd slipped by, parting the low brush as they passed. All she'd seen was a jagged series of shiny black ridges peeking over the foliage, glittering with filtered sunlight.

Even though she hadn't seen much, she'd *felt* them, as if they left a cold fog in their wake. She'd been chilled to the bone, even after running back to the village. Her instincts had screamed at her the whole way, demanding that she go faster.

Do not look back.

The words had sounded in her head as clearly as if someone had been running beside her. It could have been Brenya, who often summoned her with a voice like that, but it sounded different. Almost afraid. And Brenya was never afraid.

Torr stepped away, his footfall silent on the leaf litter. As thick as the brush was here, he could disappear within only a few steps.

The idea of being out here alone again with those things was too terrifying to even consider.

She shifted her weight to follow Torr, and before she could take so much as a step, his head turned and he gave her a hard amber stare.

Stay. He mouthed the single word, and she froze in place, a strand of fear strumming inside her—one that had nothing to do with the Hunters in the woods. This was deeper, a part of her former self that she didn't understand.

Something had happened to her that had terrified her, and there were times when a single word or movement from someone else would set her off, making her want to cower under the covers like a child. Maybe that something was what had nearly killed her. No one seemed to know, or if they did, they weren't telling her.

So she was left to deal with her inconvenient moments of fright, never able to predict when another might strike.

Torr slipped silently out of sight through the brush. Grace crouched to hide and make herself as small a target as possible. The action felt natural, as if she were used to cowering.

That idea grated on her pride. She was the weakest person here, not including the infants and toddlers, but that didn't mean she was weak-willed. She would be as strong as she needed to be. As brave as she needed to be. Whoever she'd been in her old life, she was no longer that person. She had been remade.

She pulled the dagger from her belt. It was little more than a tool, meant for digging up roots and slicing off bark. But the blade was sharp, and her grip was firm.

Seconds passed in painful silence, each one measured in frantic beats of her heart. The rustling sounded again, only this time farther away.

She turned to face it and nearly stabbed Torr in his stomach.

He grabbed her hand, lifting the dagger out of the way before it could make contact. The move pulled her hard against his front, forcing her to catch herself. Her left hand splayed over hot male flesh. She felt muscles along his chest shift against her palm as his arm came around her to steady her.

She was plastered against him from knees to breasts, which made her heart pound even faster.

"It was just an animal," he whispered.

Fear trickled out of her but was instantly replaced by something else—something hot and laced with excitement. It was as though her skin had suddenly come to life, allowing her to feel things she'd never noticed before.

The breeze swept past her, lifting fine hairs away from her nape. Each of his fingers at her back flexed slightly, as if he were trying to resist stroking her. The leather of her tunic was clinging softly to her thighs. Her legs were bare beneath the hem, and the worn softness of his pants made her want to rub against him. Or maybe it was the man beneath that created such an odd urge.

His head angled down and he stared at her mouth. She licked her lips, just in case there was some stray bit of food lingering there. She couldn't stand the thought of embarrassing herself like that in front of this man.

The bright amber of his eyes darkened until only a slender rim of color remained. For some reason, seeing that change in his gaze excited her until her insides were squirming with the desire to get closer.

Not that there was much closer to get. Not with their clothes on.

Her fingers clenched involuntarily against his bare chest. She could have sworn she could feel his pulse speed up and a wave of heat spill out of his skin.

Slowly, his fingers relaxed on hers, allowing her to pull her weapon hand from his grip. "I'm sorry. I could have hurt you."

He swallowed twice. "Not with that toy. If you want to fight, you need a real weapon."

"I'm not allowed to fight. Brenya says I'm too fragile."

"You are fragile, which is why you need to know how to protect yourself."

"No one will teach me."

"I will."

His easy agreement made her suspicious. "Why?"

"Because I don't know how long I'll be around to keep you safe. I want to make sure you know how to do the job yourself."

"That's what I keep telling the women—I should be able to protect myself."

"What do they say to that?"

"I should just stay in the village where I can't get hurt."

"I'd scoff at them for that, but I remember telling a young woman much like you much the same thing—to stay inside the walls of Dabyr where she'd be safe."

"And was she?"

"No. She almost died inside those walls." Torr released her and turned his back.

A thick wave of cold slunk along the ground, gripping her ankles. Before she could so much as gasp, that cold swelled up from the ground, enveloping her.

There was no question what it was. The Hunters were here.

Chapter 8

G race grabbed Torr's arm as she darted past him, forcing him to run. He could practically feel the panic spilling out of her as she crashed through the brush.

He spared a quick look over his shoulder and saw what had made her take off.

Hunters.

Two glittering black creatures charged after them, their target clear. Their skin looked like it had been forged from volcanic glass, chipped to a razor edge. They were tall and narrow, with sinuous, fish-shaped bodies that easily slashed through dense terrain. They traveled on four legs, the top of their backs at about eye level on Torr—just over six feet. From the tremors shaking the ground as they ran, they probably outweighed him by a lot.

Grace was ahead of him, but nowhere near as fast as the things behind him.

He drew his sword, gripped it in both hands and

powered the blade through a tree as they passed, knocking it down behind him. The Hunters weren't even slowed down. They tore right through it like it was no more than a twig, cutting it cleanly into logs.

If Grace didn't run faster, these things were going to be slicing through her in a matter of seconds.

Torr picked up speed, grabbing Grace around the waist as he went. Her feet barely touched the ground as they ran. He could hear her rapid breathing, feel her muscles straining to keep up, but she was human, and that came with a potentially deadly set of limitations.

He tried to scan ahead for some kind of cover—a defensible location where he could hold them off. But the trees and undergrowth were too thick for him to see more than a few feet in front of them.

The sounds of glass crunching grew louder. A quick glance over his shoulder proved that the Hunters were definitely gaining on them.

"Just a little . . . farther," panted Grace. "To . . . the right."

He had no idea what she meant, but he trusted her, so he angled right, taking even more of her weight as he pushed his legs to pick up speed.

The Hunters were nearly on their heels. The *thwack* of leaves and branches being severed was right behind them. A few more seconds, and it would be him and Grace being cut to shreds.

Up ahead he saw bright orange sunlight. The sky. The trees were thinning out.

At least if they were in a clearing he could see these

things coming at him—one wouldn't be able to sneak around and attack him from behind while the other distracted him. He'd shove Grace up into a nearby tree where she would be relatively safe while he took the Hunters down.

The poorly timed fear of what might happen to her if he failed rippled through him, but he let it pass, giving it no weight or value. With none of his brothers here to help him, and Grace's life on the line, his focus had to be absolute.

"Stop! Cliff!" she shouted in warning, just as what lay ahead came into view.

It wasn't a clearing that awaited them. It was a steep drop down farther than he could see. The gap was several hundred feet wide—far too wide to jump.

Torr tightened his grip on Grace's arm and hauled her sharply to the left. They landed hard, and her cry of pain tore away his concentration for a split second.

He gathered his wits enough to regain his feet, rather than seeing what was wrong with her. Whatever it was, it would have to wait until he dealt with the most pressing threat charging toward them. He lurched upright as one of the Hunters closed in for the kill.

Torr lifted his sword just in time for the creature to slam into him.

His blade sheared off a small chunk of translucent black rock. The thing screamed in pain, its voice sounding like glass grinding against stone.

The force of the blow rocked Torr back, but he kept his feet planted, knowing that Grace was on the ground right behind him. If he stepped back, not only could he hurt her, but it would put the Hunter that much closer to her.

A bone-chilling cold seeped out from the thing, freezing the sweat on his brow.

The second Hunter streaked by, its body gleaming obsidian and orange. A moment later it disappeared into the thick foliage. There was no question in his mind. The Hunter was positioning itself to charge. And they had only a few seconds before it happened.

"Get up a tree," ordered Torr. He didn't know if she was able to obey, if she was even conscious.

His blade was locked against the front ridge of the Hunter's head. Its jaws were too small to do more than snap at him, and its arms and legs were too short to reach him. The real threat was its partner, who could slide in silently at any moment, killing them before Torr even knew it was there.

The chill this creature put out grew deeper, numbing his toes. It had taken only a couple of seconds, making him wonder how much time he had before his fingers became numb, too. If he couldn't hold his sword, they were both dead.

He turned his blade until the flat of it was pressing against a serrated ridge of black glass. With one hand on the hilt and the other on the frigid blade, he used all his strength to shove the Hunter back into a thick tree.

The thing's feet slid over the leaves. It snarled and fought, but Torr was strengthened by the knowledge that he was the only thing standing between Grace and death.

The tree's metallic bark split around the Hunter's narrow body. Torr kept pushing, ignoring the tingling cold in his hands.

The trunk opened as the Hunter's wedge-shaped body was forced back into it. A layer of frost crept over the bark, and the clear sap that had leaked out began to crystallize as it froze. Wood creaked as the ice spread through the tree.

"The other one's back," yelled Grace.

Her voice, even as frightened as it was, was as sweet as angels singing. She was alive, conscious and still with him.

Until that second, he hadn't realized just how terrified he'd been that he'd lost her again. He'd kept that fear below the surface, where it couldn't affect his ability to fight, but it was there, lurking, waiting for a chance to defeat him.

Torr flicked a glance toward the sound of her voice. She wasn't in a tree. She was leaning heavily against one, holding her head. Blood trickled out from her hand, staining the knotted cords decorating her fingers. Her skin was as white as bleached bones.

She was staring wide-eyed at something in the distance.

The second Hunter.

Torr eased away from the one he was fighting, making sure his plan had worked. The Hunter didn't follow him up. It was stuck inside the tree, embedded in frozen sap. Its feet scrabbled against the ground to find traction, but as soon as it had dug furrows in the soft earth, it could no longer even reach the ground.

It wasn't dead, but it was disabled, and that was enough for Torr to move on to the next target.

That next target was sailing toward him, leaving bits of leaf litter and branches in its wake. Torr was in a bad position—too close to the jaws of the trapped Hunter. Even a few steps back would put him close enough to be killed.

The second Hunter must have seen that.

So did Grace.

She waved her arms and shouted to draw its attention. "I'm over here!"

She sprinted away from Torr, her gait unsteady and way too slow.

One of the Hunter's eyes tracked her movement, but the other stayed fixed on Torr. The deep cold that suddenly embraced him had nothing to do with the chill the Hunters put off.

He scrambled to reposition himself—to make himself a more tempting target than Grace, but it did no good. His shouts and flailing arms were no match for a sweet, unarmed human woman.

Torr charged the Hunter.

The creature charged Grace. Torr had been in enough battles to know how this one would play out. The Hunter would slam into her, slicing her in half instantly. Torr was too far away to do more than watch. No matter how hard he pushed his legs, the distance between them seemed to stretch out, leaving an impossible length to cover in a couple of seconds.

In the blink of an eye, he remembered every achingly sweet moment they'd shared. He remembered the first moment his paralysis wore off and he was able to stand again. All he'd wanted to do was find Grace and share the good news with her, to sweep her up in his arms and hold her as he'd craved to do for so long. Since he'd met her, his whole world had revolved around her visits, her touches. And now, because he couldn't run just a little bit faster, he was going to lose her.

He gathered as many tiny sparks of energy as he could and used them to speed his stride. The sting of that power coursed over his skin, but it didn't matter. He still wasn't going to be fast enough.

Torr shouted, "Get back!"

Grace backed up three long steps until she was teetering on the edge of the cliff. The creature realized too late what lay on the other side of its prey. It tried to slow down, but the shiny serrated paws slid through dirt and leaves like they were water.

She took one more step and fell from the cliff just as the Hunter toppled over the edge. Their screams mingled for a split second—hers filled with fear and the Hunter's a harsh, alien howl.

Then her scream stopped abruptly, and Torr knew Grace was gone.

Chapter 9

Torr went completely numb. He couldn't believe what Grace had just done. She'd leapt from the cliff. Killed herself to take out one of the creatures. Killed herself to save him.

She was so insanely selfless, throwing her life away as if it meant nothing. How could he have let her do that? How could he not have seen this coming? How could he not have known she would gladly trade her life for his? Again.

He should never have let her come out here with him. Fuck what Brenya had said about gaining her trust. He should have locked Grace inside one of those huts, wrapped up in a soft cocoon of blankets so she couldn't get so much as a paper cut.

He stumbled to the edge, praying that the drop wasn't as steep as it seemed, or that there was water beneath to cushion her fall.

She couldn't be gone yet—not when he'd just gotten her back.

He braced himself for what he might see and peered over the edge. The shattered remains of the Hunter lay strewn on the far bank of a narrow river. Jagged scrape marks and chunks of black glass were embedded in the opposite cliff, where it had hit as it fell to its death. Below, the edge of the river had begun to freeze.

There was no sign of Grace on the banks below, no sign of her bobbing in the churning water.

"I'm here." Her voice came from his left, strained and weak.

Torr held his breath, afraid he'd imagined the sound. "Over here."

This time he was sure he hadn't imagined it.

She sat on a narrow ledge of rock about eight feet below the edge. There was blood on her bare legs and more running down her cheek. Dirt covered her skin, along with several cuts and scratches. Leaves clung to her hair, which was a wild, tangled mess. Even so, she was the single most beautiful woman he'd ever seen.

She was alive. The sheer power of his relief knocked him on his ass. He sat there, weak and shaking as a tidal wave of gratitude flowed through him.

Grace was alive. Nothing else mattered except his burning need to keep her that way.

"How badly are you hurt?" he asked, his voice shaking with emotion he couldn't control.

"I'm sure it's not that bad. Just give me a minute and I'll try to get up."

Climb up and risk falling again? Fuck that. "No. Stay there. I'll come get you." As soon as he stopped shaking so hard. If he tried it right now, he was going to get both of them killed. He needed a minute to collect his wits and regain the strength in his limbs. The thought that he'd lost her had been enough to render even a strong man like him weak.

From the breathless quality of her voice, he could tell he wasn't the only one scared shitless by her stunt. "There's another way down here other than the one I took. Just follow the edge for a few more yards around the curve and you'll see a natural ramp in the stone."

"Okay. Just stay still and I'll be down as soon as I can. I need to take care of unfinished business."

She nodded, her body already slumping with fatigue as the effects of the adrenaline wore off. If she was more seriously injured than she looked, shock wasn't going to be far behind.

Torr pulled himself together, pushed away from the ledge and went back to where the Hunter was trapped in the tree trunk. He cut himself a long section of branch about the length of his arm and skinned the smaller twigs away, leaving him a nice thick club.

With a firm two-handed grip, he got as close to the thrashing creature as he dared and swung right for its head.

The beast shattered, its grating scream dying with it. Bits of glassy black chips showered over him. A few left shallow slices along his exposed skin, but the sting barely registered. All that mattered now was Grace.

*   *   *

Grace tried to still the trembling in her limbs. She wasn't cold anymore, but she couldn't seem to keep from shaking.

Nervous energy tumbled out of her core with nowhere to go. She couldn't even stand and walk it off—not with what was probably a sprained ankle.

The fall she'd taken hadn't been very far down, but in that moment her life flashed before her eyes.

With only four years of memory, it was a sad, lonely thing to witness.

There was more to life than what Brenya allowed her, and from this moment on, Grace wasn't going to let anyone stand in the way of her experiencing it. Weak or not, human or not, she was going to find her place in the world and milk every drop of happiness she could from life. No one was going to stop her.

Torr's steps sounded from behind her, much too fast for the narrow ledge he traveled. Before she could even scoot around enough to tell him to slow down, he was at her side, his big hot hands gliding over her.

"Where are you hurt?" he asked.

Grace was struck again by how beautiful he was. Lean animal strength poured from him, making her wish she could soak it in. Even in his concern he was stunning. His worry seemed to brighten his amber eyes and gave him the feral look of a male predator.

She shivered again, and this time it was due more to some innate feminine response to his nearness than to her ordeal.

"My ankle is the worst. The rest are just minor scratches and bruises."

His hands moved along her leg, gently unlacing the leather straps covering her calves. Once her leg was bare, his fingers stroked her skin, carefully probing as he inched down to her foot. She closed her eyes and reveled in how good his touch felt.

Right up to the point where he prodded a tender spot.

She sucked in a hissing breath. "There. I think it's sprained."

"Okay. Let's just sit here for a minute and see if the pain eases." He sat behind her, positioning himself so that his long legs spread out beside hers. He wrapped his arms around her, urging her to lean back against him and tuck her head under his chin.

Grace didn't resist. She was still so shaken and terrified that the idea of wrapping herself in his strength seemed like the best idea in the world.

Every breath she took was filled with his scent. The solid bulk of his body behind her put off waves of heat that made coiled muscles unclench. As the seconds flowed by, she began to relax. With each shuddering series of tremors, he stroked her arms and helped ease her through it. Finally, after what was an embarrassingly long time, she got control of herself enough to stop shaking.

"Please tell me you knew this ledge was here when you jumped," he said. His tone was gentle, but there was a tension in his body that told her to tread carefully with her answer.

"I didn't jump. I just stepped down." A long way down, but that wasn't something she thought she needed to remind him of.

"And you knew the ledge was here?"

Her need for honesty and her desire not to upset him started a brief war in her gut. She settled for "I was pretty sure."

He let out a short strangled sound, then cleared his throat. When he spoke, it was with exaggerated calmness. "How sure is *pretty* sure?"

"I'd been here several times. There's a cave a little farther down the ledge where some mushrooms that Brenya likes grow."

Some of his calmness faded. "That's not an answer."

"I knew the ledge was long. I thought I was in the right spot."

"But you didn't look first, did you?"

"And take my eyes off that thing?"

His arms tightened around her for a second before releasing the pressure. "Promise me you'll never do anything like that again."

Grace knew the power of a promise, the innate magic it held. That was one of the first things Brenya had taught her: never make a promise she wasn't certain she could keep. Doing so was a form of slavery she would never escape.

"I don't know you well enough to promise you anything," she said. "But I have no intention of going cliff-diving again anytime soon. It scared me to death."

"You shouldn't risk your life like that. You have no idea how valuable you are, how much pain your absence would cause."

"I'm no more valuable than anyone else, including you."

"That's why you jumped. To save me."

"I wasn't smart enough or fast enough to think of a better plan. I'm just glad it worked out."

"You're injured. That's hardly what I would call working out."

"My ankle is already feeling better."

"It doesn't look better. It looks broken."

She glanced down and saw the obvious swelling. "It's not broken. It looks worse than it is. Once I'm on my feet, I'll just walk it off."

His thighs tightened against her hips. "You can't walk off a broken bone, no matter how advanced your skills at denial are."

"I'm not an idiot. I know my own limits."

"Apparently not, seeing as how you thought you might be able to fly."

"Don't be ridiculous. I knew I couldn't fly." As soon as she said the words and felt his body tense against hers, she knew it was the wrong thing to say.

She turned her torso enough that she could look up at him. "Can we please just let it go? I did what I thought was right."

He looked down at her, which put his mouth only

inches from hers. It was the perfect angle for a kiss—at least she thought so. She couldn't remember ever having been kissed, but her lips still tingled in eagerness, as if they knew exactly what to do.

Torr cupped her cheek. His hand was so big it nearly covered the side of her face. His thumb stroked along her cheekbone, awakening some deep awareness she'd never felt before.

Once again, that odd sense of familiarity assaulted her, shoving out all other thought.

"You touch me like you've done so all your life," she told him.

His eyes darkened. He licked his lips, and her gaze was drawn to the curved indentation above his top lip. The urge to dip the tip of her tongue in the groove was almost more than she could resist. She had the strangest sense that if she did so, he would taste sweet and forbidden, like hidden memories.

Beard stubble shadowed his jaw, lending him a harsher edge. Curiosity lifted her hand until she was touching the roughness riding his skin. A strange shock of excitement rocketed along her spine until her pain was a distant, meaningless thing.

His hand slid to encircle her throat in a touch so gentle she had to concentrate to feel more than a tingling heat. His forearm settled between her breasts, and she was sure her heart sped up to match his pulse.

"You would have looked so pretty wearing my luceria," he said.

She didn't know what that was, but the way he said it, it hardly mattered. "If you want me to, I will."

A sad smile curved his mouth. "I want it more than anything I've ever wanted, but it's impossible. Like so many things."

Before her head cleared enough for her to ask him what that meant, he helped her sit up and he stood, all in one fluid movement.

With his strength and heat out of reach, the horrible cold of her shock and fear began seeping back in. She suppressed a shiver until his back was turned before she gave in to it.

He surveyed the area. "When you're ready, we'll see if you can stand, or if you're more damaged than you think. If you can walk, we'll head back to the village."

"If I can't walk, you should go back for help."

He turned toward her then, his gaze intense against the backdrop of the orange sky. "I know you hardly know me, but do you really think I'd leave you out here to fend for yourself, wounded and alone?"

"What other choice do you have? You have to be back before nightfall."

"I can carry you."

"It's too far. I'll be fine here. I'll just hide in the cave over there until you can get back."

He scrubbed his fingers through his hair in frustration and started pacing. Low, angry words spilled from his lips, too quiet for her to hear.

Seeing him mad made that old queasy fear lurking

within her lurch to the surface. Instinct took over, and she curled herself into the smallest space possible.

The movement caused her ankle to shift, and pain shot up her leg, but she bit back the scream and remained silent.

He won't find you if you're quiet.

The words came to her in a sweet but terrified voice—one she recognized but couldn't place. All she knew was that she trusted the voice absolutely and would do whatever it told her to.

"Grace? Are you okay?" Torr. That was him speaking to her, not some phantom memory she couldn't grasp.

A hand landed lightly on her shoulder and she jerked away. Terror radiated out along her limbs, until she was quivering with the need to hide.

"Grace, honey, you're okay now. You're safe. Look at me."

Until this moment, she hadn't realized that she'd shut her eyes.

His hand stroked her face, the touch achingly gentle.

Grace pulled in a shuddering breath and forced herself to open her eyes. Torr was crouched beside her, touching her, but still keeping his distance, thanks to his long arms.

"There you are," he said. "I thought I'd lost you for a minute."

She swallowed hard to shove the fear down where it belonged, only to have it replaced by shame. Her cheeks burned, and she couldn't stand to look him in the eye. "I'm sorry."

"Are you okay?"

She gave a shaky nod and took an equally shaky breath. "I'm a nutcase, but I'll be fine."

"You're not a nutcase."

She started to sit up, and Torr hurried to help ease her upright. "I don't know what else you'd call it."

"You've been through some terrible trauma." He said it like he knew it was true, rather than as though he was guessing. "You're allowed to be afraid sometimes, especially after jumping off a cliff to avoid being killed by ugly demon-cicles."

The metallic taste of fear at the back of her throat began to fade. Each slow breath was a victory, strengthening her just in time to pull in the next. "It shouldn't matter what I've been through. I don't remember any of it, so it shouldn't bother me."

"But it does, and that's okay." He wiped away a tear, and until that second she hadn't realized she'd let herself cry.

She wanted to stand up and slip away where she could pull herself together in private, but with her ankle throbbing, that wasn't an option. "No, it's not okay. I keep telling Brenya she should help me remember so I can face whatever makes me like this and move on."

"But she won't?"

"She keeps saying that some things are best left forgotten and that the things I no longer know are a gift." Grace let out a frustrated growl. "Her control over my life makes me so furious sometimes. I know she saved me, but it's *my* life. *My* memories. I should get to pick what happens in my own head."

He actually smiled at her, and for a split second she wanted to punch him in one of his amber eyes.

"That's good," he said.

"What's good?"

"That you know how to be mad."

"How can you possibly think being mad is good?"

"Because it beats being afraid."

"I don't like being either."

"Sure. No one does, but if you have to be one or the other, mad is definitely better."

"What makes you say that?"

"A few hundred years of experience in combat."

A few *hundred*? "Really?" she asked. "You're that old?"

"Yep. And Brenya calls me 'young Theronai,' which makes me wonder just how old she is. And how much she's learned in that time."

Grace had never really thought about it. Some rule in the back of her head told her it was rude to ask another person their age, so it had never come up. Until now. "So you're saying I should trust her."

"No, I'm just saying that there's a chance she's wiser than either of us. Maybe when she says that some things are better left forgotten, you should listen. And so should I."

"You? Do you have lost memories, too?"

His lips clamped together, like he didn't want to talk about it.

"I'm sorry. I didn't mean to pry."

Torr leaned down close, moving slowly so she wouldn't freak out again, no doubt.

"Put your arms around my neck," he said.

The iridescent necklace he wore shimmered with his pulse. Thick muscles and tendons stood out, drawing her eye down to the gleaming curve of his shoulders. So much of his skin was bare, dotted with perspiration. She knew if she did as he asked, he'd be hot to the touch, driving away the chill of fear that lingered just below her skin.

His altered shirt was even more tattered than it had been before their mad dash through the woods. All it managed to do was hide enough of his body to make her stare on the off chance that the breeze would pick up and she'd get more of a peek at the man beneath.

"Grace," he said, her name a dark temptation coming from his lips, "grab your shoe and wrap your arms around me."

There was nothing she wanted to do more than touch him, so she did as he asked, uttering a half-hearted, "Why?"

He lifted her into his arms, forcing her to tighten her hold. "That's why. No more waiting around to see if you can put weight on your ankle. It's time to go. I don't think we should be out here alone in the woods together. Not when there's so much danger, and not when you look at me like that."

She almost asked him, *Like what?* but she already knew the answer. She was looking at him like she wanted him, like she'd never known what it was like to want a man before he'd shown up. Because it was true. Her body was melting from the inside out, growing warm and soft in a way that made her want to lie back and give in. To what, she wasn't sure, but she knew that with Torr it wouldn't matter. He could do whatever he pleased, and she would enjoy it.

There was no reason for her body to respond to him that way, and yet she couldn't seem to make it stop. All she could do was try not to think about how good his solid strength felt as he lifted her. "I'm sure I can walk."

"I'm not. This first bit on the narrow part of the ledge is going to be tricky, so I don't think you should argue with me."

Because he was right, and because the fall to the river below was one that would kill them, she clamped her lips shut and held on for dear life.

Chapter 10

The walk back to the village was the sweetest kind of torture. After so many months of wondering whether Grace was alive or not, she was in his arms, clinging to him like she couldn't get close enough.

Part of him still couldn't believe she was safe and whole. No matter how tightly he held her, no matter how close she got, it wasn't enough. He wasn't sure it ever would be when it came to Grace. He wanted all of her. Forever.

Having her body against his made him so erect he throbbed. Each awkward step made him ache, but he didn't want the trip to end. Once it was over, he'd have to let go of her again, and he wasn't sure he would be able to.

She'd nearly killed herself today. That she would be so careless with her safety made him want to protect her and paddle her all at the same time. Though if he ever got her over his lap and put his hand on her ass, punishing her would be the last thought on his mind.

Another harsh spike of lust surged through him. His step faltered, but he regained his balance immediately and forced himself to pay attention.

He hated it that she was hurt and that there wasn't a thing he could do to ease her pain. If she'd been a female Theronai and able to wield his power, she would have been able to tap into his vast stores of magic and heal herself, or at least mute the pain.

But she wasn't a Theronai, and her fragile human body healed slowly. An injury like this could lay her up for weeks.

How many more times would she be injured because she had the misfortune of being close to him and the danger that surrounded his life? And the next time it happened, would it be something as simple as a sprained ankle?

The answers to those questions were bleak, painful things reminding him of just how dangerous it was for her to be around him.

Maybe that was what Brenya meant when she said some things were best left forgotten. Maybe she knew that if Grace remembered her love for him, it would put her life in danger. If she loved him, she'd want to be near him. And the humans who were near men like him were almost constantly in jeopardy.

There were no Synestryn here. If there had been, Brenya would have warned him. Even if she hadn't, his blood would have drawn them out that first night.

This place was as close to safe as he could imagine

finding, and within a day of his arrival, Grace was already damaged.

There were no safe places in the universe, and even if there were, Torr's vow to fight and protect would not allow him the luxury of staying there long. He would be compelled to return to Earth, where he could perform his duty. Because of that duty, danger was a part of his life, as it would be for any woman who chose to be near him.

If he truly loved Grace, he needed to find a way to let her go. And if there was one thing he knew to be true without a single doubt, it was that he loved her.

They entered the village, greeted by several children. One of them was the tiny girl with the white-blond hair who'd almost been eaten by the lizard he'd killed yesterday—the girl Tori had scooped up and saved.

The little girl wrapped her arms around his leg and held on while he kept walking toward the hut where Grace had tended his wounds. Each step had the girl squealing with delight, until a second child joined in the game and tackled his other leg.

The extra weight slowed his steps, but he welcomed the delay. He couldn't help but smile in the face of their simple joy. It had been years since he'd had much of a chance to play with children, and he'd forgotten how healing they could be for the soul. There was something about their innocence that made the world clearer, hard decisions easier and heavy burdens lighter.

By the time Torr reached the hut, Brenya appeared, gently shooing away the children.

"How damaged is she?" Brenya asked.

He set Grace down on the cot and let her go. The patch of skin that had been against hers went cold. A sickening sense of loss churned in his gut, and he had to fight the need to hold her close again.

"I'm fine," said Grace. "I think it's just a sprain."

Brenya glared at Torr. "You allowed this."

"I did," he admitted, unwilling to lie to the older woman.

"It wasn't his fault," said Grace. "I did this to myself."

"And he allowed it."

Grace looked at Torr. "Tell her that's not true."

"But it is," he said. "It's my job to protect humans. You got hurt. That means I failed."

She rolled her eyes. "For heaven's sake. If you two think that's true, then you're both messed up in the head."

"You would protect him?" asked Brenya.

"I'm just telling the truth. I stepped off that cliff of my own free will. Even if Torr had wanted to stop me, he couldn't have. End of story."

Brenya's face turned a furious shade of red. She lifted her hand in a demand for silence. "I do not want to hear more. I already know too much." She touched Grace's ankle, and the swelling and bruising disappeared.

Brenya leaned on the edge of the cot, sagging.

"Are you okay?" asked Torr as Grace said, "You shouldn't have done that."

"I did what I must," said Brenya. "Now go and help see to dinner."

Grace lowered her head. "Yes, ma'am. Thank you."

Brenya waved her away. The second the door shut, she turned on Torr. "That woman nearly died to save you once. Did you not think she would do it again?"

"She saved me before because she loved me. She doesn't even know me now. I never thought she'd willingly throw herself off a cliff."

"You make excuses?"

"Of course not. But I can't see the future. I can't predict what crazy things she or anyone else might do."

"There is no need for magic to predict her actions. She places the value of all others above her own. I am furious that you allowed her to be damaged, but she would have done the same for anyone. I would call her reckless, but her actions are too precise for that."

"So she's done this before?"

"Never from a cliff." Brenya lowered herself into a chair. "But yes." She let out a tired sigh. "I have never known a soul like hers. Genuinely selfless with no thought of her own wants or needs. No thought of reward or praise." She looked up at Torr, and her eyes were raging with silent, leaden waves. "If we had more creatures like her on our side, the war against the Synestryn would be over, victory assured."

"There is no one else like Grace."

Brenya gave a sad nod. "I know. Forged in pain,

tempered by fear, polished by years of selfless service. She is a unique and rare creation, unbreakable by anyone but herself."

"So you know what happened to her?" Torr knew she'd had a troubled life, but it was something they'd never talked about. Whenever any conversation started leading them toward the topic, Grace had deftly steered it in a different direction.

"I do. Those memories of her childhood are part of me now. I wish they were not."

"Tell me," he demanded. Grace's silence about herself had always bothered him. Even her stepbrother refused to talk. All Torr knew was that their lives had been bad. Until now, he hadn't even realized how bad.

But that was Grace. She wouldn't give anyone pain if she could avoid it—even her own pain.

"No, young Theronai. They are not mine to give. And even if I could, you would not want them."

"I want to know her. All of her. Even the bad parts."

"For what purpose?"

He tried to think of something noble, but every answer he came up with was selfish. The truth was that he wanted her all to himself in every way he could have her. Even though he knew he was wrong for her. Even though he knew he would only cause her pain. "I should let her go, but I don't know how. I love her."

"I could make you forget her."

Fury blasted him from the inside, making his voice come out in hot, seething rage. "Try and I will kill you."

Brenya lifted a trembling hand. "Settle, Theronai. I

am too weary to carry the love of another soul. I only meant to test your resolve."

"Test me? Why?"

"Because I know our sweet Grace. Her desire to serve is too strong to deny. She will find a way to fight by your side, whether or not either of us allows it."

"Why would she need to fight? We killed the Hunters."

"Not all of them."

"You weren't even there. How could you know what we did?"

"I touched Grace. Her memories naturally flow into me. I saw what she did, and the beasts you killed were only two."

"So there are more out there."

"I have no idea how many the Masons created. What I do know is that the Hunters' numbers will grow until the Masons complete the portal and you destroy all that remain."

"What does the portal look like? I can go find it and see how close to completion it is."

"Finding it will not be difficult, though it is imperative that you do so before the Masons finish construction of it so we know if the Solarc sends through more of his minions. What you should be asking is how to destroy it once the Masons leave. That is the tricky part."

"Okay. How do I destroy it?"

"There are explosively powerful crystals on this planet. When I came here, I encased them in stone to keep them safe, keep them cool. The Hunters you encountered—the Masons formed them from this stone."

"That's why they were so cold."

"The cold keeps the crystals stable."

"And if the Masons are using that stone, then it's weakening the protection you put in place. Tell me that's not dangerous."

"Of course it is, but it will also make your task easier."

"How's that?"

"Those crystals are powerful enough to destroy whatever portal the Masons may construct. You will need to collect some of them. If the Masons have already chipped away at the encasement, your work is nearly done for you."

"How will I keep the crystals from exploding once I get them out of the stone?"

She bent and retrieved a box from beneath her bed. "This will keep the crystals cool."

The outside of the carved box was wet with condensation. Torr took the box from Brenya, wiped away the drops and opened the tiny latch. The work was intricate, engraved with twisting vines and leaves that reminded him of his sword's hilt. Inside, the box was lined with gleaming black stone. Frost formed across the shiny surface the instant it came in contact with the humid air.

He shut the lid and fastened the latch.

"What happens if the crystals get hot?"

She gave him a hard, warning stare. "Do not allow

that. The energy the explosion puts out might not kill you, but it would certainly kill any animals or humans nearby within minutes."

Including Grace. "Got it. Only one last thing I need to know. Where do I find the crystals?"

Brenya sighed with weary acceptance, and instantly Torr understood.

"Grace knows, doesn't she?"

"Parts of me remain inside of her, filling the voids my healing left behind."

"Why fill them with anything?"

"Emptiness is unnatural. It will be filled with something, and I did not want that something to be chosen by another. I thought the knowledge I gave her harmless at the time. There was no fear attached to it, only cold fact. She does not even know it is there within her, sleeping, as all of the memories I gave her are."

"So I have to take one of you out there with me, don't I?"

"Yes."

"And you're too weak to go hiking around the woods."

"No, but I am needed here to keep the others safe—to keep the Hunters at bay."

"So Grace has to go—the woman who stepped off a cliff today, hoping she remembered correctly that there was a ledge beneath to stop her fall."

"You understand the situation well, young Theronai."

"How am I supposed to keep her from tossing herself into a volcano or jumping into shark-infested waters?"

"That is the puzzle you must solve. It is one of the reasons why I brought you here."

"Because you knew I'd protect Grace with my life?"

"Any of your kind would have done that much. Your vows demand it."

"Then why choose me? Was it because I was the only one you could summon?"

"No, there are others at my command."

"Then why me? If Grace will sacrifice herself for anyone, and the Sentinels would protect her at all costs, why me?"

"Because you deserve the honor. I saw you through Grace's memories, and you alone are worthy of any sacrifice she might make."

Sacrifice? Hell, no. "I don't care what she knows. She's staying here. I'll find a way to locate the portal without her help. I'm not letting her risk her life for me again."

"You will do as I command."

"Or what?"

The thrashing waves in her eyes kicked up and she seemed to grow larger. Power radiated out from her, making him realize that as weak as she might appear, it was all relative. Brenya was still strong enough to squish him flat. "Do not push me, Theronai. I lived with the Solarc for millennia. I have learned how to inflict pain."

"You're bluffing. You're not going to kill Grace, and since I know that, I also know there's nothing you can do to me. Nothing would hurt worse than when I thought I'd lost her."

"Your lack of imagination makes you reckless."

"I'm not going to risk Grace, no matter how scary you think you are."

"If you do not obey, I will take every beautiful memory of Grace you possess and tear it to shreds. I will steal your love for her and burn it to ash. And then, each day, I will give you back what you lost—the memories, the love—just long enough for you to remember what you are about to lose all over again. You will suffer her loss each day and never know why you weep, why you rage. You will live without her, except for the moments when you know that you will have to live without her again. Over and over."

Torr couldn't even imagine such a thing. As many twisted things as he'd seen, he'd never witnessed a torment so complete and devastating. "If you do that, I'll be useless. One less warrior to fight your battles."

"Not useless. An example. A warning to others to obey my commands."

"You'd really do that?"

"I hold the fate of entire worlds in my hands. Countless souls. What I do here is vital. I will not allow you or any other creature to get in my way, even if that means I become like the one I despise most."

"If I take Grace out there with me, she could die."

"If you do not, we all die. Including Grace."

Torr searched for some way out but found none. The crushing blow of acceptance left him feeling weak and diminished. "Then I guess I have no choice."

Her face sagged with weary sadness. "In that, we are the same."

"I won't forget this," Torr warned.

"See that you do not. My next lesson will not be so gentle." She pushed herself out of her chair, her body shaking with the effort. "Now go and prepare what you need to survive in the wilderness while I prepare Grace to find the crystals. You will leave at dawn."

Chapter 11

Grace didn't dare ignore Brenya's summons.

She grabbed a bowl of stew and hurried through the village, pretending there was no tingling in her ankle. There was no pain or weakness left, but healing was an exhausting process that doubtless strained Brenya's already weakened state.

The dimness of the hut blinded her for a moment. She stood still, aware of the piles of books and trinkets crowding the space.

Brenya's dwelling was the largest, but she'd filled it until there was hardly any room to move around without knocking something over. From the aged patina that darkened the metal, leather and paper objects in the hut, Grace guessed that most of the items Brenya kept were ancient and priceless.

"I brought you dinner," Grace said as she waited for her eyes to adjust.

The space smelled of the spices and herbs Brenya

used to concoct various potions, soaps and salves. In the back of Grace's mind, she knew that there were places to buy those things, but she couldn't remember ever seeing any. That was something from her old life, unimportant in the here and now.

"Sit," ordered Brenya with a snap in her tone that had Grace scurrying to obey.

She set the bowl of soup on the only clear surface in the hut, right at Brenya's elbow. The chair across the small table was filled with stacks of rolled paper, so Grace settled on the floor at Brenya's feet.

She waved her hand toward the chair. "Sit there, child."

Grace stood to move the paper, only to find that it had vanished. She didn't ask where it had gone. The mood Brenya was in was one Grace knew too well, and the sooner she was able to leave, the better.

The older woman leaned back in her chair and set down the book she'd been holding. It looked like the pages were blank, but she didn't have a pen or ink, so Grace had no idea what it was for.

"You will travel with Torr to find a weapon to fight the invasion."

The mention of the stranger's name sent a frisson of excitement racing down Grace's spine. Her stomach trembled as it had when he'd carried her back to the village. She had to lock her fingers together to keep from fidgeting.

She didn't know what it was about him that made her feel so odd, but she was starting to enjoy it. The mere idea of seeing him again was enough to make her squirm in her seat with anticipation.

Rather than ask when or why, Grace sat silently, waiting for Brenya to finish giving her orders.

"You will leave at dawn. You are not to walk off of any more cliffs or scare the young warrior again. His heart has already been battered enough."

"How?" asked Grace before she could stop herself. The need to know more about him had overpowered her better judgment, and she winced, waiting for Brenya to punish her for interrupting.

"Does it matter? Is it not enough to know that his soul is bruised and that you should do everything in your power to soothe it rather than add to his pain?"

"Of course, Brenya. I'm sorry."

"Males are powerful, but they are also delicate. Their pride is easily damaged. You must take care not to injure it, or you will rile the beast within."

Genuine fear took hold of her, tightening her throat until her words were pitiful squeaks. "I won't let him hurt me. I'll run, far and fast."

"Torr would never hurt you, child. Not in the way you mean. But, like all males of his kind, he carries a predator within. A fierce protector who will not allow his woman to put herself in danger. That is the beast you must be wary of—the one that will bare its teeth and cage you for your own safety."

Grace heard all the words, but two of them echoed in her mind, over and over. "I'm not his woman." The idea was compelling. Thrilling. But also impossible.

Brenya paused, as if thinking carefully about her words before she spoke. "For the purpose of this journey, he will treat you as such. I would demand no less from your protector."

"Are you sure he will agree?"

"He will do as I command. As will you." Even as weary as Brenya looked, she still reeked of power—power Grace would probably never understand.

"Yes, ma'am."

"Torr will guide you through the journey, but it will be your job to seek the portal the Masons build even now. Once you find it and are sure the Masons have left this world, you will destroy it."

"I will? How?"

"There is a place on the far side of the southern village. In it are large black stones. Deep within those stones are the weapons you need to destroy the portal."

"Is there a map?"

Brenya leaned forward and grasped the sides of Grace's face in her hands. Her skin was warm and dry, like sunlit parchment. A familiar scent lingered on her shaggy clothes, lulling Grace into a drowsy, relaxed state.

"You already have the map, child. I gave it to you years ago, never once thinking I would need to awaken it."

"I don't understand."

"I know. I had hoped to save you from what I took from you, but it was not to be. There can be no voids in you. They are unnatural and must be filled."

Grace frowned and tried to shake her head, but Brenya's grip held her still. "What voids?"

"Once I awaken the knowledge you need, the hole it once filled will be empty. You will reopen the memory that used to live in that hole. For that I am truly sorry."

Power seethed just below Brenya's skin. Grace could feel it thrashing against her, seeking entrance. Her head started to throb, and her stomach lurched with sickening intent.

She grabbed Brenya's hands, trying to pry them away from her head, but it was no use. The older woman was too strong, despite her fragile appearance.

"Stop," begged Grace. "You're scaring me."

Brenya's eyes brightened, frothing and frosty. "You are not yet scared, child. But you will be."

Chapter 12

Grace hid in the pantry, covering her stepbrother's mouth. Soapsuds dripped from her fingers, making Blake's skin slippery.

She'd been washing dishes when her stepfather had sloshed up the driveway, taking out one of Mom's rosebushes. There hadn't been time to dry her hands before Mom shoved her and Blake into hiding, fearing the worst.

"He won't find you if you're quiet," Mom said.

The fight started like it always did. His voice raised in anger, Mom's quiet with humble apology for something she probably hadn't even done.

Grace wanted to shout at him and force him to back the hell off, but she was a scrawny fourteen-year-old and completely outclassed. Jerry Norman was strong when he was sober. Drunk, he was strong and mean.

The fight escalated until his enraged bellowing took over, nearly drowning out the sound of fists meeting flesh, toppled furniture and muffled, hopeless sobs. One more loud clatter and the house fell silent.

Grace quivered in fear and anger, physically restraining Blake from rushing out after Mom. When Jerry was like this, there was nothing a seven-year-old could do but accumulate more bruises and broken bones.

Footsteps came closer, too loud to be Mom's. The refrigerator opened, spilling a sliver of light in through the gap under the pantry door. There was the hiss of a beer being opened and the metallic clatter of the cap hitting the floor. Heavy footsteps went back the way they'd come.

Grace waited for Mom to come get them, to tell them that the worst was over. She would wipe away any blood and hide her face, but Grace would see the pain in the way Mom walked, in the way her shoulders hunched or the way she held her ribs.

Blake pried her hand away. "Let me go."

"Not yet. You know the rules. We stay here until Mom comes," she whispered.

Jerry would be asleep soon and they'd all be safe for a few hours. Grace would help Mom clean up, get her an ice pack and pray that this time would be different.

Too much time passed. Jerry's snores sounded from upstairs, shaking the thin walls.

Grace let Blake go and opened the door. "Be quiet."

"I know," he snapped in a tone so much like his father that it terrified her.

He was a few steps in front of her when he came to a sudden halt outside the kitchen doorway. There, lying on the crumpled remains of the coffee table, was Mom. One arm was bent awkwardly behind her. Blood dripped from her chin onto the carpet.

Grace stood frozen, unable to make sense of what she saw.

This wasn't how things went. Mom was supposed to get up and tell them it was all going to be okay. She was supposed to make excuses for the pitiful man she'd married—the only father Grace had ever known.

He'll never do it again. It was my fault. I shouldn't have made him angry. *Those were the words Mom was supposed to say now—the lies she always told. And believed.*

Blake rushed to Mom's side, shaking her. "Wake up!"

His voice was too frantic. Too loud. He was going to wake up Jerry, and his next target was always Grace.

"Shh," she hissed. In that moment, shame consumed her. Her mother lay unconscious on the floor, and all she could think about was what Jerry would do to her if Blake woke him up.

She didn't dare cross the room. She couldn't stand knowing the truth. Not yet. Right now, she could still pretend that everything was going to be okay, that Mom would get up and their lives would go on like they always had.

She dialed 911 with numb fingers and held Mom's hand while they waited for help to arrive.

Jerry never woke up to help, not even when the paramedics carried Mom away.

Grace opened her eyes and saw Brenya's sad face.

"What did you do to me?" whispered Grace. Tears rolled down her cheeks, and that deep, aching sense of shame and loss clung to her.

"I released the knowledge you needed. The space it emptied had to be filled with something else, so I let you see what was always yours."

"Those were my memories," said Grace, knowing it was true. She could remember every heartbreaking minute of that night, how the doctor had come out and told them that Mom was never going to wake up again. How Jerry had told Grace that if she reported what he'd done, both she and Blake would go live in foster care and probably never see each other again. He'd told her he would get help, be a better father.

Like Mom, Grace had believed him because she'd wanted to.

"I don't understand," she said. "How did you give me back my memory?"

"I gave you nothing. You took it. For that, I am sorry. Some things are best left forgotten."

Those words made sense now in a way they never had before. Grace could remember every moment of fear, anger and grief from that night. The rest was still a dark void with no more than fluttering shadows taunting her.

She had a mother, a brother. His was the face she'd seen in her dreams. At least now she knew his name. She also knew how much she'd loved both Mom and Blake. That alone was a tremendous gift, even as mixed with pain and loss as it had been.

Grace had a family. She wasn't completely alone. They were humans like her, and they'd loved her despite her weaknesses.

That knowledge was a precious gift that helped balance out the dark burden of the memory itself.

"Are there more memories I can see?" she asked.

"The more important question is whether or not you know where to find the crystals."

Grace opened her mouth to say no, but the knowledge was there, clear and certain. "I do."

"Good. Then tonight's work is done."

"But there's so much more I want to know. What happened to my mother? Where is Blake?"

"Not tonight. I am weary. Leave me and go rest for your journey." It wasn't a request.

Arguing with Brenya wasn't an option, and Grace really did worry about the older woman's health. As much as the need for more memories burned inside Grace, she knew she would get nowhere tonight. It was best to do as she was told and bring it up another day.

She left the hut, still reeling from what she'd seen.

She had a family out there somewhere.

She looked up at the sky, wondering if she would ever see them again. Were they even alive?

Dark had fallen, and the nighttime animals had come out to play. Their chattering comforted her, making her feel grounded in reality. Wherever she'd been before in her memory—in a house she couldn't remember—she was here now, in the world she knew and understood.

The scent of dirt and leaves rose from the ground. Warm, humid air wrapped around her limbs, but it did little to drive away the chill just beneath her skin. The longer she turned the memory over in her mind, the more she realized what it meant.

This man who'd brutalized her mother and terrified

her and her brother had shaped her life. She couldn't remember him clearly, but he still had control over her. *He* was the reason she flinched and shied away from displays of anger. *He* was the reason she would hide under the covers, afraid of some nameless threat in the night. Even from a distance of both time and space, he shaped her.

The idea that she let it happen gave her a rare surge of anger.

She had to walk this off, shed the oily film of fury that left ugly streaks across her insides.

She wasn't like Jerry. Never would be. Now that she knew he existed, it was time to take away any lingering control he had over her.

There was no conscious thought to her path. Only habit guided her steps as she walked blindly along the edge of the village.

It wasn't until strong hands circled her arms that she realized that she'd almost walked right into Torr.

"Whoa—I said your name three times. Where were you?" he asked.

"Sorry. I didn't hear you."

"Are you okay? You look like you've seen a ghost."

Maybe she had. Was her family still alive? Were they looking for her?

His thumbs stroked her skin, calming her a bit. Some of the shaky fear and anger trickled out of her, giving her a little room to breathe.

"Something's wrong," he said. "You talked to Brenya, didn't you?"

Grace nodded as she looked up at him. Once again she was struck by the beauty of the band around his throat. For a second, she forgot all about her own thoughts, which helped ease some of her roiling emotions.

From the necklace, her eyes naturally wandered to the skin beneath it and the strong lines of his neck. She'd been cradled close to him only a few hours ago, and she could still recall his scent and the way it made her whole body relax and grow languid.

His expression hardened. "Did she upset you? If she did, I'll—"

Grace instinctively pressed her hand against his chest to calm his anger. "No, it's not that. I mean, she did, but it wasn't her fault."

"Of course it was her fault. That woman has got to stop playing queen and start thinking before she speaks." His tone was getting sharper, angrier.

Grace took a step back, shoving herself away from him. His body didn't even sway. "Stop it," she said, surprising herself with the force of her words. "Brenya saved my life. She can talk to me however she likes."

"Okay," he said, more gently. He lifted his hands, palms out, completely nonthreatening. "Why don't you tell me what happened?"

"She gave me back my memory," she said. "Well, I guess she didn't give it. I took it, but it feels like the same thing to me."

His face lit up, gleaming with a kind of hope she couldn't understand. "You remember?"

She nodded. "I have a brother. A family."

"What else do you remember? *Who* else?"

"A doctor whose name I don't know. Maybe I never did. And a stepfather who I wish I'd never known."

Hope fell from his expression, leaving behind a bleak stare. "No one else?"

"No. Why? Do you know something I don't?"

His lips clamped shut until all the blood was pushed from them. He looked like he ached to say something, but instead he turned around and started walking away.

Grace grabbed his arm. The instant her fingertips touched his skin, he rocked to a halt. She swung in front of him just in time to see him close his eyes and brace himself. For what, she wasn't sure.

"What aren't you telling me?" she asked.

After what seemed like a long time, he finally opened his eyes and looked down at her. In the darkness, his amber gaze seemed to glow, catching flickering bits of torchlight along the path.

"I'm glad you remembered your family. That's got to feel good."

He hadn't answered her question, but at least he wasn't running away after she'd snapped at him. "I wish I knew more about them. I don't even know if they're still alive. What if they're looking for me?"

"Are you happy here?"

"Mostly."

"Then you're doing everything you can to ease any worries your family or friends might have. Given the circumstances, that's going to have to be enough."

"But I want to find them."

"What does Brenya say about that?"

"She shooed me away before we could really talk about it."

"That should tell you something."

"She's tired. That's all."

His brows lifted in disbelief. "Then I guess you'll have to talk to her about it tomorrow."

"You and I are supposed to go hunting for some crystals tomorrow."

A swift flash of anger tightened his features before he controlled it. Instinctively, Grace backed up out of reach.

At least now she knew why she did that—it was something her stepfather had taught her. Still, she hated it that he had any influence over her at all.

"I would never hurt you, Grace," he said, disappointment softening his tone.

"Sorry. I didn't mean to insult you."

"Never mind. It's not about me." He ran his fingers through his dark hair, leaving it messy.

The urge to undo the damage ran through her, but she kept her hands to herself. She really didn't know him well enough to be touching him every time the mood struck. Which it did often.

"I'll try harder not to flinch."

"You do whatever you need to do to feel safe, Grace. I mean that."

"I don't think 'safe' is going to be on the menu for a while. We have to go out tomorrow, and who knows how many of those Hunters are out there?"

If the way his skin darkened was any indication, he really didn't like that idea. "Do you know where the crystals are?"

"I do now."

"Tell me," he ordered.

Her instincts were to obey a command given in that kind of forceful tone, but when she opened her mouth to comply, there were no words. "I don't know how to tell you. I can see a picture in my head as clear as if I were looking at it now, but it's just an image." And a feeling that she needed to head south. "I think it's one of those things I'm going to have to show you."

"In a perfect world, I'd be able to see what's in your head."

She wasn't sure how, but she didn't ask. It was either one of those things she'd forgotten or one she'd never known because she was human. "But it's not a perfect world. And as much as I'd rather stay here where it's safe, I'm glad that neither one of us has to go out there alone."

His hand lifted as though he was going to reach for her, but it fell to his side before he could. "There's no one I'd rather be with, but you're the absolute last person I want to take out there with me."

Now it was her turn to have her feelings hurt. "It's because I can't fight, isn't it?"

"If you were the fiercest warrior on the planet, I'd still want you to stay where it's safe."

"Nowhere is really safe. Animals make their way into the village all the time." After seeing him fight, she was sure that the safest place around was right by his side. But she was going to slow him down. "You know, you could show me a few moves, maybe help me prove to the other women—and you—that I'm not a complete weakling."

"You shouldn't feel the need to prove anything."

"Easy for the manly man with the invisible sword to say. All I've got is this knife." She drew it from her waistband to show him how puny it was. "That's why my only option was to step off a cliff."

"Don't remind me." He shuddered, and every muscle in his gleaming body flexed.

A tingle from somewhere deep down started to uncurl in her belly, spreading out through her limbs until she wasn't sure she could even hold the knife. She didn't know why this man had the power to make her go weak, but he definitely did.

Grace wasn't sure if she hated that or loved it.

"You need a better grip," he told her as he pulled the dagger from her limp fingers. "Hold the blade along your forearm to keep it hidden until the very last second."

"Wouldn't it be better to scare someone away by letting them see it?"

"With that little knife?" He snorted. "Not likely. Surprise is a better option for someone like you."

"Like me how? A wimp?"

"I wouldn't have said it that way."

Anger was starting to slip into her tone. "How *would* you have said it?"

"You're human. You have the strength of a human. There's no shame in that."

"Again, easy for you to say. It's not like I'm asking you to give me your sword. I just want a little knowledge."

He forced out a long breath as if seeking patience. "A little knowledge can be dangerous."

"More dangerous than stepping off a cliff?"

"You have a point." He repositioned the knife in her hand and showed her how to hold it. His warm fingers closed around her fist, making his words trickle away, unheard.

She stared up at him, watching his mouth move. The little dent above his top lip was beyond intriguing. She wanted to slide her finger along the contours to get a better feel. Or maybe even her tongue.

The thought was enough to make a mist of perspiration break out across her spine.

He went still and looked into her eyes. "You didn't hear a word I just said, did you?" There was no censure in his tone, but a demanding kind of curiosity that compelled her to respond.

"Sorry."

His gaze moved over her face, slowly, like a caress. He was so close to her like this, one of his hands covering hers on the grip of the knife, the other at her shoulder, changing her position. She could smell his intoxicating skin and feel shimmering waves of heat spilling from his body.

The need to get closer overwhelmed her, driving all

rational thought from her head. Her feet shifted closer to his. He lifted the blade so she wouldn't stab either of them. The move brought her right up against his frame, so close that the tips of her nipples brushed against him whenever he breathed in.

Torr's eyes went dark, his lids falling to half-mast. His hand glided down to the small of her back, splaying wide. She wanted him to pull her closer, to increase the pressure of his chest against her nipples. They tightened in anticipation, but he didn't draw her in.

His fingertips found the opening along the back of her tunic and slipped inside. A burst of pleasure exploded down her spine, and a soft sigh escaped her lips.

His expression hardened at the sound, and every muscle along his frame vibrated with tension.

He stared at her mouth now, and hunger lit his eyes. "You tempt me."

To do what, she wasn't sure. Nor was she sure if that was a good thing or a bad thing. "Should I be sorry?"

"I fear you will be if I give in and do what I desire."

Desire sounded good. "What's that?"

His fingers curled against her skin, pulling her fractionally closer. "Everything."

Her heart surged against her ribs. She had to swallow before she could speak. "Long list."

"Yes. It is. One that would take a lifetime to exhaust. Maybe longer."

"Sounds like you should get started on that." With her.

"Do you even know what you're asking for? Just how much of your knowledge was taken?"

"Not so much that I don't know what men and women do together, if that's what you're asking."

"But you don't know what you've done. Or haven't."

"True."

"And you don't know if there was a man in your life—one who might object to you helping me with such a list."

He was right. She didn't know. And a horrible, selfish part of her didn't even care.

Grace wanted to move on with her new life, to find some kind of meaning and happiness, but what if there was someone else? What if she was married?

She shoved away from him. Every cell in her body suffered a little death at the separation, but she ignored the agony. "I should go to bed."

Torr stood there, his arms tight at his sides as if to keep from reaching for her. "Yeah. I think that's best. I'll come get you first thing tomorrow."

She walked away, sure that she was going to be spending the night playing that scene out in her head over and over again, rather than sleeping.

Tomorrow she had to set out alone with Torr. She didn't know how she was going to keep her distance when she was so drawn to him, but she knew she had to find a way.

Tori watched the disgusting display that Grace and Torr put on. For a minute, it looked like Grace was enjoying the man's touch.

More confused than intrigued, Tori crouched in silence, her dead prey dangling limp in her grasp.

Nighttime hunting was the best. She'd been out for only a couple of hours, and she'd already scored enough meat to feed the village breakfast. The rest of the night was hers to do with as she pleased, and yet all she could do was stare at the couple who thought they were alone.

Torr's back was to her, but even so, she could still see the tension radiating out from him as he held Grace. Restraint. Control. He held her as if she were the most precious thing in existence.

Tori knew what he wanted—the same thing all males wanted. If Grace hadn't left, Tori would have been forced to intervene and protect the sweet woman from what he had in store.

The need to kill bloomed deep in her chest, pounding against her bones with the thirst for blood. The short sword strapped to her belt was in her hand before she even realized it. Its weight felt good in her hand. Solid. Safe.

Once Grace was completely out of sight, Torr stalked off, his walk stiff and awkward.

Tori didn't have to see his front to know that his penis was bulging and hard. He would have used it to hurt Grace if she'd let him.

Sweet, innocent Grace didn't even know enough not to let him.

But that was a problem Tori could fix. She had her sword, and she knew just what to do with it.

Chapter 13

It had been a long time since Torr had washed clothes by hand, but the chore came back to him easily, making him thankful for both washing machines and the Gerai who usually did his laundry.

The lake was blissfully cool. Animals serenaded his work but did little to keep his mind off of Grace. He'd wanted to kiss her so badly. He'd wanted to do a lot more than that, too, but kissing was definitely at the top of his list.

She'd grown lovelier over the past four years. He hadn't thought it possible, but it was true. Whatever magic was in this place, it suited her. A little too well.

His erection throbbed, so he took a step deeper into the lake to rinse the soap from his charred jeans, socks and underwear. The cool water helped ease his lust, but he knew better than to think it would cure him.

Nothing could make him want Grace any less. But taking her now when she was stripped of her memories and vulnerable seemed like a sort of betrayal.

As much as he wanted her body, he wanted the real Grace more—the one who loved him back. Anything less would be hollow.

His body disagreed, but they'd been at odds before.

Something slipped into the lake a few yards away—probably some nocturnal animal hunting for fish. He'd seen a lot of strange creatures here, but so far, no more of those giant lizards.

He amplified his night vision, gathering a few sparks of power from the earth beneath his bare feet. It added to the power swelling inside him but didn't hurt the way it once would have.

Ever since Grace had put that healing disk on his back, the pain from the energy he contained—the magic that his mate would someday wield—hadn't bothered him. He'd spent years in pain, feeling it grow worse every day. That growing pressure was gone now, another gift he didn't deserve.

With a few quick sloshes, he finished rinsing the clothes. They would be stiff without a dryer, but at least they'd be clean for tomorrow's trip. A little worse for wear, with a few cuts and burn marks, but still more functional than going naked.

As he tossed the socks over his shoulder and began wringing out his jeans, he felt the water ripple against his thigh.

He reached for his sword, but he was too slow. A sleek, dark form burst from the water, close enough to kill him.

He felt the sting of his skin splitting a second before

he recognized that the attacker was a woman, not some animal. And not just any woman. It was Victoria Madison. Tori.

Torr lifted his hands in surrender. Whatever she was going to do to him, he couldn't fight back. His honor forbade it.

Water sluiced from her hair, but she didn't blink it away. Her cold blue stare was that of a warrior bent on revenge.

The last time he'd seen her, she'd been raving mad. And with good reason.

The Synestryn had taken her when she was a child. They'd raised her, fed her their poisonous blood in an effort to alter her body so she could bear their young. She'd been their prisoner for most of a decade, and when she'd finally been rescued, it was too late. She'd been tortured beyond imagination. The offspring she'd delivered had died almost instantly. From the rumors Torr had heard, it might not have been the first stillborn child she'd delivered.

Tori had survived those horrors, but her mind was damaged. She was wild, violent. The taint of demon blood running through her veins had changed her into a fierce and savage creature. Only her sister's pleading and a pledge of fealty to Brenya had earned Tori a ticket to this place and a possible escape from her pain.

Looking into her eyes now, Torr could see that Brenya's efforts had failed.

"I will kill you," promised Tori, digging her knife a bit deeper into his skin.

He felt blood trickle down his ribs, but ignored it. The pain was trivial. The damage she could still do to him was the real concern.

Torr took a breath and let it out before he dared speak. When he did, he kept his tone soft and quiet, as he would when speaking to a wild animal. "You can kill me, but I'd prefer you didn't."

Her eyes narrowed. "I know what you want to do to Grace. I saw you."

His cheeks heated in embarrassment, less because of what he'd been doing than because Tori had been close enough to see them and he hadn't noticed. "I would never hurt Grace."

The knife lowered toward his naked groin. "You were stiff. You wanted to hurt her."

"That wasn't about pain. I know what you've been through, but—"

The knife dug into his lower stomach, way too close to his dick for comfort. "You don't know anything. Don't pretend like you do."

He lifted his hands wider, trying to look as nonthreatening as possible. As tall as he was, that wasn't the easiest feat to accomplish. "Okay. I don't know. But there are things you don't know either."

That caught her attention. He could feel the subtle shift of pressure traveling through the blade slicing into his skin a fraction of an inch. Her grip had relaxed. Not enough for safety, but a little.

"Like what?" she asked.

"What you saw between me and Grace was about love, not pain."

"She doesn't love you. She doesn't even know you anymore. Brenya says we can't tell her."

"You're right. She doesn't know me. But I know her, and I'd never do anything to hurt her."

"Then why were you stiff and bulging?"

Poor Tori. She really had no idea about how the world was supposed to work. All she knew was pain, blood, hunger and death.

Torr made sure that none of his pity for the girl showed on his face. While she was physically a grown woman now, inside she was still a child—a feral one who would not appreciate his sympathy for her. In the world of the Synestryn—the world she'd grown up in—pity was weakness, and weakness was to be cut out, culled from the herd.

He chose his words carefully. "I was aroused because I wanted to make her feel good, make her happy."

Tori snorted in derision and slid the blade to his balls. "You were going to hurt her. Admit it."

"No. I won't. I swear I would never hurt Grace."

"Vow it."

"What?"

"Use the words of power. Bind yourself to your lies. If you say the words, you have to obey them."

Torr looked her in the eye. "I promise I will never intentionally hurt Grace."

"Promise you won't put that thing in her."

"No. That's none of your business. You don't know what you're talking about when it comes to sex."

The blade nicked his skin deeper, and he had to grit his teeth to keep from flinching.

"Promise me!" shouted Tori.

This was not going to end well. He'd used up all the patience he could spare. If he didn't do something now, she was going to do irrevocable damage.

Torr stopped pretending he was harmless and unleashed his power. A blurring burst of speed later, Tori was disarmed and her back was pinned against his front, his arms caging her. She kicked, but the water slowed her down and robbed her of any strength behind her blows.

He felt the moment that she shifted from anger to panic. Her limbs became rigid, and the sour stink of fear poured out of her. Her screams rose an octave, and there was no more intellect to her blows, only pure instinct.

His heart broke. This poor girl had been damaged beyond even Brenya's ability to repair. There was nothing left for him to do but put her out of her misery.

He gathered a glowing pulse of power and shoved it out his fingers. "Sleep," he ordered.

Tori fell limp in his grip. He carried her to the shore, then dressed in wet clothes before taking her back to the village. He hoped that when she woke in the morning she'd be calmer, but he wasn't going to hold his breath.

A girl like Tori didn't have any calm left in her. The

Synestryn had taken it, leaving behind only fear and rage. If he hadn't already vowed to kill every one of them he could, she alone would have been enough reason to do so.

The only chance she had now was to find the male Theronai who was compatible with her. Maybe he would be able to reach past the crazed violence enough to touch the woman Tori would have been had she not been kidnapped as a child.

Then again, giving someone like Tori access to the almost unlimited power housed inside a male Theronai was one of the worst ideas he could imagine.

Maybe she was better off here where she could do only minimal damage, where she could live out the rest of her years in as much peace as someone like her was able to find. It was the least she deserved for her lifetime of suffering.

Grace slipped into Brenya's hut before dawn. She needed answers. Now.

"You should have already left, child," said the older woman. She was wrapped in a fur, huddled against the morning chill.

"I will soon. But first I need to know something."

"I've given you all the knowledge you need."

"No, it's something else. I need to know if I was married."

Brenya fell silent, but the slightest smile creased her cheek. It was gone before Grace was even sure she'd seen it.

"Was I?" she asked.

"When you came to me, there was no ring."

"You opened up those other memories. I thought maybe you'd open more, or that you'd know something."

"Why does it matter?"

Grace had hoped the older woman wouldn't ask that question. "You know why."

"So you fall for the first man to enter our borders?"

"He's . . . nice."

"Flowers are nice. A warm bowl of stew is nice. Torr is dangerous. That is why I summoned him."

"He would never hurt me."

"All men hurt women. It is their nature."

"You don't know him."

"And you do, child? How?"

Grace had no answers. "I don't know. I just . . . He makes me . . ."

"Tingle?"

"Yes. Exactly." Grace beamed, pleased that Brenya understood.

"Ignore it."

"That's not the kind of thing a girl ignores."

"Tingling comes right before sorrow. That man lost the woman he loved. Such pain is bound to leave its mark. You do not want to be the thing he uses to erase it."

"You really do hate men, don't you? The girls all say it's true, but I never believed it before now."

"I do not waste anything as powerful as hate on men. They are not worthy."

"So you're not going to help me figure out if I'm married, then, are you?" asked Grace.

"You are not. But you should not let that make you stupid, child. Guard your heart."

Grace laid her hand on Brenya's arm. "I'm sorry he hurt you so much."

The waves in the older woman's eyes frothed with anger. "There are no words for what he did, child. I wished it had been only hurt he caused."

Grace didn't dare ask. She didn't want that kind of thing in her head.

Brenya's tone was calm again, as if nothing had angered her. "Go fetch Victoria for me. She and I must speak. She was a naughty child last night and must be punished."

Tori hated Brenya's hut. It was dark and cluttered, reminding her of dank caves filled with the bones of dead friends.

"What do you want?" she asked as she entered.

"Respect is a good place to start. After you have found that, I think we should discuss what you did last night."

"Torr told on me, didn't he?"

"He did not need to. I know you. I am part of you now."

Tori hated the reminder, hated that the old woman had been in her head, rooting around for what she thought should be there: flowers and candy and fuzzy puppies. Those were the things that real girls thought about—girls who grew up in houses, with parents and television and food.

Tori had been raised by demons who kept her locked in tiny, cramped spaces with no light. Her entertainment was watching her captors fight to the death over who would hurt her next. She was fed the blood of monsters. And worse.

Brenya thought she could somehow change all that—that she could reach into Tori's mind and scoop out all the bad stuff. It wasn't until the older woman started stomping around inside Tori's skull that she realized the truth: bad stuff was all there was.

"You are more than your past, child," said Brenya.

Tori stalked forward, her hand on the grip of her blade. Anger seethed in her veins, burning her from the inside out. Her head pounded with the need to kill. "You have no right to invade my privacy like that. Get the fuck out of my head!"

"You are overwrought. Settle." Power pulsed from Brenya's order, forcing Tori to collapse where she stood.

The packed-dirt floor was cold, hard. She could smell the soil, feel the grit of it clinging to her skin. Very little light streamed in through the single window, covered with a layer of heavy leather. None of that light reached Tori, and she felt herself collapsing inward as terror crushed her.

She hugged herself and rocked, unable to hear anything beyond the demon blood pounding in her ears and her own pitiful wails of anguish.

She wouldn't go back to living like that again. She

would dig her own heart out of her chest before she'd let those demons touch her again.

A warm, dry finger pressed into the center of her forehead. She flinched, striking out in reflex.

Brenya let out a sharp rush of air but didn't even rock from Tori's blow to her gut.

"You will calm yourself, Victoria." It was a command, as powerful as the ocean and as bright as the moon.

Tori's heart started to slow. Her breathing evened out. With no energy left to fuel her panic, that began to fade, leaving her dizzy and nauseated.

"That is better. Now, let us go outside under the suns and discuss what you did to Torr and why you are sorry."

"I'm not," snapped Tori. The heat of her words lost a little force in her breathlessness.

Brenya offered her hand to help Tori to her feet. Her face was stoic, but her stormy eyes gave away just how angry she was. "Perhaps you are not sorry for your actions yet. But before we are done, you will be."

Chapter 14

Torr tried to keep his eyes on the path, but with Grace leading the way, the temptation presented by her sweetly curved ass was too much for him to resist.

She dressed like all of the other women here, in a sleeveless leather tunic that fell to mid-thigh. A long slit ran down the back, adding both ventilation and an enticing glimpse of smooth skin and supple spine. Strips of some kind of animal hide held thick leather soles on her feet and wound around her calves, protecting her from low brush and brambles. She was bare from knee to thigh, making him wonder just how much she had on under that tunic. He hadn't seen any underwear hanging up to dry in the village, and the idea that she might be naked under her clothes made him break out in a hot sweat.

She started up a hill, leading him to the crystals Brenya had ordered them to find. With each long stride, the hem of her tunic inched up a tiny bit more. He held his breath, wondering if the next step might finally make his heart explode in anticipation.

Grace stopped at the top of the hill and looked back down at him. "Am I going too fast for you?"

"Not if I remember to breathe."

She frowned at that and held out her hand to help him get up the last few feet. He didn't need the help, but he did need to touch her skin again, so he wrapped his hand around hers and let her pull.

Her skin was hot and damp from the hike. Little rough patches proved she was used to hard work here, but they did nothing to detract from the silken softness of the rest of her. He could still remember just how warm and smooth the small of her back had been under his fingers.

The last step put him close to her. The two of them balanced in a narrow clearing amid the brush. From this distance, he could see fiery chips of gold in her brown eyes. A dash of freckles decorated her nose. Her cheeks were pink with exertion, and her lips were as dewy as the surrounding forest leaves.

The need to kiss her consumed him, made him shake.

Concern drew her dark brows together. She reached up and pressed her hand to his forehead. "Are you okay?"

The movement brought her close enough that he could smell the sunshine warming her skin. He wanted to bend down and slide his tongue along the slender curve of her neck, just to see what she tasted like there.

A low moan of need burst free before he could stop it.

"What's wrong?" she asked. "Are you sick?"

He covered her hand with his, unwilling to let her pull away. He wanted to tell her that he needed her, that he loved her, that if she would just look deep enough into his eyes, she'd remember how much she loved him, too. Instead, words jumbled on his tongue, tangling together until nothing would come out.

Her other hand found his wrist to gauge his pulse. "We should go back. Your heart is racing."

Of course it was. It always did when she was near.

"I'm okay." He shoved the words out, his voice thick with his untimely need.

"You feel feverish."

No surprise there. He *burned* for her. "I'm fine. Really."

She stared at him for a long moment, as if deciding whether to believe him. Torr forced himself to back away from her touch and pulled a water skin from his pack. The liquid cooled his tongue and eased some of the tightness in his throat.

He offered it to Grace, watching as her mouth covered the spot where his had just been. He knew if he took another drink, he'd be able to taste her, but not in the way he was dying to.

When she was done, she licked her lips, causing another spike of lust to punch through him.

He turned away to put the water back and took some time to rearrange his load so that his damn erection was hidden from view. The thing was going to make hiking uncomfortable, but there wasn't a whole lot he could do about that—not when he still had to follow along in Grace's wake, her shapely legs and sweet bottom right in front of him.

There was no way he could look anywhere else—he wasn't that strong a man—so he was stuck with the raging hard-on for the foreseeable future.

"Do you want to sit a minute?" she asked.

"No," he said, a little too fast. Just the idea of trying to bend his body to sit on the ground hurt. His jeans had dried overnight, leaving them nice and stiff. If he tried to sit now, he would unman himself. "Let's just keep going." *And I'll try to keep my damn eyes off your backside.*

"If you're sure. We can stop anytime you want. It's going to take a while to get where we're going."

They hiked for another two hours before Grace came to a stop at the crest of a ridge. From here, the break in the trees allowed them to see to the forested landscape below. To the left was a lake, and on the right were several plumes of smoke from small fires. A few of the trees had been cleared away, but he couldn't quite make out anything else.

"That's the southern village," said Grace.

"Doesn't look very big. Why don't they live with you?"

"Brenya says it's not safe. If we're attacked, she wants at least one group to survive, so we've separated ourselves."

"Are you attacked often?"

"No, and it's always been animals wandering too close. But Brenya was always worried, like she knew something was coming."

"Guess she was right. The Hunters are definitely out there. Does this village have adequate protection?"

"What do you mean?"

"Is there another Brenya guarding them the way she does your village?"

Grace shook her head. "There's no one else like Brenya, but the Athanasian women who come here seem to be able to protect themselves. This is where they live until their time comes."

"Their time?"

"To have their babies. They come to Brenya to deliver their children. Then they leave."

"Where do the babies go?" he asked, but seeing the children of various ages in the village, he suspected he already knew the answer.

"They stay with us. We raise them until they leave."

The ultimate sacrifice. That's what Brenya had said. Now he understood.

"Where do they go then?"

"Some of them go to Earth. Others . . ." She shrugged.

"You don't know where?"

"Brenya doesn't say. She sends them into the light. We never see them again." Tears shimmered in her eyes, catching fiery rays of sunshine.

"You miss them, don't you?"

She nodded, sniffing away the tears. "It's just sad

that the few people in my life I *can* remember have to leave. I know it's important, but it's hard sometimes."

Torr ached to pull her in for a hug, offering what comfort he could. The only thing that stopped him was his worry that what started as a hug would become more. He couldn't resist this woman, and if she opened herself up for more than comfort, he knew better than to think he'd be strong enough to walk away.

Honor demanded that he remember why he was here, that he was a stranger to Grace, and that taking advantage of this situation would be a kind of betrayal of his vows.

He couldn't do that to her. He was supposed to be earning her trust so she would have someone to lean on when she went back to Earth.

So instead of forcing himself on her, he forced himself to focus on gathering what information he could. He had no idea what might be useful to know someday. "Does Brenya arm the women she sends away?"

"No. Some are given an amulet with their name on it, but that's all." She looked back out toward the southern village. "The women who live there train hard and know their way around a fight. Even unarmed, they're more dangerous than any animal I know of in these woods."

"Should we stop and check on them?"

"It's harder to get there than it looks because of the terrain. By design. If we go, we won't make it to the crystals before dark."

"Maybe on the way back, then?" He really didn't

like the idea of a bunch of women living alone with no Brenya to protect them, no matter how tough they were. He didn't even know if they were aware of the threat the Hunters posed. If he could stop by, warn them, and see with his own eyes that they were safe, he'd feel a lot better.

"Sure. There's a better way to reach them from the western side. I've gone that way a couple of times with Brenya, so I think I can find the trail."

They headed east, down a steep, rocky slope. By the time they reached the bottom, the air was steamy from the heat of the twin suns. Even in the shade, humidity wrapped around him, pressing heavily on his chest.

A little stream ran through the valley, and they stopped at its edge. The clear water called to him, but he waited, keeping watch over the area while Grace cooled off in the water.

She unwrapped the leather strips from around her calves, letting the thick hide soles of her shoes fall away. Her feet bare, she stepped into the stream and knelt on the sandy bottom.

She scooped up water in her hands and splashed it over her face and neck. While her leather tunic was modest and opaque, when it was wet it conformed to her body, displaying every one of her tantalizing curves. Even her tight little nipples were visible beneath the thin leather, puckered against the cool water sluicing over them.

Torr's mouth watered as desire heated his body further. Sweat trickled down his spine, warming the metal disk Grace had put on him. The narrow slit running down the back of her tunic showed him flickering glimpses of the matching disk she wore.

She'd said she could feel him through that disk. She didn't know that it was him feeding her those emotions when they were worlds apart, but he wondered now just how much more of him trickled through now that he was close.

A compelling idea took over, tempting him beyond resistance.

He let go of his restraint, let himself feast on the sight of her, let himself imagine what it could be like if she were to turn to him and welcome him into her arms.

Her tunic would be little more than a fleeting nuisance. He'd studied the garment and knew that the only thing holding it closed was a single leather tie at the nape of her neck. Whatever lay beneath it wouldn't stop him from reaching the bare flesh he so desperately craved.

He could have her naked, spread out in the shallow stream, feasting on her honeyed flesh while the water lapped around them to cool their fevered skin. In his fantasy she didn't deny him anything, not even the sweet, clinging wetness of her body as he thrust deep within her.

A delicate shiver raced over Grace, shaking her frame. She crossed her arms over her chest as if to hug her aching breasts. Her head turned enough for him to see how slumberous her eyes had become, how flushed her skin had grown.

Her gaze caught his, and he knew she'd felt him—
felt his lust as her own. The disk that connected them
could transfer more to her than sadness and anger. It
could give her pleasure, too.

There was nothing he wanted more in this moment
than to please her.

The urge to grip his cock in his hand and see if he
could make her come when he did was almost too
much to bear. Only the thought of how scandalized she
might be watching him jack off kept him in control. For
now it was going to have to be enough to know what
he could do to her without so much as a single graze of
his finger across her skin.

Part of him felt cheated that he didn't have the contact,
but the smarter part of him realized the gift this was.

Torr could make her burn for him. He could make
her feel good. That alone was enough power to make
his head swell with feelings of conquest.

Grace was his. She always had been. And now he
knew just how he could remind her of that without
saying a single word.

His vow to Brenya might restrain what he said, but
nothing else. Including his tongue. And the things he
wanted to do with his tongue were enough to make his
blood heat even more.

Before they left this stream, he was going to know
exactly how every inch of Grace's body tasted.

Some distant warning sounded in his head, but he
no longer cared. He was going to possess the woman

he loved. Now. If he didn't, he knew he'd regret it for the rest of his life.

Torr took a step toward her. His boot sent out ripples at the edge of the stream. Her hands fell to her sides, revealing the puckered tips of her breasts beneath the wet leather. Her thighs clenched together in a movement he knew all too well. Feminine desire rolled off her in waves, shimmering in the air between them.

A thick fog billowed down the far hillside, muting the forest noises and hiding them from the world.

He took another step, forcing himself to move slowly and give her time to catch up with the need raging through his blood.

Her gaze slipped down his chest, lingering as it passed over his lifemark, visible between the edges of his open shirt. Then lower, her stare was caught by the sight of the bulge in his jeans.

He didn't even try to hide it. Let her know what he intended, let her see what she did to him.

Grace's breath misted out, forming a silvery cloud around her head.

Something about that was wrong, but he couldn't figure out what. His mind was too focused on her to worry about a little bad weather.

She reached for him, her palm up, her hand outstretched in anticipation of his touch. He'd dreamed of a moment like this for far too long not to tremble under the sheer beauty of it.

A sound somewhere between a crack and a hiss rose

up from the far bank of the stream. The water seemed to lighten, and a silvery gray cast began to spread across the surface.

The water was freezing. The air grew cold and brittle.

The languid, inviting smile Grace wore iced over, turning to terror.

The Hunters—the ones that froze everything around them—they were here.

Chapter 15

Grace realized the danger too late. She'd been so enthralled by the feelings singing through her body that she hadn't been paying attention to her surroundings. She hadn't seen the Hunter approach.

She saw it now.

It was perched on a rock outcropping only a few yards away. Its glossy black body sparkled, and its eyes moved one at a time until both were fixed on her.

Panic set in, solidifying the air in her lungs. Sweat froze along her skin, and she swore her heart was trying to beat its way free of her rib cage.

The urge to flee set in, stealing all other rational thought. She tried to stand, but ice had already hardened around her knees, locking them in place. She slammed her fists down on the frozen surface, but it was already too thick to break, and growing thicker by the second.

The stream kept running, piling more water on top of the ice. Layer by layer, her legs were being encased faster than she would have thought possible.

Torr let out a cry of rage. One second his hands were empty, the next they held a gleaming sword.

He charged toward her, his face twisted into a fierce battle mask.

For a second, she thought he was going to cut her down. That old, greasy fear slithered through her, urging her to hide and cower. But instead of hurting her, Torr leapt over her, landing on the opposite side of the stream.

The creature's attention shifted to him. Its flat body curved around and reared back to prepare to charge. Every time it moved, she heard the sound of broken glass chips grinding against one another.

Torr attacked. Steel met black stone in a shower of sparks. Small shards of shiny rock flew out from the blow, but that didn't slow the thing down.

He shoved the creature away from Grace, causing it to slide over frozen, crunchy foliage.

A few feet to her right, the stream ran free of ice. A branch had fallen there—maybe one she could use to pry the ice away from her legs.

She leaned sideways, reaching out as far as she could. The tips of her fingers barely brushed the wet bark, causing it to shift away from her.

To her left, a horrendous crashing sounded in the trees. She spared only a quick glance—long enough to see that the creature had shoved Torr into a tree hard enough to knock it over. He roared in pain and fury. The creature screeched, letting out a sound like pottery smashing on stone.

If she didn't get free, there was nothing she could do to help Torr. It was taking all his effort just to keep the thing from coming after her.

She pulled the short dagger from her belt and flipped it so the blade was in her hand. The ice was up to her thighs now, and her lower legs had gone numb.

She reached for the branch again. The small cross-guard on her dagger caught the rough bark, and she dragged the end of the branch close enough that she could grasp it.

Water cascaded over her as she lifted the branch and started bashing it against the ice. A small crack formed, only to be immediately filled with more rushing water that froze on contact.

A terrifying screech exploded from the creature. Her head whipped around to see what had happened, but all she saw was a rain of glassy black shards falling over Torr's body. Each one left a small cut in his skin, but he didn't seem to notice the pain. His gaze was fixed on a point over her head.

She looked where he did and saw another of the Hunters inching closer to her across the ice. She hadn't even seen it approaching.

A fresh wave of fear shook her, making her arms go weak. The branch fell to the ice and stuck. She struggled to push herself up, but it was no use. As water ran over her fingers, it began solidifying, trapping her hands, too.

Her panic made her stronger. She ripped her hands free, cracking the thin layer of ice that pinned her fingers. Blood swirled in the water sliding by for only a second before it, too, became part of the ice. Several of her braided rings tore loose, but she was too numb to feel them go.

The Hunter prowled closer, its shiny black teeth easily visible now. Water droplets coated its body, but it shook like a wet dog, spewing pellets of ice.

Torr came to her side. He was careful to stay on the edge of the ice where no water was flowing to trap his feet. He moved slowly, as if he had all the time in the world. His sword spun in a graceful circle as he approached the creature, drawing its attention away from her.

"Can you pry yourself free?" he asked her, his voice as calm and even as if he were asking about the weather.

"No."

"Okay. Hang on. I've got this."

Before she could ask what he meant, he charged with brutal speed. She had no idea how he kept his balance on the ice, much less accelerated. But he did.

A moment later, he bulldozed right into the creature, sending it back over the ice and into the brush along the stream. The pommel of his sword slammed down on the thing, and chips of gleaming black rock flew out.

The creature screamed, the sound like shards of glass in her ears. It set off another one of those spurts of panic that made her try to shove herself free.

Her bloody hands clung to the ice. She didn't feel any pain, only a searing numbness at the ends of her wrists.

By the time she had the sense to think of lifting her hands away before they got stuck, it was too late. Ice formed over her fingers, pinning her. She was completely trapped. Completely helpless.

As the realization set in, so did the cold. She started shivering uncontrollably. Her rapid breaths misted out, clouding her vision. She caught fleeting glimpses of Torr in combat with the creature, but she couldn't tell if he was winning.

Lethargy weighed her down. Every few seconds, she'd feel a warm breeze sweep past, taunting her with hope.

The sounds of combat grew distant as Torr drove the creature away from her. No more ice formed over the old, but it was already too late. The ice was up to her breasts now, chilling her every breath.

She was going to freeze to death in the middle of summer, and her sluggish brain couldn't think of a single way to stop it.

Battle crashed in the woods. The fight seemed to last for hours, and each one was filled with shivering cold.

The world grew quiet, with only the sound of water rushing by. Everything was dark, but she was too confused to tell if it was night or if it was just that her eyes wouldn't open. She could smell the forest, but it was crisper and sharper than it should have been.

"Stay with me, Grace." Torr's voice. Then a heavy pounding and cracking sound.

Her whole body was numb, but she could tell she was moving. She didn't know how.

"Open your eyes, honey. Show me you're okay." Was that panic she heard in his voice?

Grace tried to comply but couldn't remember how. She couldn't even remember how to tell him she was sorry she'd let him down.

Lethargy fell over her like a lead blanket. She had to sleep now. There was no other choice.

It had been a long time since Torr had needed to build a fire without matches. The one that burned now in the mouth of the shallow cave he'd found wasn't his best work, but it was putting off plenty of heat, and that was all he needed.

He stripped Grace free of her wet clothes, doing his best to ignore how beautiful she was. The paleness of her skin and the bluish cast of her lips were more than enough to keep his head where it belonged. He laid her close to the fire, then shed his own wet jeans. The boxer briefs stayed on to remind him of boundaries in case the danger of the situation didn't do the job.

He curled up behind her, wrapping his arms around her torso in an effort to give her as much of his body heat as possible. Her fingers still bled, but the damage didn't seem to be too bad—certainly not worse than hypothermia.

Slowly, her skin began to warm. A pink flush bloomed in her cheeks, and she was no longer frigid to the touch. Once she started shivering, he knew she was going to be okay.

Relief would have laid him out if he hadn't already been horizontal.

Grace shifted, turning in his arms until she faced him. Naked, fire-warmed breasts flattened against his chest, branding him in a way he was sure he'd never forget.

She lifted one leg over his, giving his thigh plenty of room to slide between hers. Damp, womanly heat seared him, making his whole body clench against the need to lay her back and fill her up with his cock. As hot as it was, he could almost justify the act as another way to warm her.

His erection flexed against the cotton of his underwear, leaving a damp spot he couldn't control. Everything about her called to him, beckoning him to take, claim, possess.

Her shivering began to slow, evening out into waves of fitful restfulness. It was fully dark outside now, and about time for him to build a screen of brush to hide the light of their fire.

As he moved to peel himself away from her, she opened her eyes.

So pretty. All he could do was stare.

A haze of sleepiness still clouded her features, but it was soon burned away by confusion, then a harsh layer of fear.

Her body tensed, causing her thighs to clench around his and her mound to grind even closer.

Torr breathed through the blaze of lust, letting it trickle out until only a slow burn remained.

"What happened?" she asked.

"I broke you out of the ice, found some defensible shelter and warmed you up."

"Defensible . . . ?" She looked around and saw their location.

It was a shallow opening in a rocky hillside, only a few feet deep, overlooking the forest floor below. He couldn't stand up inside the space, but nothing could sneak up on them from behind either.

As shelters went, it was the best he could do on short notice.

He saw it in her face the second she realized she was naked. And that all of that nakedness was pressed firmly against his. It was a moment of wide-eyed shock, followed closely by her pupils flaring with awareness.

"Your clothes were wet," he explained.

"I remember." She didn't try to move away or hide herself. Instead, she took a deep breath that pressed her breasts even more firmly against his chest.

Torr's heart rate kicked up. "I'll get them for you."

"Are they dry?"

"I doubt it. They're laid out, but I had no way to hang them without leaving your side." Something he was not about to do while she was unconscious and vulnerable.

Her fingers slid over his shoulder. She could have done it just to get more comfortable, but it still felt like a caress. And his body responded accordingly.

He stifled a shiver and swallowed hard, struggling to think of the most unsexy thing he could.

His mind went blank, but his vision was filled with swaths of naked skin. Smooth curves, gently sloping lines, flickering shadows hiding feminine secrets he yearned to discover.

Her gaze flitted over his face, landing again and again on his mouth. Each time the tip of her tongue would glide just inside her top lip, tempting him with the need to taste what she did.

Would she welcome his kiss, or would she shove him away like the stranger she thought he was? And did he really want to know for sure when lingering within such delightful possibility was so much sweeter?

"I should get up," he said. "Put out the fire so we're not glowing like a beacon."

She didn't release him. If anything her fingers curled into his skin as if to hold him in place.

"Are you warm enough now without the fire?" he asked.

"I'm warm," she said, but the way she said it made him think of the slick heat that waited between her thighs.

He wanted to feel that intimate warmth so much that he had trouble pulling in his next breath. Even if he couldn't claim her the way he wanted, he still needed something. A touch, a taste. Anything he could get. He was dying for it.

His cock throbbed and lurched toward her. He couldn't have done a thing to control the involuntary reaction, and with only his thin underwear to cover him, there was no way she hadn't felt it.

Color stained her cheeks, but it wasn't embarrassment he saw. Not even close. It was desire, pure and unrehearsed.

Grace stroked the side of his face with one finger. Her touch was light, gentle, but it sliced through him all the same.

How many times had he dreamed of her being with him like this? Naked, touching him. Wanting him.

And she did. The proof of that was gathering against his thigh, slick and hot and scented with her growing arousal.

"I should get up," he said again, trying to convince himself.

She stared into his eyes, her expression so sweet and unguarded. She didn't even try to hide what she felt—it was all there on her face for him to see. The innocent hunger, the open curiosity.

Maybe she didn't know how to hide her feelings, or that she should. Maybe she had no way of knowing what her vulnerability did to him, how it inflamed him and made him want to protect and possess her that much more.

If he ever got inside her, she would hold nothing back. He'd know just what she liked, what drove her wild. She would be an open book—*his* open book.

"I really should get up," he said yet again, wishing that saying the words aloud might make him move his ass.

Her finger traced over his chin, reminding him that he hadn't shaved since he'd come here. Stubble roughened his jaw, and all he could think about was how badly he wanted to leave beard burn on the delicate skin of her neck, her breasts and her inner thighs.

There were no other men here for him to warn away from her, but the idea of marking her was compelling all the same. He'd make sure she felt too good to hold his lack of a razor against him.

Grace swallowed and wet her lips. In that instant, Torr knew he was too late. Moving away was impossible now. She was going to kiss him, and there wasn't a being in the universe powerful enough to make him move away now and miss it.

His body clenched in anticipation. He remained completely still, letting her come to him. He desperately wanted to move in and take over, but he had to know this was her idea—what she really wanted. It was the only way he would be able to live with himself.

The first touch of her lips on his was butterfly soft, but potent enough to steal his breath. He couldn't believe this was happening, that she was real, safe and in his arms. He hadn't lived a good enough life to deserve this kind of reward, and he prayed that God wouldn't figure that out before Grace was done with him.

She pressed her lips to his and let out a long, sweet sigh.

Torr drank it in, his body rejoicing at the contact. He wanted to let her go at her own pace, explore, but his good intentions burned away in the face of so much longing. He'd wanted this for too long not to take over and lead the way.

Grace was human. Not his kind. He shouldn't have been so drawn to her, but he couldn't help it. She was so beautiful, both inside and out. Kind, selfless, brave. Human or not, she was everything he'd ever wanted in a mate, and if all he ever got with her was this one, single kiss, then he would still count himself lucky to have had that much of her.

Her hands tightened on his shoulders, her fingers grazing his luceria. His muscles clenched as his instincts roared at him to force her to take the necklace. He knew it wasn't possible, but that didn't change the need pounding inside him to claim her as he would his Theronai mate.

He couldn't bind her soul to his, but he could claim her body as his own personal playground, taking her over and over until even the idea of touching another man was an impossible concept for her.

Torr rolled her onto her back, ready to take control of her tentative kiss. His knee spread her thighs wider to make room for him to settle between them. He was hard. She was wet. He'd spent forever imagining this, longing for it. He was done waiting.

He shifted his weight to angle their bodies together, and she let out a sharp cry of pain.

Torr pushed off of her, holding his weight up so he wouldn't crush her. Tight lines creased her forehead, and the hot flush of pleasure evaporated, leaving her pale.

"What's wrong?"

She arched her back and reached behind her. "The disk. Hard ground. Bad combo."

Her words made sense, but any meaning was lost the second he caught sight of her breasts thrust toward him. Full, round, tipped with the most delectable nipples he'd ever seen. Had he known that such beauty had been pressed against his bare skin, he would have come without so much as touching her.

Torr shut his eyes and rolled away, giving her his back. Her wet clothes lay in a soggy heap near the fire. He tossed them toward her without looking. "You should get dressed."

If he caught sight of her again before she was dressed, he knew he was going to finish what they'd started, rock-hard ground or not. He would put her astride him, riding his cock, and not think twice about the reasons why he shouldn't.

Of which there were many.

She was human. She deserved a full, human life with a husband and children and a job that didn't involve hunting monsters every night. She deserved a man who would grow old with her, who wouldn't make her feel like her life was a fleeting blip of time. She deserved safety, and that was one thing he knew for sure she'd never have at his side.

So many good reasons to find a way to let her live her own life, and yet not one of them could compete with the one reason he had to hold on tight and never let go: he loved her.

Torr pulled on his wet jeans, glad of the chill he needed to get his dick to calm the hell down. The last thing he wanted was for her to see his erection and give him that hungry look again, like she wouldn't be able to pull in her next breath if he didn't give her what she wanted.

Because he knew that, in the end, he wouldn't be able to deny her anything, even if he knew she'd regret it. That made him less of a man, but it was the truth and one he had to accept if he was going to protect her.

"I'm going to patrol the area," he told her. "Stay here, and yell if you see anything you don't like."

"Um, okay. Sure."

He didn't look her way as he stalked off, but he didn't need to see her face to hear in her tone that he'd done the very last thing he ever wanted to do.

He'd hurt her.

If anyone else had done that to her, he would have beat them to a bloody pulp, but since he couldn't do that to himself and still keep her safe, he put as much distance between them as he dared and prayed he would find a way not to hurt her again. No matter how much she wanted him.

Chapter 16

Torr had been gone for hours when Grace finally gave up and let herself drift off to sleep. Nearly freezing to death left a layer of lethargy over her that she couldn't seem to fight. It also gave her strange, sad dreams in which he was weak and helpless and she was his only hope.

She couldn't imagine a man being less helpless than Torr. His body was so casually strong and solid. She'd felt that strength up close and on an intimate level she could only have dreamed about.

Even now, with the suns rising and the night animals growing quiet, she could still remember just how nice it had felt to have his sleek, hot strength caging her in.

He'd held her like he couldn't stand the thought of letting her go, like he'd been dying to hold her for years. A feeling like that had a way of going to a girl's head, making her forget what was real and what was fantasy.

As she opened her eyes, she saw that Torr was both. He crouched at the farthest edge of the opening away from her, watching her. He was real, solid and so intense it almost hurt her eyes to stare at him. Definitely the stuff of fantasy, with his good looks and that whole gentle-warrior vibe.

If it hadn't been for the hard disk digging into her spine, she could have had him last night. She wasn't sure exactly what she'd do with that much man once she got him, but it would have been fun to enjoy him as her own for as long as it lasted.

"Hungry?" he asked, his bright amber gaze unblinking.

She was, but not in the way he meant. She'd heard some of the women talk about men, after visiting Earth to make their babies. They'd talked about need and hunger, about desire and want, like they were living, breathing things that consumed a woman and made her lose control. The women had sighed and laughed, sharing stories of conquest over who'd found the best father for her progeny, or at least the best lover.

Grace had never really understood what they meant before, but she did now. She hadn't even known that she could want something as much as she'd wanted Torr.

The slow burn was easier to bear this morning, but it was still there, one single breath away from igniting all over again.

She cleared her throat. When that didn't loosen her words, she just nodded.

He untied a cloth that held some bread they'd brought with them and set it next to a small pile of fruit he'd gathered. "Eat up. We'll leave as soon as you're done."

Within seconds, he was gone, slipping into the forest as silently as a predator.

That slow burn of desire sent out a few sparks, but she held herself together long enough to shove down some food and get moving. The sooner they found those crystals, the sooner they could be back around other people—people who would keep her from doing anything she might regret.

The only real question left was which she would regret more—taking what she wanted or denying herself something amazing.

That thought was the one that stuck with her as she led the way through the dense woods. She'd never gone this far before, but there was no question that she was headed in the right direction. The whole path was one long, familiar trail. Each step she took put the next one firmly in her mind, as if she'd come this way every day for years.

By the time both suns were halfway up the horizon, she'd found the spot she'd been searching for—a giant forked tree so old that its bark had taken on the same metallic shimmer as its leaves.

"Just over this next rise," she told Torr.

She didn't need to look over her shoulder to know he was there. She'd felt his silent presence all day, heating her back and making her spine tingle.

Grace started up the hill, but he grabbed her arm and pulled her to a stop. "I'll go first and scout. Stay here," he whispered.

She instinctively mimicked his tone, keeping her words quiet. "I've led the whole way and got you this far. I think I know where I'm going."

"I'm not worried about your sense of direction. I am, however, worried about the sounds I hear coming from the other side."

"I don't hear anything."

"You're human," he said, as if that explained it all.

"A human with ears."

"Mine are better. Stay here and stay silent."

He was gone before she could argue further, leaving her feeling more than a little inadequate. She'd never thought he would have better hearing than she did; it made her wonder what else he could do that she couldn't. What else she hadn't considered.

Was he just being nice and pretending that she wasn't lacking, the way someone might do with a child too small to reach up high?

The notion grated on her as the seconds ticked by in slow progression. If he ran into trouble on the other side of the hill, would she even be able to help him? Would she even know he needed help before it was too late?

Anxiety pushed her into action. She didn't care if she wasn't as strong as he was or if her hearing was worse. She wasn't weak or stupid. If he needed help, she'd find some way to give it.

Grace tiptoed up the hill, lowering herself to belly-crawl as she neared the summit. She crawled, inching forward over scratchy leaves and sticks. The leather of her tunic protected her torso, but the skin above her sandal straps was bare and raw by the time she peeked over the top.

The air here was distinctly colder. The land sloped down into a shallow bowl about a half mile across. The ground was charred and burned to a crisp, with a shimmering sprinkle of rough black sand covering everything. Little pools of frozen water dotted the area, as if the last rainfall had been unable to soak through the hard crust on the ground before it froze.

It looked like something had slammed into the planet years ago and cauterized the ground so that nothing could grow again. Single, infant strands of new plant life crept over the edge of the sand but were frozen wherever they touched the charred earth.

The forest had tried to reclaim this land and failed.

Several large boulders of glossy black rock sat at the bottom of the crater. They varied in size and shape, but each one was made up of jagged angles and razor-thin obsidian blades. In the closest one, she could see a depression that had vaguely the same shape as one of those Hunters that had attacked her and Torr. Beneath that indent, deep within the center of the boulder, was a pulsing light.

As she stared, she felt her own pulse slow to match the pace of the glow. A heavy sleepiness washed over her, tempting her to close her eyes.

Torr was still down there. She couldn't give in to the need to take a nap when he was in danger.

Grace forced herself to look away from the light and concentrate. She couldn't see him anywhere, but she could now hear what he had heard. Voices, low and rumbling. They were speaking in the same flowing language that the Athanasian women did, but there was no smoothness to the sound. The rough words were punctuated with a rhythmic clinking that set her teeth on edge.

Her sleepiness faded more as she looked away from the light longer. Whether that glowing was some kind of magic or technology, she wasn't sure, but it was definitely potent stuff.

She scooted back down the hill and moved a few hundred feet to her left, hoping for a better angle that might allow her to see Torr. By the time she was nearly back in position at the lip of the crater, the clinking sound had changed pitch. It was higher now, but it still made her skin crawl.

As she peeked out from the brush hiding her, she saw the source of the noise. Two huge creatures were chipping away at the glowing stone with heavy chisels and hammers. The workers were shaped like humans, but the similarity ended there.

Their skin was a smooth, flawless surface without a single hair anywhere. They were a muddy gray color with the same sheen as freshwater pearls. Their skin was granular, like fine-packed sand. Their eyes were tall, narrow slits filled with the same glossy black as the stones they chiseled. Completely naked and apparently sexless, they worked in perfect unison. Thick, bulbous hands gripped the tools, making their forearms bulge with visible strength. Each of them had in the center of its chest a bright circle that seemed to glow with its own inner light. Swirling plumes of yellow and white rose from that mark, bursting out like solar flares.

Between heavy blows to the boulder they worked on, their lipless mouths defiled a language Grace had once thought beautiful. She could feel power vibrating in those words as the cold air turned them to fog. As the strange men neared the end of their sculptural project, the black glass they were carving into the shape of a Hunter began to move.

These two gray creatures had to be the Masons that Brenya had talked about—the ones that were trying to kill the people Grace loved.

Torr sneaked out from behind one of the glowing boulders near the pair. His sword was in his hand, as lethally beautiful as the man himself. He moved silently, his breath misting in the cold air.

Grace stared in a surreal kind of trance. She knew his life was in danger and that he was going to try to kill those gray men. She knew that no matter what she did, there would be pain. And yet she still couldn't pull her gaze away from the scene, as if her watching could somehow alter the outcome.

Torr slipped behind the large boulder they were working on. In a blur of flesh and steel, he moved in for the kill, cutting cleanly through the waist of one of the gray men. It fell into two pieces, but there was no blood, only a spray of fine sand spewing through the air in the wake of Torr's blade.

The second man screamed in rage and panic, and slammed his hammer down with brutal force. The Hunter he'd been chipping from the stone was broken free, missing one of its legs.

Its jaws snapped as it lunged for Torr. He leapt out of its path, but because of its incomplete form, its aim was off, causing it to veer toward Torr anyway. He brought his sword up at the last second, lodging it in the thing's jaws with two hands.

Blood leaked from Torr's palm where he braced the blade with his bare hand. The Hunter's body bowed and its single back leg scrambled awkwardly, trying to gain traction.

Grace couldn't breathe. She was terrified for Torr but even more terrified that anything she might do would distract him and make things worse. She hated being stuck here, able to do nothing but watch and pray, but the alternative—getting Torr killed—was unthinkable.

The tall gray man knelt next to his fallen partner, aligning the two severed halves of his sandy body. There still was no blood. Whatever made up those guys, it wasn't flesh and blood—not as she understood it.

As she watched, the gap between the two halves of the gray man's body began to close. The whole one picked up his heavy hammer and moved around to angle himself behind Torr.

One blow from that hammer, and Torr would be

dead. She didn't care how fast he healed. A crushed skull was going to be fatal.

She had to do something without making things worse. And she had to do it now.

Grace rose from her hiding place and took a step out onto the charred ground. A chill sank through the thick leather protecting her feet, as if she were standing on ice. Without making any noise that might distract Torr, she began waving her arms.

The gray man who was about to bash Torr's brains in saw her and started to come her way. That was exactly what she'd hoped for, but she certainly hadn't realized just how fast legs that long could run.

Holding back the squeak of fear that rose to her throat, she sprinted into the woods. There was no way she could outrun him, but she could hide and give Torr a fighting chance.

Chapter 17

Torr was going to throttle Grace. Assuming he lived.

He'd seen the Mason sneaking up on him, knew it was a threat. He'd had another seven seconds to kill the wounded Hunter, which was more than enough.

If she'd been a Theronai, connected to him in the way his mate would have been, she would have known his plan. She would have seen his thoughts and stayed silent and hidden.

Of course, if she'd been a Theronai, she probably would have already used magic to shatter the Hunter to splinters.

Now, not only did he have to disable the Mason but he had to find it before it had time to kill Grace first.

With a spurt of brutal rage, Torr wedged his foot between himself and the Hunter and shoved the creature back. The move gave him room to regain his balance and fix his grip. He held the sword in both hands and swung hard just as the Hunter came back inside his reach, forcing it backward.

As he moved forward, with one hand he picked up the giant hammer the fallen Mason had dropped, and with the other hand he sheathed his sword.

One wicked slam of that hammer against the side of the Hunter, and it shattered, screaming as it died.

The Mason on the ground had nearly rebuilt itself, but Torr didn't give it a chance to finish the job. Instead, he smashed its head with the heel of his boot and crushed its chest with the hammer until it was a pile of sand.

Let it rebuild that.

Anger and fear fueled his steps as he raced in the direction Grace had gone. His heart pounded, but it was less a sign of exertion than of his terror that she would get herself hurt.

He could not lose her again. He *would* not.

His ears drew him in the right direction. The sounds of thrashing brush and Grace's heavy breathing grew louder.

She let out a breathless cry of fear—the kind of sound that only a woman who knows she's trapped can make.

Torr forced his legs to move faster. He slashed at the branches that barred his path.

In the distance, he caught glimpses of the sandy-skinned Mason between the trees. It had stopped and was now circling a single location.

Torr looked up and saw that Grace had climbed a skinny tree and was struggling to get higher, out of the Mason's reach.

It grabbed the tree in both hands and began shaking it.

Grace screamed and hugged the narrow trunk with her whole body. She was flung around, slammed into the branches of nearby trees.

She slipped down a couple of feet, and Torr could see the bright stain of blood left behind on the trunk where her skin had been torn by the rough bark.

A red haze the same color as the blood flooded his vision. Rage took over his limbs, giving him seemingly endless strength. He bellowed as he charged. His attack was less about killing the thing than it was about getting it the fuck away from Grace.

Torr's face must have been scary, because the Mason looked over its pasty gray shoulder and then set off at a dead run.

Torr ran faster.

He tackled the Mason from behind. It flipped over, trying to slam its hammer into Torr's head, but he was already inside its reach, making the tool nearly useless.

He didn't waste much time dispatching his foe, not with Grace bleeding and in need of aid.

The Mason's body was heavy, smooth and hard to grip, but Torr managed to get a firm hold on its throat and started squeezing. Sand crumbled in his hand, cutting off the Mason's cries of pain. A whooshing rush of air blew dust into Torr's eyes, blinding him.

The hammer fell against his calf with enough force to send a riot of pain up his spine. Two huge, rough hands gripped his shoulders and started twisting. He felt like he was going to be ripped in half, but it didn't stop him from clawing his way through the Mason's thick neck.

More sand fell away from the thing, and with every additional fistful, the Mason's strength drained away a little more.

Finally, Torr felt fallen leaves slide against his fingertips, and the Mason's hold on him failed completely. The heavy body went still.

Torr pushed himself to his feet and wiped the sand from his eyes. As soon as he could see again, he saw the Mason's crushed neck being rebuilt, one grain of sand after another.

He slammed his boot into the thing's head, kicking it into a tree, where it burst into a shower of dust.

The rush of battle was still pulsing through his body with each beat of his heart. He'd destroyed three creatures in the last three minutes, but he wished there were more waiting for him to kill. An entire army would have been welcome, and perhaps even enough to quell his rage.

Grace had risked her life. Again.

How dare she? Did she have no idea how precious she was? How fragile?

When he was done with her she'd know. And she would never again even consider being so careless. He was going to make sure of it.

*   *   *

The man stalking toward Grace was not the one she'd thought she knew. This Torr was different. Furious. His amber eyes glowed with murderous intent.

Panic hit her hard, knocking the wind from her lungs. Her pulse kicked up, speeding so fast she could barely tell when one heartbeat stopped and the next started.

She slid the last few inches down the tree, wincing as the raw skin along her thighs rubbed across the bark. As soon as her feet hit solid ground, she started backing away, putting as many trees between her and him as she could.

It did no good. He was faster than she was, and he didn't even look like he was exerting himself.

Maybe he was saving his strength for what he was going to do to her when he caught up with her. And he would catch up. She had no doubt how this would end.

At the last second, she couldn't hold back the panic exploding in her chest—the need to turn and flee.

She now knew why she flinched when people moved too fast in her presence and why certain looks on the faces of others made her want to crawl into the smallest, darkest hiding space she could find. Her stepfather had taught her those behaviors, and while he was nowhere near her now, he'd left his mark.

And now the lessons he'd taught her took over, ripping rational thought away and forcing her to run.

She had made it only a few yards when her feet left the ground. Torr's thick arms wrapped around her, pinning her against his chest.

Grace kicked him with every bit of strength she had. The move tore at her abraded skin, but she landed a couple of solid blows against his shins—hard enough that he let out a grunt of pain.

"Stop it," he growled in her ear. "You're going to hurt yourself."

"No, I'm going to hurt you if you don't put me down." Her words were too breathless to hold much force, but at least she was able to get them out.

"You need to stop. You're bleeding. This is only making it worse." His voice was calmer than she would have expected for a man who wanted to kill her. The shock of that helped snap her out of the need to run and never stop.

"Put me down!" This time her words were not breathless, flighty things. They had enough weight to make him listen.

"Are you going to run again?" he asked.

She didn't dare struggle. This was her opening, and she wasn't going to do anything to set him off again. "Are you going to keep looking at me like you're going to kill me?"

He set her down, held her long enough for her to steady herself, then let go. She spun around to face him, ready to run again if that look of rage was still on his face.

She hated it that she was so ruled by panic, by something from so long ago, done to her by a man she could barely remember. But just because she hated it didn't mean she wouldn't respond to that blind panic in exactly the same way if provoked.

She shifted to put a thick tree between them, just in case.

He ran his hands through his hair in frustration. His wide shoulders lifted several times as he pulled in a series of deep breaths.

Grace waited, torn between wanting to ease his obvious distress and wanting to run and hide.

"I'm sorry if I scared you," he said.

She wasn't falling for it. "Words are easy. Apologies mean nothing coming from a man who knows he'll hurt you again."

He froze, then turned slowly to face her. The anguish in his expression was painful to witness. "I hurt you?"

Afraid that he would fall on his own sword if she said he had, she decided to tell the truth. "You scared me. That was bad enough."

He swallowed twice before responding in a tone laced with tiny tremors of shame. "You scared me, too."

She hadn't been expecting that. "How? By running away from you?"

"You let that *thing* chase you. You drew it away. *On purpose.* It could have killed you."

It would have. If it had been six inches taller, it would have been able to reach her in that tree, and she'd be the one lying in pieces on the ground instead of it. "It could have killed you, too."

He scrubbed his face with one hand and sucked in a long breath. "I can take care of myself."

Arrogance. "It was sneaking up on you."

"I saw it."

"So? You were already a little busy."

"I've been fighting for centuries longer than you've been alive. I had time to do what needed to be done. You should have trusted me."

"I was trying to protect you."

"Well, don't!" His shout was so loud that the leaves over her head shivered.

Grace backed away, unable to stand her ground in the face of so much rage. Her whole body was shaking now, and a chill took root just beneath her skin.

His gaze flicked down to her thighs, where she could feel a sticky film of blood from her scratches. His mouth hardened as he saw the damage. "*Shit*. I'm sorry, Grace. I'm scaring you again, aren't I?"

She didn't want to give him the satisfaction of knowing how easily frightened she was, so she pretended she was like Tori—impervious to fear and ruthless enough to know she could flatten him if he tried anything.

Her chin went up and it didn't even wobble a little. That victory alone was enough to make her proud and to strengthen her resolve. "You're not even the scariest thing that's chased me today."

He shoved out a heavy sigh and his body relaxed visibly, as if he'd simply willed it to do so.

"We'll talk about what you did. Later," he said. "You're bleeding, and that's more important. Let's get you cleaned up."

Her chin was still up and Tori's fierce essence was still

guiding her. "I don't need help from someone who thinks he has the right to shout at me. I'll manage on my own." She wasn't sure how she was going to walk with the blood making her thighs stick together, but she'd find a way to fly before she would accept his help.

"I don't have the right to shout, but I do have a duty to protect you. Letting enemy combatants chase you is exactly the opposite of that."

"I didn't ask you to do anything for me, including protecting me. I've been fine here without your help for years. I'll be fine here after you're gone."

His eye twitched. His fists tightened.

The need to run away quivered through her legs again.

He must have sensed it, because he did that forced-relaxation thing one more time. His voice came out calm and quiet. "You'll be fine only if we do as Brenya says. She brought me here for a reason, and part of that reason was because you all needed my help."

"*All* of us need your help. Not just me. That means that it's my duty to keep *you* safe so that you can do what Brenya brought you here to do."

"There you go again, acting like my life is more important than your own."

"It is. I don't like it, but that's the truth. You have skills I can only dream of having, and if anything were to happen to you, I'm afraid Brenya would be too weak to summon more help. Like it or not, you're our only hope. I won't let you die and make the people I love suffer because you're too arrogant to accept my help."

"And I won't let you die, period."

She shrugged, trying her hardest to pull off casual nonchalance. "Humans have short lives. Not much you can do about that."

One second he was too far away to reach her and the next, his hands were around her arms, holding her close. His touch was careful but unbreakable. "You have no idea what you're doing to me, Grace." His thumbs slid along the tender skin under her arm. "Please, just let me keep you safe. I need it like I need to breathe."

"Because of your vow," she said, suddenly remembering that he'd taken a vow to protect humans. "I'm sorry. I didn't think what it would do to you if I risked my life."

Vows were serious things. If he thought he'd broken his, she had no idea how much pain it might cause. She was safe, but she was finally starting to understand why he would freak out over one human trying to help him in combat.

"Then you'll promise me that you'll never do it again." It wasn't a question. In fact, it was nearly a demand.

Grace shook her head. "I'm not binding myself to you with promises. Brenya warned me."

"She would want you to stay safe."

"You don't know her as well as I do. She would want me to do whatever I needed to do to make sure *you* stay alive. The lives of all those children in the villages depend on it."

He stared at her for a long time, and she was sure she could see him working hard to gather patience. His jaw clenched again and again, and his fists flexed. Finally, in a tone that seemed far too calm, he said, "If that's the case, then you need to continue to be my bodyguard. So sit down and let me take a look at those cuts. I need you in top fighting form."

She tried to find a reason to argue with him, but his logic was too sound. She couldn't even find a hint of condescension in his tone. "You mean it? You're going to stop harping at me to be careful?"

He lifted one dark eyebrow. "Hardly. But now that I understand your motivation, I can deal with it."

"What's that supposed to mean?"

"It means that you're going to sit down now so we can get those cuts cleaned up."

He'd given in, but somehow it felt more like a trap than a victory.

Grace found a downed tree and perched on the trunk. Blood seeped from the deep scratches along the inside of her thighs. It wasn't enough to be serious, but as her adrenaline faded, the pain increased fast.

Torr had left his pack behind somewhere. Grace was still toting hers on her back, proof that in the event of a fight she really didn't know what she was doing. If she'd dropped the pack, maybe she could have run faster.

He pulled the bag's strap over her head. The leather left a damp mark between her breasts where her sweat had soaked her tunic. The swirl of cool air felt good, easing a bit more of her body's stress.

He ripped a piece of fabric from the bottom of his makeshift shirt and wet it with clean water. She held her hand out for the cloth, but he ignored that and started wiping the sticky blood away to assess the damage.

"I can do that," she told him.

"So can I." He pressed gently against her knees to get her to widen her thighs.

Grace felt the blush sweep over her cheeks. "I really don't think you should be—"

"Hush. I've already seen you naked. Besides, if I was going to take you, it certainly wouldn't be while your thighs are raw and battered." His gaze caught hers and held on tight. "I want only pleasure for you, Grace. Never pain."

The sheer power of the hunger in his eyes nearly did her in. She'd never seen blatant want like that before.

But she had felt it. Was starting to feel it again now.

Her mouth went dry.

He went about cleaning her wounds, his hands far more steady than hers.

"I wish I had the power to heal you," he said. "You've suffered too much."

"They're just scratches. Nothing to worry about."

"Anything that causes you pain worries me. And there's nothing you can do to change that."

One big hand settled on her knee. She could feel the heat of each of his fingertips, feel the rough line of flesh along his palm where his sword had left its mark. Each swipe of the cloth was gentle, but even so, he winced more than she did.

Grace couldn't take her eyes off his hands. The stark contrast of his skin against hers was oddly thrilling. His careful strength made something deep inside her loosen up. The fear from her ordeal drained away, leaving her relaxed and floaty.

He soaped up a clean section of cloth. Apology was clear in his tone. "This is going to sting."

She hardly felt a thing. As long as she kept her focus on the man, the pain of what he was doing was distant and completely drowned out by the shimmering pleasure his touch gave her.

Cool, clean water trickled over her skin as he rinsed the soap away. He looked up from where he knelt between her thighs. "You okay?" he asked.

A fluttering feeling spread out from her stomach. She nodded, not trusting her voice to remain steady.

His fingers settled on her cheek. "You're flushed. There's not some kind of poison in that tree bark, is there?"

She shook her head.

"Would you even tell me if there was? Or would you be more worried about us completing our mission?"

A little spurt of anger burned off some of the dreamy haze he'd given her. "I'm fine. We should go back and get those crystals."

"Did you see them?"

"Inside the black stones. Those pulsing lights? I'm sure those are the crystals we're after."

Torr went back to where the Mason had fallen. He picked up its heavy hammer. "Guess we're going to need this, then."

The tool was huge. The handle was made from some kind of pale pink wood she'd never seen before. The metal head gleamed bright, its intricate carvings flickering with reflected sunlight. There wasn't a scratch or nick anywhere, making her wonder just how hard the metal was. Each of the carvings was perfectly formed, reminding her of the runes carved into the Sentinel Stone in the village. As she watched, a faint blue strand of light snaked across the surface, connecting the runes with tiny shards of lightning.

The muscles in Torr's forearm bulged as he balanced the hammer on his shoulder. The sight shouldn't have done anything to Grace, but she was a mess right now. Weak. She couldn't stop the little spike of desire that sliced through her.

"Do you want to stay here and wait for me?" he asked.

Grace stood and tested the thin layer of cloth bandages he'd tied around her thighs. The fabric held as she walked toward the crater. "What do you think?"

Chapter 18

It had taken every bit of self-control Torr could summon to bandage Grace's wounds. All he'd wanted to do was press her thighs open wide and kiss her all better—kiss her until the last thing on her mind was pain.

Thanks to her dip in the frozen stream and the need to get her warm, he had now solved the mystery of what she wore under that tunic—a thin strip of cloth that wove around her waist and over her sex, covering less than it revealed. One single tug and the whole thing would have unraveled, exposing her to his fingers and his mouth.

For a second, he had been convinced that she would have let him pleasure her. But then he'd questioned her honesty, and all that languid, womanly heat had evaporated from her expression. Her thighs had clamped shut, and he knew he'd lost his chance at heaven.

It was for the best. He tried to remind himself of that. They were exposed out here. She was wounded.

They had a job to do, and every hour they took doing it was one more hour that the women Brenya protected would be in danger.

Taking a break to explore Grace's body would be as selfish as it was foolish. Still, a man could dream.

By the time they reached the rim of the black crater, he'd gotten his libido under control and his head back in the game.

Grace was about to break the plane of the summit when he stopped her. "What are you doing?"

"Going to get the crystals."

"We don't know if enemy reinforcements have arrived. We need to be careful."

She nodded and eased to the ground. She might have been wearing a brave face, but he could tell that her wounds were painful by the way she moved.

As soon as they got back to the village, he was going to demand that Brenya heal her. He didn't know if she operated like the Sanguinar, taking payment in blood for their services, but whatever she required of him, he would pay the price. He couldn't stand letting Grace hurt when there was something he could do to make it stop.

He scanned the area below, watching long enough to satisfy himself that no more enemies had arrived and that the Mason in the crater hadn't yet had time to rebuild itself.

He whispered to Grace, "I'll run down there and bust out some of those crystals. You stay here and keep watch."

"You just want me out of the way."

"That assumes you were ever in the way, and I can assure you that's not true. I couldn't have found this place without you." And while that was true, he wished like hell there had been any other way.

"Fine. I'll keep watch over you. What do you want me to do if I see trouble?"

"Yell a warning and then take off toward the cave we were in last night. I'll meet you there."

She let out a long-suffering sigh. "You don't catch on very fast, do you?"

"What's that supposed to mean?"

She shook her head. "Nothing. Just go do what you need to do. I'll do the same."

The longer they stayed here talking, the more likely it was they would be found. Before that could happen, Torr picked up his pack from where he'd left it and ran down the slope. He found the glossy boulder that seemed to have the easiest crystals to extract, picked up one of the Mason's chisels, and went to work with his hammer.

Cold permeated this whole area, sucking the heat from his skin. He was slamming the hammer down hard, working as fast as he could, but not a single drop of sweat had survived the chill.

The closer he got to the crystals, the more aware he became that the light they gave off had a strange effect on him. It made him feel heavy, almost sluggish. He did the best he could to keep his eyes averted, but when he was only a few inches away from the target, that became nearly impossible.

Finally, he closed his eyes, checking every few blows to make sure he was still on track.

The hammer and chisel broke through the final layer of black rock. In the center was a cluster of pulsing crystals each about the size of one of Grace's slender fingers. They sat in a hollow core, attached by a thin filament of whatever this transparent black rock was.

Torr took out the heavy box that Brenya had sent with them to house the crystals, opened it and set it on the ground. He didn't dare touch the black stone, afraid his fingers would freeze and snap off. Instead, he pulled off the tattered remains of his shirt and folded it until it was several layers thick. A quick twist of his wrist and the thin finger of glasslike rock snapped, freeing the mass of crystals.

He dropped them into the box, closed the lid and bound the thing shut with his shirt so he could carry it safely. The last thing he wanted was to have the box open and get his ass blown off by a pile of rocks.

As he turned to leave, his instincts warned him of danger.

He could see the top of Grace's head along the ridge-line. As he stared, she moved enough that he could tell she was fine. A quick scan of the area revealed no enemies in plain sight.

Still, something was definitely wrong.

Grace stood and pointed, making herself an easy target.

Torr drew his sword and turned to face the threat. Nothing.

He kept scanning the area, searching for what she'd seen.

The wind quieted, and he heard a scratching sound. It was close. Right in front of him.

He took a step back and watched as the sandy remains of the Mason he'd smashed re-formed. As each grain of sand took its place, the surface of the creature hardened into a smooth mass.

It was rebuilding itself, as Brenya had said it would, but he'd never imagined it would be so fast.

If the one at his feet could do that, then so could the one in the forest—the one that was only a few yards away from Grace.

Torr slammed the hammer down on the Mason, crushing its progress. More sand crumbled away, but it was obvious that the destruction was only temporary.

He scooped up as much of the sand as he could carry and sprinted toward Grace. Maybe if he got a piece of the thing far enough away, it would stop the healing process. It was the only thing he could think of without more time.

And with Grace up there, no way was he slowing down to ponder the situation.

He hit the tree line running and flung the sand out as far as he could. His fingers were numb from the cold work he'd done, but he forced them to move enough to grab Grace's hand.

"Run!" he yelled, pulling her into compliance.

"You killed it."

"For now. There's still the other one." As he said the words, he saw a grayish shape lumbering through the trees up ahead.

He veered to the left, heading toward a stream he'd spotted earlier.

Their progress was slow. Grace was trying hard to keep up, but there was only so much she could do.

He fell behind her, urging her to keep going as fast as she could. Her bandages kept snagging on low branches until they were loose enough that they fell around her feet. They tripped her up twice. Finally she stopped long enough to strip them away, then picked up speed again.

By that time, the Mason was right behind them, crashing along in their wake.

"Left!" Torr shouted, hoping she would understand what he meant.

Without hesitating, she banked sharply to her left, heading down a steep slope. She fell and slid halfway down, but regained her feet just in time to splash across the shallow stream.

Torr drew his sword and turned to face the Mason. This was where he would make his stand.

"Keep going," he ordered.

He didn't know if she obeyed, but he no longer had time to find out.

The Mason charged, but Torr was ready. He dodged the first heavy blow that came at him. The Mason had no hammer, but its fist flew past his head so fast that the wind ruffled his hair. He stepped to the side and swung his sword in a complete arc that sliced right through the Mason's thick wrist.

It roared as its hand fell in a sandy pile on the bank of the stream.

Torr's rush of victory lasted less than a second. The Mason's foot slammed into his knee, bending it sideways.

Pain attacked his brain, blinding him for a moment. His body instinctively went on defense, protecting his vital organs while he regained his vision.

As soon as he did, he saw Grace with a thick stick in her hands, closing in.

Like fucking hell.

Torr let his body take over, giving his rage just enough rein to strengthen him. He wasn't as mobile with only one functional leg, but that wasn't going to stop him from killing the thing before it could lay so much as a single grain of sand on Grace.

Each swing of his sword cut away another crumbling section of sand. Defending himself was no longer a priority. It made him reckless but deadly.

Grace drew the stick back like a baseball player at bat.

The Mason saw her and swung its uninjured arm right toward her head.

Torr launched himself at the creature, ignoring the wrenching pain in his knee. His sword struck first, cutting a hole through its chest. His fist tore through the hole, forcing it open enough that the rest of his body could fit through.

The Mason's scream died as it disintegrated into a waterfall of sand over Torr's body.

He landed hard, unable to control his fall with a busted knee. Sand clogged his eyes and filled his mouth. He spat it free and shook his head to rid himself of the rest.

"Are you okay?" she asked.

Frigid rage made his body lock up. Regardless of what he did or said, Grace was determined to put herself in harm's way. Now that he was injured, she was going to be even more likely to believe he couldn't take care of himself.

He couldn't speak right then—at least not about her actions. If he did, if the anger pounding through him broke free, he knew he'd scare her off forever.

"Dump as much sand as you can in the stream. Spread it out."

"Your knee—"

"Will heal," he snapped. *"Move the fucking sand!"*

She ducked her head and hunched her shoulders, looking like a scolded puppy.

Instantly, Torr felt like a dick. No matter what she did, she didn't deserve to hurt. Her whole life had been about suffering, and he wasn't about to be the asshole who added to that burden.

It took a good five minutes of deep breathing before he trusted himself to speak. She was scraping a pile of sand together with her hands when he found the guts to open his mouth. "I'm sorry, Grace. Again. I shouldn't have raised my voice."

"No, you shouldn't have. But you're in pain."

"That's no excuse. Pain doesn't excuse bad behavior."

She looked up at him, surprised. "Most people would say it did."

"They'd be mistaken."

She took a tentative step closer. "How bad is it?"

Something was definitely torn, though he couldn't tell what. His jeans were growing tight over the swelling, and he would bet his sword that the whole knee was already turning black and blue.

He'd managed to straighten his leg so it would heal right, but that was going to take more than just a few minutes. "I'll be fine."

"Yes, you *will* be, but how is the knee now?"

"It's uncomfortable," he admitted. "But at least I can feel it. That's a blessing."

She frowned. "Why would you say that?"

"Because I was paralyzed once. Couldn't feel anything below my neck. I was completely helpless. *That* hurt. This is just pain."

Compassion welled up from her, as natural as breathing. She knelt at his side and put a hand on his shoulder. "What happened? How were you paralyzed?"

"I was attacked by a demon. Poisoned. It destroyed my spinal column."

"But you heal so fast."

"Not from that. No one could help. At least that's what I thought."

"But you're better now, so you must have found some kind of cure."

She was so beautiful—his eyes burned because he refused to blink and miss even a second of looking at her. This was his Grace, the woman he loved. That he would have yelled at her made shame seep into his soul.

"A woman saved me," he told her. He ached to say that she was his savior, but his vow forced his silence.

"You loved her," she whispered, the words part awe, part sadness. "I can see it in your eyes."

He nodded. "Very much. She nearly died saving me. She's the reason it makes me crazy every time you risk your life. I can't lose . . . another woman."

"Where is she now?"

He touched her cheek. Her smooth skin was a warm temptation. "She's moved on. Lived her life."

"Without you," she guessed.

"Exactly."

"Brenya shouldn't have brought you here. She should have let you stay to fight for her."

"If it weren't for Brenya, she'd be dead. For that, I owe the woman everything."

"But she brought you here, tore you away from the one you love."

Torr ached to say that the woman he loved was right here, close enough to touch. Or at the very least, tell her that Brenya had saved his love's life but taken her memories. Surely that would have been enough for Grace to figure out that she was the one he loved.

It was too close to the truth for him to say the words aloud. Even thinking about doing so made his throat clamp shut.

He swallowed to ease the tightness. "We should figure out our next move. I don't want to send you back to the village alone, but I'm in no shape to protect you, and it's only a matter of time before the Masons rebuild themselves again."

"I'm not leaving you here, not when you're too injured to fight. How long do you think it will take for you to be able to walk?"

"It's hard to tell for sure, but at least a few hours. Could be tomorrow before I can hike over rough ground."

Grace surveyed the area. He could see her mind spinning as she assessed their options. Torr waited for her to reach the same conclusion he had—that she needed to go on without him.

"I'll mix up something to help ease the swelling. It will make you sleepy, but when you wake up, we'll make some kind of splint and get you mobile."

"You're not serious. You can't stay out here when I'm not even able to protect you. The moving water may or may not slow down the Mason's healing process, but even if it does, the other one is still out there. It will heal and when it does, it could decide to come after us."

She gave him the same look she might give an errant

child. "I've been protecting myself in these woods since before you came along and I will keep doing so long after you've gone. What I won't do is leave a helpless, wounded man out here as bait for who knows what kind of creatures that might come along."

"Helpless?" He forced himself to one foot, refusing to let her think of him like that. The move made his damaged knee throb, but it also eased his pride. "I'm far from helpless."

"Good," she said, then picked up a sturdy branch from the ground and tossed it at him. "Then carve this into some kind of crutch you can use."

Torr caught the branch and nearly fell over when his balance went askew.

"Sit down. Elevate your leg. I'll be back in a few minutes."

"You sound like Brenya."

She beamed. "Thank you."

"I didn't mean it as a compliment."

She came to his side and grabbed his arm. "Then you should have chosen your words better. Now sit down."

He wasn't quite sure how she'd managed it, but he found himself on his ass, his leg elevated on the trunk of a fallen tree.

"I'll be quick. Call out if you need me."

He stared after her, trying to figure out what had just happened. His sweet, quiet Grace had just stepped up, completely taking over the situation. Just like he would have expected any female Theronai to do.

She'd always been insistent when she thought his safety was at stake, but there was something different about it this time. More confidence, more assertiveness. Her time here had changed her, and while it was going to make his life more difficult, he couldn't help but enjoy it. Bossy or not, Grace had grown a stronger backbone. And it was sexy as hell.

She came back with her hands full of purple leaves, spindly roots and what looked like pale gray bark shavings. She shoved the ingredients into one of the water skins and gave it a good shake.

"Drink it all," she ordered, handing it to him. "It's going to taste like the bottom of a dirty foot, but you will drink it."

With an order like that, what could he say but "Yes, ma'am."

Torr drank. It tasted worse than she'd described, but he was blissfully distracted by the sight of Grace moving around the area, clearing space for a fire. The smooth efficiency of her efforts proved she'd done this before.

"Do you spend a lot of time in the woods?" he asked.

"I used to. Some of the women and I would go foraging for berries and herbs. It's been too dangerous to do it lately."

She pulled a small stone from a pouch and set it on a pile of dried grass, like an egg in a nest. With the end of a stick, she bashed the rock, and it exploded in a tiny ball of fire. After a few seconds, the fire grew to consume the smaller twigs she'd laid out. In no time, there was a tidy fire crackling away safely inside a ring of damp stones.

"How's the knee?" she asked.

"Better," he said, amazed by how well her concoction had worked. The deep, hot throbbing he'd felt before had faded. There was still pain, but it was a distant thing he had no trouble ignoring.

"You sound surprised."

"Guess I am. Where I'm from, the healing is mostly done by the Sanguinar, and they always want to drink blood as payment."

Her lip curled in disgust. "Eww. And here I was thinking it was time to eat."

A swooping wave of dizziness spun his head around. "What was in that stuff?"

"Plants. Brenya taught me what to look for as soon as I was able to walk." She smiled. "She said she wasn't about to let me sit around and be a burden."

"And remembering that makes you grin?"

"I *was* a burden. It took her ten times longer to do everything because she had to drag me around with her. Even longer to teach me what she knew. I was so slow, so weak. She never once lost patience, though. The fact that she said she wouldn't let me be a burden made me feel like I wasn't one."

That crazy spinning sped up, and his eyelids got too heavy to hold open. "You could never be a burden to anyone, Grace."

"There's no possible way you could know that, but you're sweet to say it, anyway."

The water skin left his hand. He could smell her scent and knew she was nearby.

His words were a slurred mess. "You're going to remember who you are soon. Remember everything." *Remember me.*

"Some things are best left forgotten, Torr. You need to learn to accept that. I have."

It wasn't fair to lie to a man who was too intoxicated to think straight, but it was for the best.

She wasn't completely sure how long Torr would sleep, so she went to work right away. A few careful slices through the leg of his pants, and his swollen knee was free. The fabric had been so tight it had left impressions in his skin. Deep bruises colored his knee and ran halfway down his shin, but they were already the color of days-old wounds.

As she watched, she swore she could see the sickly colors fading.

Careful not to hurt him, she probed the area, searching for signs of broken bones. The feel of his skin under her fingertips distracted her, and she had to start over and force herself to pay attention.

He loved another woman, and because of that, she shouldn't have let herself feel anything for him at all, not even some girlish distraction.

She still couldn't believe she'd kissed him. Even more surprising was that he'd almost kissed her back. If not for the spike of pain the disk had given her, chances were he'd have done a lot more than just kiss her.

And she would have let him.

She felt guilty enough that she'd kissed a man who loved another woman. If she'd had sex with him, she probably wouldn't have been able to live with herself.

Whoever the woman was, she was an idiot not to hold on to Torr with both hands and never let him go. He was an amazing combination of sweet and fierce, ruthless and gentle. His anger had scared her, but she believed him when he said he would never hurt her.

Maybe that made her as much of a fool as her mother had been to believe her stepfather.

For the thousandth time since having that single memory restored, Grace wondered where her family was. If they were still alive. If they were searching for her.

If she proved herself to Torr, maybe he'd take her back to Earth, where she could have at least a chance of finding them.

She knew how bad things were there. How dangerous Earth was. Synestryn demons roamed free, hunting for even the slightest drop of Athanasian blood and the magic it carried. Brenya had told her that she had some of that running in her veins. Somewhere on Grace's family tree there'd been an Athanasian ancestor. That made her vulnerable to attack.

While part of Grace wanted to stay here in the world she knew and understood, she still ached to go home. Yearned to make a life for herself with her own kind.

Torr was the key to that.

If she could convince him that she wasn't weak, that

he didn't have to protect her from the Synestryn, that she wouldn't be a burden to him, then maybe he would take her home.

She watched the firelight flicker over his body. He was shirtless again, giving her eyes a visual feast. The silvery necklace he wore danced with swirling patterns of light and color. Each breath expanded his ribs and drew her attention to his lifemark and the intriguing masculine planes of his body.

The desire to touch him was overwhelming. The only thing holding her back was respect for him and his love for the lucky woman. Even if she was out of reach to him, he still cared deeply for her. And while Torr had been obvious in his attraction to Grace, she refused to be a substitute for the woman he truly wanted.

Down that path lay her destruction.

It was better to keep her hands to herself, guard her heart, and hope that there were more men like Torr out there.

Sadly, if there weren't, she was sure she'd end up alone, because from this point on, she knew she would compare all other men to him. And chances were that when she did, they'd come up lacking.

He shifted in his sleep, letting out a low moan of pain. The sound wrapped around her, bringing with it a memory of the smell of antiseptic and the hum of machines. Those echoes of memories faded fast, leaving her wondering what had triggered them.

His pain called to her on a level so deep she couldn't

deny it. She knelt by his side, taking his hand in hers. She wished there was more she could do to ease him, but she'd done everything she could. All that was left to her now was watching over him while he slept and healed.

For a moment, she allowed herself to wonder what it would be like to have Brenya's power to heal. She knew the act wasn't fun—that it took its toll—but she didn't care. Power like that was worth the cost. Being strong enough to help people would go a long way toward making up for her physical weakness.

She gently laid her hand on Torr's knee. Her fingers tightened. Heat spun up her arm, curling through her body until it dissipated as it flowed into the metal disk on her back.

As she stood to take her place guarding his sleep, her own knee began to ache as if she'd been kneeling on a rock.

She tried to walk off the pain, but a slow trip around the perimeter of their tiny camp did no good.

Grace limped to the bag where Torr had put the box holding the crystals. Frost covered the leather surface. She pulled out the box, wincing at the icy chill that seeped out from the container wrapped in his shirt. She used that shirt to tie the box to her knee and let the cold help ease her pain.

She would be better soon. She had to be. He needed her to protect him while he slept so that he could protect her village and everyone she loved once he woke.

She kept a constant watch for Masons and Hunters,

listening for any sign of their approach. She heard nothing.

The chill against her knee began permeating her blood as the air cooled and the sky darkened.

She scooted closer to the fire.

The movement woke Torr. His eyes opened, blinking away the haze of drug-induced sleep.

He should have slept much longer, but maybe he'd thrown off the effects of the anti-inflammatory potion as fast as he healed.

Grace shifted her body to hide her knee and quickly untied the box. She didn't want him to worry.

He was at her side, looming over her just as she opened the lid.

Blue light pulsed out, instantly slowing her heart to match its pace.

"What are you doing with that?" he asked.

"Just looking at them." The lie felt like acid on her tongue, but it was better than admitting her weakness.

"They're dangerous. They need to stay cold. That's why Brenya gave us the box."

She shut the lid and tied his tattered shirt back in place to hold it closed. She handed him the box to keep from having to get up and put it away in his bag. "Are you feeling better?"

"Yes. My knee seems fine. I thought it would take longer to heal than that. Your dirty-foot potion packs a wallop, but it worked wonders." He tucked the box back where it belonged.

"Glad to help."

"I'd say we should get moving, but it's probably too dangerous for you to walk through the woods at night."

She wanted to snap at him, telling him she would manage, but he'd just handed her the perfect excuse to stay here, off her sore knee. "Probably smart not to risk it."

He gave her a funny look, like he was expecting her to say something else. "What? No argument? Are you sick?"

"Of course not. You are capable of having good ideas, aren't you?"

"I always thought so. I just wasn't sure you did."

If he prodded more, he might figure out what was going on. Before that could happen, she needed to distract him. "I'm going to sleep for a while. Wake me when you're ready to go?"

"Sure. Okay. Whatever you want."

"Just sleep."

She rolled over, facing away from the fire and the light it put off. A moment later, Torr's big feet filled her vision.

He crouched next to her. "I will figure out what you're hiding."

"I'm not hiding anything."

"You are, but that's okay. It'll give me something to puzzle over while you sleep."

"Really, Torr. I'm just tired. It's been a crazy day."

He gave a slow nod that wasn't at all reassuring. "Sleep, then. I'm sure I'll figure it out by the time you wake up. Then we'll talk."

Grace closed her eyes before they could give her away and prayed there'd be nothing to talk about by morning.

Chapter 19

Tori paced, waiting for Brenya to free her from her punishment.

Cutting Torr wasn't right. She knew that. But this—this torture was more than she deserved. If she'd known she was going to end up here, she would have cut him deeper.

She covered her ears, trying to ignore the pitiful screams. She knew that it wouldn't take much to make the noise stop, but her vow to Brenya stayed her hand.

She couldn't kill it. Not today.

Finally, when she could take no more of the noise, she stalked over to the wooden box and looked inside.

The baby was red-faced, its chin wobbling with its misery. Each long scream ended in a breathless vibration that set Tori's teeth on edge.

Willing to do anything to make the noise stop, she picked up the wailing child and held it at arm's length.

The smell of piss sharpened the air. It was wet.

A stack of clean, soft cloths sat waiting to be used.

Tori had never changed a diaper before, but if it would get the child to shut the hell up, she'd figure it out.

She set the baby on the bed, pinning it there with one hand while she reached for what she needed. The screaming went on, drilling its way into her ears. All she could think about was the way the children locked in those caves with her had screamed while they were being hurt.

The sour taste of bile rose in the back of her throat. She swallowed it down and stripped the squalling infant naked. The clean cloth went on the way the dirty one had come off, and in a few seconds Tori had managed the task.

She held the baby against her chest to check the back of her work, and instantly the screaming stopped.

Blissful silence filled the nursery and gave Tori some space to breathe.

She set the baby back in her box, and the screaming started again.

Tori's skin crawled up her neck, trying to work its way into her ears to block the noise. She was desperate enough that she even put the baby back against her chest, hoping it would quiet again.

It did, which was more than a small miracle.

Tori went to the door where her captor stood guard—one of Brenya's soldiers, who was willing to obey any order given.

She pushed the door open enough to say, "The baby is quiet. I'm ready to come out now."

"Is she asleep?" asked the guard.

"No."

"Then you're not done yet." The guard shut the door.

Tori looked down at her punishment. "Sleep," she ordered.

The tiny thing blinked, but that was all.

Tori could make it sleep. Cover its nose and mouth. Just long enough to get it to close its eyes.

She moved her hand to do just that, but found herself frozen, unable to complete the motion.

"Stupid fucking vow," she snarled. "What the hell am I supposed to do with you now?"

The baby blinked again.

It was kind of pretty for a screaming, bald creature. Long black lashes swept out from its eyes, wet from its crying fit. Its irises were the palest green, like newly sprouted plants on Earth. If Tori looked hard enough, she could see the slightest bit of motion in them—a kind of lazy swirling of silver and green that gave away the child's heritage.

Tori didn't know what color her baby's eyes had been before it died. She hadn't bothered to look.

A surge of rage swelled beneath her skin. Her hold on the child tightened. But instead of screaming in pain and dragging Tori's guard in here, the child yawned.

She hadn't hurt it. Her vow had kept it safe.

Tori backed up to the only chair in the hut and sat. The chair rocked beneath her, reminding her of a time when she'd rocked her dolls to sleep as a child. She'd been a real girl then, not the empty, pitiful thing she was now.

Whatever she was, the baby didn't seem to mind. It just stared up at her as she cradled it in one arm and began rocking.

The slow, rhythmic motion had a calming effect. After a few minutes, the rage she lived with every day trickled away, leaving an odd blank feeling.

If she hadn't known better, she would have thought it was peace.

Tori leaned her head back and kept rocking. She had no idea how much time had passed when she finally looked down.

The baby was asleep. Tori was freed from her punishment. All she had to do now was stand up and set the child in its box.

Why, then, didn't she get up? Why was she still sitting here when there was hunting to do? Killing was more fun than this torture.

Wasn't it?

She wasn't sure anymore. All she knew was that there was a kind of quiet inside her for the first time in years. Even the screaming in her head was silent, and that had been part of her for so long that she hadn't even realized it was there until now.

Maybe hunting could wait. There were always going to be things for her to kill. This precious silence was going to end soon. Then it would be just her and the tortured screams in her skull.

*   *   *

It had been a long time since Torr had practiced with any weapons other than his sword, but he went through the motions of fighting with a war hammer, repeating drills from his youth. His technique was a bit rusty, but the knowledge was still there. With each swing, his body flowed more easily, settling into a familiar rhythm.

When the time came, he would be ready to face the Warden.

Dawn spread through the sky, turning it from black to crimson. The animals of the forest began to quiet, and the scent of dew-damp leaves filled the air.

Grace lay sleeping on the far side of the dead fire. As soon as he'd sensed she'd fallen asleep, he put it out so as not to attract company.

She'd barely shifted through the night, but every time she did, she let out small pain-filled sounds that tore at his heart.

She wasn't meant for this life. She deserved to be safe, surrounded by soft, beautiful things that made her happy.

Once again he was reminded of just how wrong he was for her—how far apart their worlds really were.

He didn't know how to let her go.

She opened her eyes and looked at him. His whole body reacted to her gaze. A slight shiver of pleasure raced across his skin, and a sizzle of excitement coursed along his spine, vibrating the carved disk as it passed. He wanted to slide in beside her and take her in his arms, while at the same time he felt the need to push her away for her own safety.

"Sleep well?" he asked.

She stretched and yawned. The move thrust her breasts toward him in a completely innocent, completely intoxicating way. The urge to peel that tunic down and suckle her nipples was strong enough to make his legs shake.

"I did. Did you get any rest?"

"I don't need much."

"Must be nice." She sat up and ran her fingers through her tousled hair. She looked like he imagined she would after a long night of marathon sex. The image had his cock swelling with painful speed.

When he spoke, his voice was thick with lust he couldn't control. "It's time to head back to the village as soon as you can see well enough to travel."

"What about the crystals?"

"I'll use them after I drop you off," said Torr.

"What are you going to do with them?"

"Close the portal."

"You don't even know where it is."

"I'll find it."

"How?"

"I'll follow the Masons. They were sent here to build it. My guess is that they will only spend as much time as they must building Hunters. Once they think they have enough to protect them and their work, they'll go back to their primary task."

"Do you think they're going to open a doorway to Earth?"

"Maybe. It could open to Athanasia, but I promise you that wherever it leads, there are all kinds of nasty things we don't want coming here. Brenya controls the Sentinel Stone in the village, but she won't have any control over what flows through this one."

"Once we destroy the portal, what's to stop the Solarc from sending another group?"

"Brenya seems to think that if she has no direct hand in destroying them, the Solarc will assume she's not here."

"Because if she was here, she'd fight back."

"Exactly."

"I don't like it," said Grace.

"Neither do I, but I tend to believe that Brenya knows what she's doing. If she thinks this is our best shot, then that's my plan."

"I want to help."

"I know, but the way you do that best is by staying out of danger. If I'm worried about you, I can't think straight."

She looked at the forest floor, frowning. "That's the way I feel, too." When her gaze lifted, it was blazing with determination. "Which is why I'm going with you to follow the Masons. I know you think I'm weak, but I can help. I *will* help, Torr."

"I don't think you're weak, but there are some jobs that you're not suited to. Battle is one of them."

"The lives of everyone I love are in danger. You can't ask me to just sit around and hope for the best."

"And you can't ask me to put you in harm's way."

"What if you get injured? Or worse? How will Brenya even know she needs to summon reinforcements?"

Torr decided it was best not to tell her that he didn't think Brenya still had enough juice to summon anyone. "I'm sure she has her ways."

"She's weak, Torr—stretched too thin from keeping the village protected."

"And she's probably worried sick about you right now. That's not going to help her recover her strength."

Grace got right up in his face and poked her finger against his chest. Her expression was fierce, reminding him of the battle maidens from his youth who helped slaughter entire armies through sheer force of will. "These are my people. I'm helping, with or without your permission. You can either let me work with you, or I'll figure out a way to be helpful on my own—even if it means drawing the Hunters away from the village by crashing through the woods so I'm easy to find."

She'd do it, too. Torr could see she wasn't bluffing.

"I should tie you to a tree."

"Maybe. But you won't. You vowed to protect humans, which means you'd be too worried about what might happen to me if one of those Hunters came slicing through it."

"My vow also means taking you back to the village, where you'll be safe."

"But I won't be safe there, because I won't stay there. And you can't make me stay if you're not there with me. Even Brenya couldn't make me stay. That means the safest place for me is by your side." She cocked her head and smiled. "How's that working for your vow?"

"Not well at all," he said between clenched teeth. "You're not playing fair."

"No, I guess I'm not. I'd tell you I feel bad about manipulating you, but that would be a lie."

"So you won't lie, but you will manipulate."

"To save your life? Absolutely."

"You clearly have little faith in me if you think I can't handle this on my own."

"Actually, I'm sure you can handle it. But things go wrong. People get hurt. Remember your injured knee? I don't want one little mistake being the difference between my entire village surviving or not. At least if I'm here with you, I can run away and warn the others that danger is on the way."

She wasn't going to budge. He'd seen this exact look on her face before, and while she was the sweetest, most selfless person he'd ever met, she also never let anyone get in the way of her doing what she thought was right.

Obviously she thought putting herself in danger was right.

"Will you do exactly what I say when I say it?" he asked.

"Probably not."

Not the answer he thought he'd get. "What?"

"I've already played this game with Brenya enough times to know how it goes. First you get me to agree to something. Then you convince me to make some vague promise that seems harmless. Once you've got that, then you tell me to do something I don't want to do and I'm forced to comply. I've scrubbed enough pots to have learned my lesson."

"What lesson is that?"

"Don't make promises to those more powerful than I am."

He wanted to throttle her, or better yet, toss her over his shoulder and carry her back to the village, where he *would* tie her to a tree.

"You might as well accept defeat," she said. "You can't force me to do what you want without hurting me, which I know you won't do."

She was right, and while her trust that he wouldn't hurt her was humbling, the fact that she knew his limits left him in a weakened position.

"You *will* do what I say," he warned.

She smiled sweetly. "Anything is possible."

Grace waited until Torr's back was turned before she dropped her smile.

Her knee was killing her. She'd done her best to cover it up, but she knew she wasn't going to be able to hide her pain for much longer.

They packed up camp, and she waved for Torr to lead the way back to the stream where they'd temporarily killed the Mason. If he was in front of her, she didn't have to hide how hard it was for her to keep up.

Each step shoved a bolt of lightning up her spine, but she managed to keep up with the pace he set. When he finally stopped by the edge of the stream, she was sweating and shaking from the pain.

Something about his posture tipped her off to danger. He was too still.

"What's wrong?" she asked.

"The Mason is gone. I don't see even a single grain of sand."

"We could go see if they're back in that crater, making more Hunters."

He turned and looked her up and down. "How are the cuts on your thighs?"

Okay. So he could see she was in pain, but hadn't guessed why. She could work with that. At least he didn't know she had yet another injury.

"They're sore, but I'm okay. I can keep going."

His mouth twisted a bit as if he were holding back a curse. "I'm going to help you into a tree. Then I'm going to run over to the crater and check things out. You will stay where I put you, or so help me God, I will find a way to convince the biggest, strongest woman in the village to sit on you and hold you hostage."

Because her knee hurt too much to argue, she didn't. "Fine. I'll stay, but if you don't come back fast, I'll assume something went wrong and come find you."

"Agreed," he said. "I'll be back within an hour."

Torr helped her climb a thick tree. The dense canopy of metallic blue leaves hid her position well.

He loped off and was back inside of fifteen minutes. His expression was grim.

"What?" she asked.

"I was too late. The Masons are gone, and I have no idea which way they went."

Chapter 20

Brenya greeted Torr by grabbing his ear and dragging him into her hut.

"Nice to see you, too," he told her between gritted teeth.

The older woman's tone was crisp and frosty. "You were gone too long. I worried."

He stepped back, nearly ripping his ear off to get her to let go. "I'm sorry about that. We ran into trouble."

"Of course you did. Why else would I have need to send you if not to deal with trouble?"

"We got slowed down a couple of times. First there was Grace's near hypothermia to deal with, then my busted knee. And both Grace and I felt it necessary to stop and warn the women in the southern village about the danger the Hunters pose. We did the best we could. Just be glad we made it back in one piece."

"One piece? Grace was limping."

"I noticed that, too. She tried to hide it, so I played

along. She's got it in her head that she's weak, and I didn't think it would be nice to make her feel that way."

Brenya's mouth tightened with her scowl. "Foolish games. I sent her with you so that she would learn to trust you. How can she do so when I am no longer certain you are worthy?"

"Wait just a minute. What the hell is that supposed to mean?"

"Did you ask her to heal you?"

"No. You know Grace. She just decided to do that on her own. I couldn't have stopped her from making that nasty concoction if I'd tried."

"Concoction?"

"Yeah. The knockout juice she forced me to drink—the one she said you taught her how to make."

Brenya's anger faded between one second and the next. She seemed to deflate, growing shorter and older in an instant. "You did not ask her to use the disks to heal your injuries?"

"Hell, no. I'd never do that. I didn't even know it was possible."

"It is. As long as she is connected to you, she can choose to take on your ailments. I had hoped it would take her longer to learn the trick."

Suddenly the pieces clicked together in Torr's head. "You're telling me that the reason Grace is limping is because she healed my knee?"

"Yes. That is the way the device works. She takes the injury upon herself."

"But what about the other times I've been wounded? She wasn't hurt then."

"Healing must be a conscious choice. Once that choice is made, it cannot be stopped. And the more she comes to care for you, the easier it will be for her to activate the disks' magic."

Torr could see Grace now, sitting beside him, wishing she could do more to ease his pain. "Fuck," he spat, furious that he hadn't seen this coming. "What do we do now?"

"Hope she does not already understand what she has done. Hope she remains ignorant long enough for you to rid Temprocia of the Solarc's minions and get her settled in her rightful home."

"She's smart, Brenya. She's going to figure it out fast."

"Then I suggest you try harder to limit your injuries. Your body can withstand much more abuse than hers. If she decides to heal the wrong wound . . ."

He held up his hand to keep her from saying any more. "Believe me, I know."

Grace wasn't going to stop. As soon as she figured out what she could do for him, she would do it. Over and over until it was too late. He'd lose her, all because she had no sense of self-preservation.

"I see you understand the situation clearly," said Brenya. "We have the crystals now. All that is left is for you to discover where the portal is being constructed, wait for its completion, then destroy it. There is a place you must go. A lake miles from here."

"Can you handle things here if I leave?"

"I will do what I must, as I always have." Her expression changed in an instant, going from weary acceptance to fear. "My defenses faltered. I was not exerting enough energy. You must go to the western perimeter. Now!"

"Why?" Torr asked.

A child's scream of fear tore through the air and he no longer needed an answer.

His response to the sound was both primal and immediate. He burst through the hut door, racing toward that terrified sound—one he'd heard too many times before to mistake it for anything else.

As he cleared the Sentinel Stone, he saw a woman's body lying on the ground in a pool of her own blood. Nearby stood the little girl with the white-blond hair who'd nearly been eaten by the lizard when he'd arrived. She was staring at the gory sight, screaming and immobile.

A few feet away from her was a sleek stone Hunter. One of its eyes rotated until it was looking at Torr. The moment it saw him, it charged the little girl, still wearing the blood of its first kill.

One second Grace was getting a drink from the well, the next she was standing in Brenya's hut, dripping ladle in hand. The flash of light from the portal was still blinding her when the other woman grabbed her arm.

"I cannot be seen by the Hunter," she told Grace. "I will take the others to the southern village. You must not let the invaders find us there. Keep them busy."

"How?"

Outside, the screams of fear mingled discordantly with those of battle. Of all of them, Tori's high, ferocious cries were the loudest and easiest to recognize.

Dry fingers settled on Grace's brow just as her vision was beginning to clear. Instantly, all of her aches and pains vanished.

"This is all I can teach you," said Brenya. "There is no more time."

Pressure built behind Grace's eyes until she was sure they would soon pop out of her head. As fast as the sensation came, it passed, leaving her dizzy and disoriented. "What was that?"

"Knowledge. It will unveil itself as you need it. I am sorry. I had hoped to spare you this."

"Spare me what? I don't understand."

"I know, child. But you will. Too soon." She picked up the box of crystals Torr had collected. "Come for these if you live. I will protect them until the time is right."

Before Grace could ask more questions, Brenya disappeared in a flash of light.

All the screams outside suddenly stopped.

Panic tore through Grace, shoving her forward on numb feet. She flew past the door so fast some of the sticks it was made of broke. She was sure that everyone outside would be dead—killed by whatever had attacked.

Instead, she saw no one but Torr and one of the Athanasian women who had only recently come here to have her child. She had been so horribly slain that her body was nearly unrecognizable. Everyone else had vanished.

Brenya. She'd done this. That's what she'd meant by taking everyone to the southern village. She'd teleported them there, leaving only Grace and Torr behind.

But why?

As soon as her thoughts touched on the question, the answer blazed in her mind in vivid detail.

The Hunter had killed one of the Athanasian women—one of the Solarc's daughters. The Hunter would report this kill back to the Masons, who would then report back to the Warden, who would report to the Solarc. If this Hunter didn't die, then the Solarc would know his daughters were sneaking through the gate. By nightfall, this whole world would be invaded with a force so powerful that even Brenya's magic wouldn't be able to hold them at bay.

"You have to kill it," she yelled at Torr.

His muscles bunched with the effort of combat. "Working on it."

The Hunter began to back away toward the tree line. If it got much farther, it could disappear into the woods and they'd lose it.

Grace couldn't let that happen.

She grabbed the closest weapon she could find—the ax used for splitting firewood. She'd spent enough hours with this tool in her hands for it to feel comfortable there. And while she knew that she was no match for the Hunter, she could at least keep its attention.

She sprinted toward the creature, weapon raised, screaming like a crazy person. One of its eyes swiveled toward her.

"Stay back!" ordered Torr, but she ignored him.

Getting close enough to the thing for it to slice her in half wasn't an option, but that wasn't her plan. All she had to do was get a little closer.

From the corner of her eye, she saw Torr's body speed as he launched a series of graceful blows. She didn't dare look at him directly. She couldn't afford the distraction.

Her lungs were burning by the time she got close enough to hurl the ax at the side of the Hunter. It provided a huge, flat target that even she couldn't miss at this distance.

The hard head of the ax slammed into the top edge of the Hunter, knocking it off balance. Small chips of black rock rained down from where she'd hit it, freezing the ground wherever they touched. It regained its footing and turned to face her and charge. Torr was faster and shattered it with one brutal blow from the Mason's hammer.

Red gashes opened in his skin wherever the shards struck him. He scanned the area, searching for more enemies. His chest moved heavily with each breath, and the expression on his face was terrifying enough to have Grace backing away.

"Stay where I can see you," he snapped.

She clamped down on the urge to run, though she wasn't sure if it was because she wanted to ease his worry or because she didn't want to provoke him into chasing her.

That was one footrace she knew she couldn't win.

When he was satisfied that there were no more Hunters here, he turned to her. He was furious. His face was red, his amber eyes practically bulging with the force of his anger.

He took one long step forward.

Now she wished she'd run.

She stumbled back and tried to pull in a breath despite her hammering pulse. The cold air caught in her throat. She couldn't scream, couldn't breathe.

She'd felt this way before, and as that knowledge came to her, so did the memory.

Her home had been invaded by demons. She and her step-brother were desperately trying to stay quiet. He had a golf club in his hands, his young, scrawny body quivering with fear. She held the pistol her stepfather had kept in his sock drawer.

He didn't need it anymore. He was dead in the living room, demons feasting on his flesh.

It was better than he deserved.

She still couldn't believe what she'd seen, still couldn't find a place in her mind for those creatures to fit. They were too twisted and scary to be real.

As terrifying as they were, what really frightened her was the comatose body of her mom, lying helpless in the back room, surrounded by the machines and tubes that kept her alive. Once the demons were finished with her stepfather and came searching for more food, the only thing standing be-

*tween them and Grace's mom was her, her baby brother, a
shaky golf club, and an even shakier gun.*

*The door to the back room flew open. The demon was
huge, with rows of yellow teeth coated in red blood. That, and
the eyes. Glowing, sickly green.*

*She stepped in front of Blake and fired. Each bullet pushed
the monster back a few inches and made it more furious.*

The gun clicked. Empty.

*Blake's squeaky scream of rage bellowed out of him as he
charged. Grace grabbed him around the middle and flung
him back onto Mom.*

*A loud crash sounded in the living room. Low male grunts
and the wet slap of severed flesh hitting the hardwood floor.*

The demon charged.

Grace blinked, shocked to realize that she was in her
little village, standing only a few feet away from the
tiny hut she called home.

But this wasn't her home. It wasn't even her world.

Torr stood in front of her, holding her shoulders as if
he feared she'd topple over. Concern lined his face and
made his amber eyes burn bright. "Breathe, honey."

She wasn't sure what he meant until she felt the
burning in her lungs. She'd been holding her breath
against the terror of her memory.

She forced her mouth open, forced air into her lungs.
It was a strange mix of summer warmth with swirling
tendrils of cold from the Hunter's presence.

He slipped her hair behind her ear and tipped her
chin up to look at him. "Better?"

She nodded. Swallowed.

Mom. She'd been so helpless. Had the monsters gotten to her? Had they reached Blake?

"I think my whole family is dead," she whispered.

A shocked pause passed. "You had another memory?"

"Yeah. Demons broke into our house. Ate Jerry. Blake and I were protecting Mom." She had to force another breath. "I don't know if they survived."

His expression went blank. He let her go and stepped away to where the Sentinel Stone had stood only moments before. A shallow depression was left in the dirt. Small insects scrambled for cover from the suns.

Brenya had taken that, too.

Torr scanned the forest, making it impossible for her to see his face. "I'm sure they're fine," he said.

Facing her worry was somehow harder without his touch. It made her feel completely alone. Weak. "You don't know that."

"You should try to stay positive. Things here are tough enough without you borrowing trouble."

"I just wish I knew the truth."

"Maybe you will," he said, his voice oddly flat. "Maybe one day you'll remember everything."

"Every memory I have is crappy. You'd think there'd be at least a couple of good ones in there, too."

He looked at her then, finally shedding whatever chill had come over him. There was blatant need on his face, so stark it was almost desperation. "I hope so, Grace."

She had no idea what to make of his odd behavior.

Maybe all Theronai were like him, running hot and cold after a battle. She couldn't be sure. The only other one she'd met was Tori, who was always burning hot, her every action fueled by rage.

Torr made a full circle of the area before he came back to where she waited, trying to pull herself together. "I saw the light when everyone vanished. Brenya?"

"Yes. She said she was taking everyone to the southern village."

"She didn't take everyone. You're still here."

"She wanted me to tell you that she has the crystals and that we should come get them when the time is right."

"I would have figured that out on my own without her using you as a messenger."

Grace refused to let his curt tone insult her. She'd helped him in that fight, and nothing he could say would change that. "That's not the only reason she left me behind. She gave me information."

"What information?"

Knowledge about the Hunter and its connection to the Solarc had come to her suddenly, as she'd needed it. Just like Brenya had said.

While that little piece of the puzzle was now in place, Grace could feel more of them, still hidden in her mind. They were there—their weight was easily recognizable—but she couldn't reach them at will. Like all the bits of memory she'd recovered, the knowledge would come to her when it came, and there wasn't a thing she could do to speed up that process.

Rather than telling him she didn't know what the information was, she lifted her chin. "I'll tell you when you need to know."

He stalked up to her, his jaw set in a way that made her want to turn and run. Only the certain knowledge that he wasn't going to hurt her made her hold her ground.

"You'll tell me now," he ordered.

"Nope."

His big hand circled her throat. The touch was firm but careful. His fingers were so long they reached all the way around to her nape, where the heat from each fingertip branded her. His thumb grazed across her pulse, making an army of tingles march down her spine.

He stared at her mouth for just a moment too long—long enough to make her think about kissing him again—then looked into her eyes. "I can make you tell me, Grace." It was a threat, but not to inflict pain. This threat was much more deadly, his gaze and touch promising her something far more potent than pain.

Pleasure.

Her voice shook when she spoke, and she knew he could feel that weakness vibrate against his palm. "You can try. I'm sure I'd enjoy your effort. But everyone is counting on you to drive back the invasion."

He was quiet for a long time, his only movement the steady rise and fall of his chest. She wondered if she should step back, away from his touch, but she liked the feel of his hand on her skin too much to move. Even angry and covered in cuts from battle, he still possessed a mesmerizing kind of beauty that made it hard to look away.

"Apparently they're counting on *us*," he said. "Whatever information Brenya gave you, it has some purpose."

Grace nodded. "I've never known her to do anything without at least three reasons."

"And she probably never tells you any of them when you ask."

"Now you're catching on."

He closed his eyes and let out a long breath. Then he nodded to himself, as if he'd made some difficult decision. "First we bury the dead. Then I'll take you as far as the southern village. If Brenya isn't willing to answer our questions, then we won't cooperate with her until she does."

"Everyone does what Brenya wants. That's just the way the world works."

"Well, I'm from a different world. She needs me. It's time she starts acting like it."

Grace stifled a groan. His plan could end only one way: badly.

Chapter 21

Torr gave Grace a list of things to collect from the village while he dug the grave for the Athanasian woman.

It didn't seem right to bury her so far away from her home and family, but it was the best he could do for now. Maybe Brenya would be able to send her home, but even if she did, chances were it would bring up questions better left unasked.

He felt Grace approach a moment before she spoke from behind him. Her presence burned through him like a brush fire, destroying all other thoughts. Even the bad ones.

There was a kind of quiet magic in her that he'd never encountered in anyone else. She gave him peace in a life that had been filled with far too much war.

"I like the spot you picked," she said. "It's pretty here."

The small clearing just inside the tree line had a thick carpet of ground cover the color of sapphires. It was far enough away from the village not to risk contamination of their well water, but still within sight of where the Sentinel Stone had recently stood. A canopy of shimmering leaves shaded the area, and the rest of the forest gave it a sense of privacy.

"I thought so, too. Do you think she'd approve?"

"I didn't really know her, but I'm sure she would."

"You didn't know her?"

"She just arrived through the stone this morning. I would have gotten to know her over the next few months, while she carried her child to term."

"She was pregnant?"

Grace nodded. "The women who come here almost always are."

Torr grieved for both the lives lost here today, but didn't allow himself to linger or wallow in it. There was too much to do, too many more lives at stake. "Did you get what I asked for?"

"I got the food and water, along with a few medical supplies." Her gaze fixed on his chest, and the blood and dirt covering him. "You should let me use a few of them on you. Some of those cuts are deep."

As he watched, a hairline cut opened along her arm, in the exact spot where he was injured.

She was healing him again without even trying. He didn't dare call her attention to it for fear that she would realize that they were connected by the healing disks and start asking questions. Worse yet, she might start using the power purposefully. So far, her accidental healing of him had been minimal. That could change at any moment.

"I've had worse. They'll heal fast," he said casually, hoping she'd forget all about his wounds. "What about weapons? Did you find any?"

"I searched Brenya's hut. There were no more crystals or anything that looked like a weapon. Mostly just books, jars and bottles. All unlabeled."

"I was sure she'd have some kind of stash in there."

"If so, it's hidden. There were a few spears in the practice area and a couple of swords that Tori uses."

"Not exactly the magical artifacts I was hoping for."

"Do you want to search it yourself?" she asked.

"No time. We have to find the location the Masons are using to build the portal before it opens and we're screwed."

As soon as he said the words, Grace went pale and got a distant stare like the one she'd had right before telling him she thought her family was dead.

It had taken all his willpower not to tell her the truth. Blake was still alive. She still had a brother who loved her and missed her. Her mom hadn't survived the Synestryn attack, but Torr had managed to save both her and her brother that night.

The night he was paralyzed.

Dark, furious emotions seethed just below the surface. He couldn't think about that time now—not when there were so many people who needed him to be at the top of his game.

Torr reached for Grace, both to comfort her and to soothe himself. There was magic in her skin, and he wasn't above using physical contact to stay strong and steady for her.

"What is it?" he asked.

She gave a tiny shake of her head. "Nothing. We should get going, though."

"That wasn't nothing. Tell me."

"You said yourself there's no time. Let's just do what we need to do and get moving. East."

"East? You sound sure. Did Brenya tell you?"

"Let's talk about it later. I'll go back and search her hut again for hidden storage."

She scurried off before he could stop her. As fast as she was moving, he knew there was definitely something on her mind.

He tried to ignore the sting of insult her silence caused. There had been a time when she would have trusted him enough to tell him anything.

Clearly that time was over, but he would earn her trust again. It was too precious a thing for him not to crave it.

Torr went to the lake just long enough to wash the blood and dirt from his body. The shallow cuts had mostly healed, but every time Grace looked at him, her gaze went right to the blood smeared over his skin and the dirt of the woman's grave.

That wasn't what he wanted her to see. Not even close. She'd experienced too much blood and pain for one short lifetime.

By the time he was done, she was waiting for him by the water's edge. He came out of the lake soaking wet but clean. Grace tracked his movements, her color deepening with every step he took closer to her.

He'd never known a more beautiful woman. Even the Athanasians he'd seen couldn't compare to the light that shone out from Grace's soul. If he lived another thousand years, he would never tire of looking at her, never tire of the desire that reddened her skin and made her dark eyes glow.

She tracked him all the way to the shore. Even though the water was cool, he felt warm everywhere her gaze touched.

His wet, charred, tattered jeans had seen better days. He needed a needle and thread to repair the opening Grace had cut along the leg, but at least they covered him and kept his swelling erection in check. As much as he wanted to lay her down and see if the languid expression on her face was the invitation it appeared to be, there were more important things they needed to do. Less pleasurable but definitely more vital.

"Did you find anything good?" he asked.

A smile built along her lips, slow, lazy and brimming with the promise of paradise. She didn't have to say a word for him to know what she was thinking.

"I meant in Brenya's hut."

She blinked a couple of times, casting off all traces of the delightful ideas that were running through her head. "No. Nothing. I did find another shirt for you, though. I think one of the women made it for you." She held up simple sleeveless shirt made from some kind of loosely woven fabric. "It's not hemmed yet, but I figure it's better than nothing."

Torr slid it on over his head. The fabric was softer than it looked, and it fit perfectly. "Remind me to thank whoever made this."

"Let's just hope we all live long enough to make that happen."

He strapped his gear to his body, sliding the Mason's hammer into a simple leather loop he'd tied on his belt. The heavy weight of it tugged at his jeans, but it was a small price to pay for having the weapon handy. "Are you ready to go?"

"Yes. We need to head east. To the lake."

"The village is to the south."

"I know, but Brenya's map is headed east. To the lake." She tapped her temple. "And you can't find it without me."

"I can. And I will."

"How long do you think that will take? How long do you think the village has? How long can Brenya keep doing what she has to do to keep everyone safe?"

He hated that she was right. "I'd rather take you south, back to the others."

"If Brenya had wanted me with the others, she would have taken me along. She didn't because you need me to help you find the building site."

Torr didn't see any plan to refute her logic. "Fine, let's go. But as soon as we find where they're building the portal, you're going right back to the others."

She said nothing, but her satisfied smile spoke volumes.

He made sure they had what they needed and that Grace wasn't carrying too much weight. As soon as there was no more reason to delay, he set a steady pace east.

Within a few hours, he began to see frequent signs of Hunters passing this way. The forest was crisscrossed with sheared paths in the foliage and gouge marks in the ground.

He could hear Grace at his back, only an arm's length away. She kept up with him, but he could tell when he was pushing her too hard by the change in her breathing. He slowed down as they banked up a steep hill, pausing several times to listen for signs of danger on the far side.

"Rest a minute. I'll be right back," he whispered, then slipped off to scout the other side of the hill before she could argue.

He saw nothing but dark, glittering trees stretching out across the valley. The angle of the suns made the metallic leaves shine and shielded the forest floor from sight.

Even though he couldn't see any danger, his instincts whispered to him that it was here.

He waited, patiently scanning the area, giving whatever was down there time to make itself known. He gathered a few sparks of power from the earth beneath him, marveling at the way it felt so different from the energy back home. These sparks were hotter, with more sting to them, but it took more of them to do what he needed.

Finally, when he'd gathered enough juice, he amplified his vision. Everything looked closer. Details were in perfect focus. Still he saw nothing.

Grace scooted up the hill on her stomach, taking a position beside him. "Everything okay?"

"I'm not sure."

She fell silent and shielded her eyes from reflected sunlight.

Every time a breeze blew past, it brought with it her scent. Torr closed his eyes and breathed her in, wishing he could have more even as he cursed the distraction she created. He had no idea how long they lay there, but when he regained his control again and searched the area, the angle of the suns had changed enough that the glare from the leaves was no longer blinding.

He amped up his vision once more, this time gathering enough power that it stung his fingertips and made his skin burn. Still he saw nothing.

Beside him, Grace squirmed and rubbed her arms.

"Are you okay?" he asked.

"I think I must have been bitten by some bugs or something. No big deal."

It wasn't bugs that had bitten her. That sting was his—he'd inadvertently hurt her because of the damn disk that connected them.

He needed to get the thing off before he did more than irritate her skin. Like it or not, Brenya was going to help him find a way to free Grace. She may not have known a life without it, but she was strong. She would adapt.

"I still don't see anything," he told her. "We'll keep going, but we need to be careful."

He helped her to her feet, lingering a bit too long with her hand in his. He'd give anything to have her back at Dabyr, safe inside the walls where he would be able to relax and enjoy her. Thoroughly.

It was a selfish fantasy, but one he couldn't control.

Torr led the way down the hill, moving more slowly than he would have liked. There were a few open spaces where trees had fallen. Nothing new had had time to grow in their place yet, leaving little pools of sunshine on the forest floor. The clearings made travel easier, but also left too many openings for ambush.

He skirted them and stuck to a path animals had cut through the trees with their passing. A thorny bush had invaded this area, making travel between trees more than just uncomfortable. Each two-inch thorn dripped with something thick and wet, like syrup.

"Watch out for those," said Grace. "They're poisonous."

"What kind of poison?"

"The kind that makes you wish you were dead."

He knew that kind all too well. "We should go back and find another way through."

"There is no other way. All the other paths lead to the swamps where those giant lizards live."

He glanced over his shoulder at her. "You've been this way before?"

"No, but Brenya has. I seem to know what she does."

"Great. What's up ahead on this path?"

"A narrow strip of rock that will keep us out of the swamp."

No wonder the path was so obvious. The animals the lizards preyed on would have learned to cross here and stay out of danger.

"When we get there, we'll need to cross fast."

"Why's that?"

"The lizards are territorial."

"This just keeps getting better."

"Well, if you were going to build a magical device you didn't want anyone to find, wouldn't you put it on the other side of a bunch of territorial, man-eating lizards?"

"Good point."

A few hundred yards later, Torr saw the pale strip of stone stretching between two stagnant pools of water. Several of the huge lizards lounged in the last rays of sunlight. He could see more of them just beneath the surface of the water.

Before they got too close, he stopped. "Let me have your gear."

"Why?"

"You'll be able to run faster."

"What about you?"

"I'll be fine. All you need to keep is your water, just in case we're separated. Head straight east and I'll catch up with you as soon as I can."

He removed one of her bags and settled the strap over his shoulder.

"Catch up with me? What are you going to do?"

Torr gave her what he hoped was a reassuring smile. "Don't worry. I'm just going to distract them."

Grace was almost certain that was the worst idea in the world. "I'm not letting you distract them. There's too many. Fighting one nearly killed you. I count at least seven."

"I wasn't ready for the fight then. I am now. Besides, I'm not going to get that close. When I say, you start running and don't look back."

"No."

"I know what I'm doing, Grace. Trust me."

"Of course I do, but there's got to be another way."

"Can you think of one?"

She couldn't. And while she would have rather had both of them run across at the same time, that was much more likely to get them both killed.

She'd seen him fight. She knew what he was capable of. If either of them was going to face off against a pile of angry reptiles, he was the safe bet.

"Okay, but if you don't come across immediately, I'm going to do a little distracting of my own." She pulled Tori's practice sword from where it was strapped to her body, making her intentions clear.

"I won't make you use that. All you have to do is get across and wait for me."

"You should try throwing them some food before using your own skin as bait."

He cupped her face in his hands, leaned down and

kissed her. She had no time to anticipate his action, no time to prepare herself for the blissful shock of his kiss.

The second his lips met hers, the whole world melted away. He was there and gone before she could do more than register the heat of his mouth. Still, the brief kiss rocked her to the soles of her feet and left her reeling.

She blinked up at him, unsure what to do or say. The urge to grab him and demand more was strong, as was the strangest feeling that she'd felt that before, only in a different way.

Breathe for me, Grace. Don't give up on me. I love you.

His voice was in her memory, but she'd never heard him say those words.

"For luck," he told her, before stepping back and shedding all signs that he even knew how to kiss.

It was the warrior side of him that stood before her now, tall and fierce. He opened a pouch of dried meat, drew his sword and gave her a nod. "Stay here until I say, then run. Got it?"

She gave a mute nod and struggled to gather her wits.

Torr moved quietly along the line of thorny brush, skirting the edge of the lizards' territory. When he was a few yards away, he stepped forward and yelled, "Now!"

Grace took off at a dead sprint.

She made it all the way across the narrow land bridge before she gave in to the urge to look over her shoulder.

Torr was holding his own, fending off snapping jaws

and powerful tails. He danced between the animals, grace and strength on blatant display.

This wasn't like the attack he'd fended off when Brenya had summoned him here. He was ready for this, and his skill shone through.

Part of Grace gloried in the sight, completely enthralled by the way he moved. The rest of her was terrified that something would go wrong and he'd get hurt, or worse.

By the time she was released from the mesmerizing show long enough to look where she was going, it was too late. Something thin caught against her shin, sending her into an uncontrolled fall. She hit the ground hard. Tiny filaments made from some kind of transparent fiber wrapped around her body. They seemed to be spring-loaded, and at the end of each one was a small, clear crystal.

Several of those crystals smashed together, sending a beam of light into the sky. It cut through leaves like a spear and glowed bright against the dimming sky.

The second Grace realized what had happened, bits of the knowledge Brenya had given her flooded her brain. She knew instantly that this was a trap set by a Warden. That beam of light was going to lead it right to her, and once that happened, both she and Torr were dead.

Chapter 22

Grace screamed Torr's name. The sound was one of sheer terror.

He immediately disengaged from the group of lizards he'd been holding at bay and ran toward her. He tossed out every bit of food they had, hoping it would keep the animals occupied long enough for him to reach Grace.

He saw her dangling a few feet off the ground, her body bundled inside a net. Several pencil-thin beams of light shone into the sky. Crystal shards littered the area, giving off a low hum of energy that he'd felt only a few times before in his life.

There was magic here, and that couldn't be good.

One strong swing of his sword cut her down. She landed hard, letting out a whoosh of air.

"Warden trap," she wheezed.

Definitely not good.

Torr didn't waste time asking how she knew. It made too much sense for him to question.

The strands binding her body were too tight for him to risk slicing with his sword. From the redness in her face, he worried that they were also making it hard for her to breathe. Still, that wasn't the worst of their worries.

Those glowing beacons were going to bring every nasty thing hiding in these woods right to them. He had to ditch the beams and get her away from here before it was too late.

The light seemed to be pouring from broken crystals. He cut through the strands attaching the crystals to her body and lifted her over his shoulder.

"Sorry about this," he said as he set out at a fast jog.

Her poor body was bouncing on his shoulder. He knew it had to hurt, but whatever pain she suffered now wasn't as bad as what any Warden would do if it found her.

As soon as he'd put a little distance between them and those beacons, he set her down to check on her.

She was still conscious, but barely. Her breathing was shallow, and each breath seemed to give the strands room to tighten.

"I'm going to give you some room to breathe," he told her. "Just hang on."

A flare of recognition lit her eyes for a second before they closed.

Frantic, he patted her cheek to wake her up, but she didn't respond.

The time for careful was over.

Torr used the tip of his sword to slice through the

strands over her tunic. The leather split open, but so did the strands. He tried to avoid the places where there was no leather to protect her. He hoped that opening even a few of the tough fibers binding her would be enough to give her relief.

She pulled in a huge gasp of air.

In the distance, the sounds of crashing leaves and wind chimes filled the air.

The Warden was here.

"We have to run," he told her.

She nodded weakly.

"Try to stay quiet. I'll get the rest of your body free as soon as I can."

"Cave," she choked out. "Not far."

"Which way?"

She frowned for a second. "North. Under the big rock."

That had to be good enough for now.

"Hold on, honey. I'll get you free as fast as I can."

The trail Torr had left behind was created in a panicked rush and easy to follow. As soon as the Warden found it, they would be screwed.

At least he only had one set of tracks to hide. With Grace over his shoulder, he was going to be slower, but he had centuries of experience in hiding his trail.

He kept careful tabs on her pulse as he moved as fast as he dared. The farther upslope he went, the thinner the brush became. The sound of wind chimes was distant, but he could still hear it whenever the wind died down.

"You doing okay?" he asked.

Her voice was strained, but she said, "Yeah."

He made use of the paths the Hunters had cut through the trees whenever he could. When he couldn't, he moved slowly, being careful not to break the small branches and leaves surrounding them. He checked behind them every few yards, making sure there was no visible path to follow and that nothing was on their tail as he headed toward the big rock she'd talked about.

Finally, he saw a rock big enough to be named for its size.

It looked like a glacial boulder deposited here millennia ago. The surface of it was smooth from wear and covered with tiny fossils. It was the size of a house, perching precariously on a hillside. In the gap between the boulder and the hillside, he saw a small opening.

He wanted to scout out the space first, but he didn't dare leave Grace out here, completely unable to defend herself or even run away. Instead, he carried her up the steep slope and angled himself so that he could peer into the opening. A few sparks of power later, he saw nothing inside except some dry grass and sticks that appeared to have once been the nest of an animal. As old and scattered as the debris was, he doubted the animal had been here in a long time.

He ducked as he walked through the opening, making sure not to bump Grace's head. As soon as they were out of sight to anyone who wasn't standing on the hillside, he eased her to the ground.

Her skin had a greenish cast to it that told him he hadn't been gentle enough. He'd made her sick. "I'm sorry about the rough ride."

"It's okay."

The clear filaments binding her had left deep creases in her skin. She was even bleeding in a couple of places where the pressure of the strands had been too much.

"It's going to take a few minutes to get you out of this thing, but I'll go as fast as I can."

He started at her head, using his sword as carefully as he could to break through the tough fibers. When the length of the blade became too unwieldy, he worked her short sword free of her belt and used that. After a few painstaking minutes, the top half of her body was free.

She took several deep breaths. He could practically feel relief radiating from her in waves. "I've had better days."

"Me too, honey. Almost there."

He nicked her knee trying to cut it out of the binding. She didn't flinch, but he could hear her nearly silent hiss of pain.

"I'm so sorry."

"Not your fault. I'd rather have a few cuts and be out of this thing."

The leather bindings around her calves helped protect her legs and he was able to make quick work of the rest of the net. Once it was all the way off, he bundled it up and tossed it into the refuse pile in the corner.

Her skin was covered with angry red marks and

more than a few cuts. Between his efforts and the filaments, she was bleeding in several places.

He removed his bags and started searching for the medical supplies she'd packed. "We'll get you cleaned up and then I'll secure the cave."

"I'll do it," she told him. "You can go do whatever it is you need to do."

She seemed steady now, so he left her side and moved deeper into the opening.

As caves went, it wasn't much of one. It only went about twenty feet into the hillside before ending in a crack just wide enough to let rainfall drain out. The floor slanted down the deeper it went, but it was still level enough that he didn't have to worry about sliding down and getting his foot stuck in the opening.

Because of the angle and the boulder that hid them, he didn't think they could be seen by someone passing by below. At night, the opening would look like little more than a shadow in the rocks.

Night wasn't far away.

They had no food, no light, and Grace wasn't going to be able to travel once it got dark.

"We'll stay here tonight. It's defensible, hidden and about as safe as we're going to get with a Warden roaming around out there."

"Is there a back door?"

"No, but it won't come to that."

"You should keep going. I'll be fine here without you."

"Even if I was willing to leave you alone—which I'm not—you're the one who knows the way."

She dabbed some kind of thick cream on one of the cuts on her thigh. "We're not far away. I can see the rest of the path from the big rock now. Travel over the hill we're in and head southeast over three more hills, each one progressively higher. In the valley after that last one, you'll find the lake there." She closed her eyes as if seeing it in her mind. "At the bottom of it are a bunch of stones—the kind Brenya used to carve the portal to Earth. They have some kind of innate magic, like those crystals we found. They're what the Masons will use to build the portal."

"How do you know that?" Torr took the small pot of antiseptic cream from her and applied it to the shallow cut on her cheek.

She tapped her temple. "A gift from Brenya."

"So if we find the source of the Masons' building material, we can wait for one to come for more stone, then follow it back to wherever they're building the portal."

"That could work, but I don't think that's why Brenya put the map to the lake in my head."

"Then why?"

"The stones the Masons are using are drawn to each other. If we get one, it can lead us to the others."

"Like a kind of compass."

"Exactly."

She held her hand out to take the cream from him

again, but he kept it. She had a dozen small cuts, most of which she wasn't going to be able to easily reach.

"I'll do it," he said. "Turn around."

She looked confused for a second, like she couldn't believe he'd help her, but then did as he asked.

The backs of her arms and shoulders had taken the worst damage from the Warden's filament. While none of the cuts were deep, he was sure they had to sting.

Grace gave no sign that he was causing her any kind of pain. In fact, she kept talking like nothing had happened. "There's no way to know how long the Masons have been at work or how much more time we have. One of us needs to find them and check on their progress before it's too late and we have an army to fight. And you know that someone can't be me. I don't see in the dark like you do, and we can't risk carrying a light source."

He didn't want to leave her. He didn't know this world or what dangers might lurk in the night. She was too precious to risk, and while he couldn't tell her why, he also couldn't pretend she didn't matter.

"We'll go to the lake together tomorrow," he said, hoping the finality of his tone would end the conversation.

She was quiet for a minute as he finished cleaning and treating her cuts. Her breathing became slow and deep, as if she was trying to deal with the pain.

Torr wished that the healing disks worked both ways, but his research into the devices had proved otherwise. They were meant to transfer health from one person to another, not the other way around—a one-way street.

When he was done, she let out a long breath. "I'm slowing you down."

Torr closed the jar of cream and tucked it back in her bag. "I never would have been able to find the location of the lake without your help."

"But you can now. I told you where it is. You should go."

"No. I'll be too distracted, wondering if you're safe. You've gotten me this far. Morning will be soon enough."

"And if it's not? If they finish the portal and open it before you reach it?"

"Then I'll kill whatever comes through. I've been beating back evil invasions since I was old enough to hold a sword. I've got this." He hoped.

She stared at her lap. Her whole body seemed to deflate, and even without a luceria connecting them he could feel her sadness and frustration. "Brenya should have picked someone else to guide you. I have no idea why she chose me, a weak human."

"She must have thought you were the best choice."

"Or maybe my brain is just so simple in comparison that it was easy to shove information into it."

"I promise you that human minds are anything but simple. But even if that were true, Brenya is powerful enough not to let a little thing like that get in her way. She chose you because she thought you were their best hope. She knew you were brave and that you'd give your last drop of blood to save them."

"Of course I would. Those women and children are important. Earth's survival depends on them."

"And their survival depends on you. Not exactly a task Brenya would have given to some weak human."

"Desperate times . . ."

He took her by the shoulders, resisting the urge to shake some sense into her. "Stop it. I know plenty of humans. Some of them are weak—they break vows, they give up when things get hard, they toss each other aside like bags of garbage and spend their lives as victims, waiting for someone to save them from their own laziness and poor decisions. I know you, Grace. You're not like them. You're special."

"You've only known me for a few days."

He bit his tongue against the urge to correct her. "In those few days you've proven yourself over and over. Now stop bashing yourself and have a little faith in you the way Brenya and I do."

She stared at him, her gaze direct. He could see the exact moment her mind changed, and it was a beautiful thing to behold. She shed her insecurity like an old skin and let a bright new confidence shine through. "You're right. Brenya wouldn't have risked everything she's worked for all these years on someone she thought would fail."

"Now you're catching on."

"I won't let her down, Torr. Or you."

"Honey, you couldn't let me down if you tried." *I love you.*

He didn't dare say the words, but he let them swell

in his heart, hoping that some of his intense feelings would spill through the disks that connected them.

Her eyes fluttered shut, and the sweetest smile warmed her expression. When she looked at him again, her eyes were brighter and filled with newfound hope.

He had to kiss her. There was no more holding back. No more resisting her pull on him. She was the woman of his dreams, everything he'd ever wanted. He didn't care if she wasn't a Theronai. He didn't care if he couldn't have her forever. She was here now, and he was going to love her for as long as he could, even if it was only for one night.

One night with Grace was more than he'd ever hoped to have. A lifetime with any other woman couldn't compare.

There was little light left outside, but plenty for him to see by. The deep orange glow cast russet shadows across her body, highlighting the delicate lines of her frame.

He traced that line between light and shadow with his finger, following it up her arm, along her neck and across her mouth. Each inch he traveled made her brown eyes grow darker as her pupils flared in a way that had nothing to do with the dim lighting.

He cupped her face with one hand, being careful of the shallow cut on her cheek. His thumb glided across her skin, reveling in her soft warmth. There was something about the texture of her skin that was uniquely hers. Perhaps all those hours she'd spent holding his hand had somehow imprinted the feel of her skin in his mind, but he had no question that he would know the feel of her anywhere, even in utter darkness.

Her lips parted, and the slick, glossy inside of her bottom lip inflamed him. He wanted to taste that skin, to feel it glide under his tongue until he knew it as well as he did the shape of her hand in his.

There was so much of her he wanted to memorize, so many intriguing textures to experience.

Sweat broke out along his spine but did nothing to cool him down. His heart beat faster until he could feel it pounding through him in a mad rush. He felt like a young man again, giddy and eager for a first kiss.

Grace pressed her hand to his chest, right over his heart. His abdomen clenched hard. A flood of desire raced through him, so powerful it was hard to breathe through it.

Everything about her deepened his need. He wanted to control his lust and bank it until only low embers remained, but she made that impossible.

He tipped her head up and fitted his mouth against hers.

Grace melted into the kiss. Her fingers dug into his chest. A little breath of excitement eased out of her in the form of the sexiest sigh he'd ever heard.

He wasn't exactly sure how it happened, but one second she was sitting on the cave floor, and the next she was straddling his lap. His hands were on her ass, holding her close, so chances were he'd simply picked her up and put her where he wanted her.

The hem of her tunic slid up to make room for her to

spread her thighs around him. He could feel the leather bunching under his grip and wanted nothing more than to shred it away from her body.

He'd had her naked before, but had done his best to respect her privacy and keep his eyes to himself.

This time would be different. He would look his fill. He'd linger over every sweet curve and hollow, making sure he didn't miss an inch.

She lifted up on her knees and grabbed his head, angling it to please her. Each kiss was a sweet little gift, but not nearly as much as he wanted.

"Open for me, honey," he said against her mouth.

Her lips parted instantly, giving him the access he needed.

The taste of her drove him wild. Made him hotter. The cave air had been cool only a moment ago, but his body was in overdrive, unable to shed heat fast enough.

As if sensing his need, Grace grabbed the bottom of his new shirt and pulled it over his head. Their mouths separated only long enough to get the job done before she came right back to him.

The feel of her supple leather tunic grated on him. He needed her flesh on his, bare and hot. Maybe he was rushing things, but he'd wanted Grace for so long he couldn't seem to stop himself from taking what she offered.

He slid his hands under her tunic, cupping the mostly bare cheeks of her ass. The thin fabric she wore over her sex was far too rough for such delicate skin. She deserved silk. Or better yet, nothing at all.

"Need you naked," he told her as he pulled on the leather tie that held her tunic closed.

The garment fell forward. She pulled back, holding it against her breasts. Her lips were already puffy from kissing him. A deep flush covered her face and neck. Her hair was a wild, dark mane around her head. Her eyes stayed fixed to his as she moved her hands and let the tunic fall.

Torr lost all ability to speak. Or think. The sight of Grace's mostly naked body straddling his was more than even a strong man like him could take.

So beautiful. So tempting.

Her breasts were the perfect size for his big hands. Her nipples were tight buds that made his mouth water. The curve of her waist and the flare of her hips were enough to make him fight the need to come in his jeans.

"More naked," he managed to rasp out between labored breaths.

Grace rose to her feet in a move so fluid it made him think of lazy rivers and dew dripping from blades of grass. She let the tunic fall. A swift pull on the knot at her waist and the fabric wound between her thighs unraveled around her ankles.

More of Torr's brain cells sputtered and died as he soaked in the sight of her. He'd intended only to look, but his hands gripped her hips and tugged her closer.

The dark hair shielding her sex was visibly damp. Her sea-salt-and-woman scent went straight to his head, intoxicating him further. He knew if he touched her and found her wet for him, he would mount her and be thrusting inside her before he even had time to find out if it was what she wanted.

He prayed it was what she wanted.

Rather than let himself get carried away, he slid his shaking hands over the leather ties at her calves until he found how they were fastened. A few quick tugs of his fingers, and even those were gone, leaving her completely naked.

Torr got to his feet in an uncharacteristically clumsy move. He needed to put a few feet between them before he dove in headfirst and took what he wanted from her. His sweet Grace was too precious to treat like some kind of whore.

His cock swelled and throbbed, beating in insistent demand. He ignored it and simply looked his fill.

"I want to see you," she whispered. "Before all the light is gone."

"If I take off my jeans, there won't be anything to slow me down."

She took a tentative step forward. Her voice was a sultry temptation. "I don't want slow. I want you."

He couldn't let her change her mind. She could have whatever she wanted—whatever got her off so long as she didn't change her mind.

Torr stripped off his boots, unbuckled his sword and shucked his jeans in record time. He stood before her naked and blatantly aroused. She was only a few steps away. Even as low as the last light of the setting suns was, there was no way she couldn't see what she did to him.

Her chest stopped moving for too long. He was so

attuned to her that he hadn't even realized he'd been keeping tabs on her breathing. It must have been habit from all that time he'd spent at her bedside, hoping she would recover from healing his paralysis.

"Breathe, Grace. Or I'll do it for you." He'd done it before, filling her lungs with air to keep her alive. He'd do it again in a heartbeat if she needed it.

Her breasts lifted with a deep breath, giving him an awkward mix of relief and arousal. His erection twitched, lunging toward her like it had a mind of its own.

"You're beautiful," she told him, awe plain in her voice.

She took a step forward. Then another. She was within his reach now, but he kept his hands at his sides.

Her fingers traced the branches of his lifemark. A hard shiver raced through him, making every muscle clench as it passed.

"Did that hurt?" she asked, pulling her hand away.

"Only if you don't touch me again."

She did, only this time the caress was lighter. "It's moving, isn't it?"

He couldn't answer. His throat was clogged with need so huge it nearly choked him.

He wanted her to be his partner. Forever. He wanted her to take her place at his side and draw strength from him. In this moment, he would have made a deal with the Solarc if it meant she could be his other half.

Grace pressed her cheek to his chest. "I swear I can hear it move. Is that even possible?"

He didn't know. Couldn't think. Her head was over his heart, and there was nothing he could do but wrap his arms around her and hold her there, wishing it could be the place she laid her head each night.

This woman was meant to be his, and it was a cruel twist of fate that he couldn't keep her—at least not as long as he wanted.

Before bleak thoughts could slip in and ruin what they had here and now, Torr lifted her chin and kissed her. He put the full force of his will into it, holding nothing back. He let her feel his need. Didn't even try to hide it. He knew that feelings this strong would blast their way through the disk she wore and give her a tiny fraction of his need.

By the time he lifted his mouth from hers, she was gasping for air, clinging to him. "I feel like I've done this before," she said, "but I know if I had, I would have remembered it."

He didn't want to talk about memories or the past. He wanted to grab on to the present and wring from it every drop of pleasure he could. For both of them.

Her nipples grazed his chest. He bent her back over his arm just enough that he could reach them with his mouth. The high cry of surprise she gave him was the sweetest kind of music. If he got his way, he was going to be hearing a lot more of that before he let her rest.

She gripped his hair in both fists and held on tight. He felt the moment her legs weakened, but he simply accepted more of her weight, thrilled to his core that she would trust him not to let her fall.

He suckled her, making note of what made her thighs clench, what made her let out those musical sighs. It was only when his own legs got a little shaky with lust that he decided to move the fun to the ground.

He arranged their discarded clothes into as smooth a pallet as possible and eased Grace onto it. "I don't want to hurt your back again."

She looped her arms around his neck. "I don't think I'd notice this time."

When she pulled him down to kiss her again, he had no choice but to go where she led. If he ran the show, he'd already be inside her.

His cock grazed her stomach. He felt the hot, slick wetness welling from him as he rubbed against her. The movement was involuntary. His poor lust-hazed mind couldn't seem to slow down and ease off the throttle. He'd wanted this—her—for too long.

All those months of being trapped inside his wasted body had left him little to do but fantasize. She'd come to him every day to feed him, bathe him and generally keep his ass alive. She was so sweet, so wounded. He knew she'd been abused. The marks were all over her when he found her. Still, as scared as she was, she still came to him, trying to repay him for something that needed no thanks.

Because of the demon that had poisoned him, he'd been too weak to hurt her. He knew that was what gave her the courage to show up every day, but he still cherished his time with her. And as time passed, he stopped seeing her as the sweet girl he'd rescued and started seeing her as a kind and loving woman—one with a body that made him lie awake at night, sweating and dreaming of what he'd do to her if he ever had the chance.

That chance was now, but all of those fantasies were jumbled up, too tangled for him to pull out a single one to make it come true.

He traced the line of her arm, lingering as his path led him down her ribs. She shivered at his touch, which only made him want to touch her more—something he hadn't thought possible. The lower his fingers ran, the more powerful her reaction became. She arched toward him, breathing faster, growing warmer.

Her hands splayed against his back, her fingers digging into his skin like she couldn't get enough of him. The idea went to his head, giving him a feeling of power that not even the magic flowing through his veins could match.

She broke the kiss. Her mouth moved across his jaw, down his neck. She placed hot, open-mouthed kisses along his skin, biting and nibbling just enough to leave a pleasurable sting in her wake. When she reached his luceria, she slowed. Her tongue delved beneath the magical band, touching flesh that was more often covered than not. He was ultrasensitive here, and each flickering swipe of her tongue made him burn hotter.

"Enough," he said as he eased her onto her back. "It's my turn to make you burn."

Chapter 23

Grace didn't know what Torr meant. She was already about to combust.

Her skin danced with tingling flames. Every inch of her body ached to get closer to his. She wanted him to cover her, consume her. There was too much space between them, and if he didn't give her what she needed, she was certain it would kill her.

He rose above her, supporting his weight with his arms. Muscles bulged beneath his tan skin. A mist of sweat glistened across his chest. His scent filled her head, making her insides melt, but it was his eyes, bright and gleaming with wicked intent, that were her undoing.

He stared at her body, devouring her inch by inch. She felt that stare like a physical touch. When his gaze moved over her breasts, her nipples tightened until they were almost painful.

She needed his mouth on them again, soothing them with his tongue.

Grace tried to tell him that, but as soon as her lips parted, he kissed her again, robbing her of all ability to speak.

His hands roamed her body. They were so big, leaving wide swaths of heat wherever they went. He was gentle but gave her no chance to resist what he wanted to do. By the time he pulled away from her mouth, his hand was covering her mound, with just the tip of one finger sliding between her labia.

As soon as he felt how wet she was, he went still and pulled in a hissing breath. His eyes shut tight, but when he opened them, his gaze locked with hers.

"Sweet Grace. You have no idea what you do to me."

"Is that bad?"

"No. Not even close."

His finger slid along her folds, gliding easily to her core. If anyone had ever touched her like this before, she couldn't remember. Didn't even want to. Her entire world was right here, right now—just her and Torr.

He watched her while he moved inside her, as if expecting her to tell him to stop. She couldn't even imagine such a horrible thought, not when his hand was between her legs, his skin lightly grazing across her clit as he entered her.

The sensation was almost too much. He'd barely even begun to touch her, and she was already feeling a steady kind of pressure building where he moved.

She grabbed his wrist, unsure if she wanted to make him slow down or move faster. Instead, he froze.

Sweat lined his brow. "Do I stop?"

"No. It's just . . . a lot."

A dark smile of conquest spread across his face. "Not yet, it's not."

He pressed deeper and stroked some magical spot inside her that made her see stars. Her fingers dug into his wrists, but all that did was allow her to feel his tendons shift with whatever it was he was doing to her.

He slid out, just long enough for her to mourn the loss of his touch before he gathered her juices on a second finger and moved within her again.

The stretch was good. Really good. She forgot all about trying to restrain him and simply let go and gave in. By the time he had a third finger easing inside her, it wouldn't have mattered if she wanted to stop him or not. She was too boneless, too breathless.

His mouth latched onto her nipple. He blew across the wet tip, making it tighten more. When his teeth grazed across her, biting just hard enough for her to feel it, that pressure he'd built within her detonated like a bomb.

She shattered, flying apart into a million sparkling pieces. Just when she was sure that the pleasure was over and what was left of her was going to drift off on the slightest breeze, the next wave of her orgasm crashed against her, shocking her with its intensity.

Torr's hand kept moving, kept urging her through the next shimmering pulse until she was shaking and unable to catch her breath.

His head lifted and he wore an expression of complete male satisfaction. "You are such a miracle. Utterly stunning."

She couldn't speak. There wasn't enough air in her lungs for anything more than her rapid panting breaths.

He cradled her body close, stroking her while the storm eased. As soon as she felt whole again, he lifted her and moved until he was lying flat on the ground with her sitting astride him. His erection lay heavily on his abdomen. She could feel its thick length hot against her sex, see the tip of it rising past her mound. Wetness welled at the end of his penis, forming a pearly drop. His big hands cupped her hips, and she could feel her own juices clinging to his fingers. More coated him as she rubbed her labia over his hard length. Blatant male need tightened his jaw, giving him an almost feral expression.

Grace had just had the first orgasm she could ever remember, but seeing him look at her like that—like she was the answer to his prayers—made need rise in her again.

She moved her hips, experimenting with the feel of his slick skin on hers. Every few strokes her clit would slide against him just right, making her whole body clench and shiver.

Torr groaned, and a rush of feminine power swept through her. Before she was done here, she was going to make him feel as good as he'd made her feel.

She leaned down, covering his body with hers. The brush of her nipples against his hard chest sent a riot of sensation cascading along her spine.

His groan deepened, and his fingers tightened around her hips. A strand of restraint vibrated through him, taunting her to find a way to make it snap. Just the thought of Torr completely unrestrained with her was enough to make the wetness between them thicken.

She kissed his mouth. His erection pulsed against her, hitting her clit. She sucked in a breath that tasted like him, and then suddenly had a remnant of memory flash in her mind.

His mouth on hers. Him breathing for her.

The feeling was gone so fast she wasn't sure if it had been real or something she'd imagined. And when his tongue swept in to tease hers, all she could think about was finding a way to get more of him.

He was right there, hot and hard between her thighs. All she had to do was shift her hips, lift up and take him inside.

She was more than ready for it.

Grace broke the kiss and sat up. The image of the tree on his chest seemed to sway madly with his rapid breathing. She gripped him in her fist, holding his gaze while she centered his erection.

She couldn't remember having ever done this before, but her instincts guided her, urging her onward.

She eased down. The pressure of his broad tip made lightning dance in her veins. He was slick, hot and so incredibly smooth that it didn't take long before her tissues parted and let him in.

Her breath caught in her chest. An aching stretch strung her taut. She already felt consumed and she'd barely accepted any of him. She truly wasn't sure how she was going to take more.

Torr must have sensed her hesitation. He sat up and cradled her in his arms, dropping soft kisses over her cheeks and eyelids.

"I'll wait as long as you need, honey. And if you want to stop"—his words cut off in a strained, choking sound—"then that's what we'll do."

"No stopping now," she said, easing down to take another inch of him.

His breath came out in a long hiss of pleasure. He took her mouth with his, staking a claim without a single word. There was a kind of fevered franticness to his mouth, his hands, as if he had to gather as much of her as he could before she slipped away.

Grace wasn't going anywhere. Not now, not when he surrounded her and filled her so completely.

She started moving, lifting and lowering herself in small increments. Each sweet glide of skin on skin was better than the last, pushing her back toward that glittering place where she'd been ripped apart and reformed.

The stretching pressure of him filling her was her whole world. Her body kept surprising her with its hungry need, its ability to accept more than she would have thought possible. It wasn't just his physical presence in her body, but also the shimmering pleasure he gave her with each stroke of his hand, each hot, wet kiss.

He seemed to know just where to touch her to make her need more. He never pushed or hurried her, but the glide of his mouth on her neck made her want, and the gentle tug on her nipples made her hunger.

Finally, when they were joined as deeply as possible, he went still and simply looked at her. Some kind of declaration burned in his amber eyes, but he said nothing. Instead, he stroked her face with the tips of his fingers, touching her as though she were the most precious thing he'd ever beheld.

Her body burned, but it was her heart that she felt most in that moment. It seemed to expand and swell, as if it had been waiting for him to fill a void she hadn't even realized she had. When he looked at her like this, she felt strangely complete.

"I'm going to love you now," he told her. "I can't wait any longer."

She wasn't sure what he meant until he started to move. His powerful body flexed, lifting her up. The clinging glide of her skin on his made her nerve endings sing. The feeling of emptiness barely registered before he slid back home again.

Grace clung to his shoulders, holding on while he moved her. Each stroke tightened her belly and wound her up until she couldn't think of anything but pure sensation.

Sweat coated their skin, allowing her nipples to slide over his chest. The added sensation was too much for her to hold.

She opened her mouth to warn him that she couldn't take any more, but all that came out was a breathless cry as her body exploded. One wave of pleasure crashed into the next until all that was left were demanding ripples that squeezed the last of her energy from her body.

Torr's muscles bunched, clenching hard. His voice came out in a strangled roar, and she felt his erection swell and pulse inside her as his semen erupted from him.

He collapsed back onto the ground, bringing her down with him to cover his body. His heart hammered under her ear. His arms tightened around her as if he was afraid she'd run away.

Not likely.

Even if her legs could support her weight—which she knew they wouldn't—there wasn't a single place she wanted to be more than where she was right now.

When their breathing evened out, he rolled her beneath him and brushed her hair away from her sweaty brow. "You okay?"

"Never better."

"I got a little carried away."

"I loved every second of it."

His erection was relaxing inside her, but she felt it twitch with interest. "That's good, because I have every intention of doing it again. Soon."

She didn't think it would be possible for her to want more. She already felt boneless, weak and completely sated. Still, her body knew a good thing when it heard one, and a little rush of excitement flooded her. "Now works for me."

He flashed her a breathtaking smile as he eased from her body. "I'm going to feed you first."

"With what? I saw you drop all our food."

He pushed to his feet, putting his gorgeous body on gleaming display. For as long as she lived, she would never forget how he looked now, with only the faintest glow of sunset painting his nude body. "Don't worry. I've been hunting longer than you've been alive. I'll find us something."

Suddenly, the idea of being alone in this cave was terrifying. Maybe it was clingy of her, but she didn't want him to run off—not after what they'd just shared.

Her unease must have registered in her expression, because he leaned down and kissed her, long and slow. When he came up for air, that familiar look of hunger was back in place, tightening his jaw and mouth.

"I'm only going because we need to eat. I'm not running away. I promise."

His vow took her by surprise, its weight settling gently over her shoulders like a warm blanket. "Okay."

"I won't be long." He pulled on his clothes and set a short sword within her reach. "I'll stay close. If you need me, call out and I'll come running."

She nodded.

He swept her hair behind her ear and gave her a look so filled with delicious intent it made her thighs squeeze together. "When I get back and have fed you, I'm going to spend the rest of the night inside you, Grace. And I'm going to see to it that you love every second."

About that, she had no doubt.

Chapter 24

Torr had been lying about not running away, just a little.

Grace overwhelmed him. Made his head spin. Made him wish for things that were impossible.

Just the idea of being with her like that every night for the rest of his life was enough to scare him. Not because he couldn't imagine it, but because he *could*. He could also imagine the lengths he'd go to keep her at his side.

Now that he'd gotten a taste of her, he knew he'd never have enough. Anyone who tried to stand between him and Grace now was in for a world of pain.

He would die for her, kill for her, raze entire worlds for her.

For a man with his abilities, that was a dangerous way to feel.

He knelt on the damp ground and simply breathed in the thick night air. He had too much emotion rioting inside him—too much love, lust and territorial greed.

Grace was his. No other man would ever touch her, human or otherwise.

He could keep her here on this planet where there were no other men. He could stay and spend the rest of his years loving her. Or at least the rest of her years.

Even as the idea sparked to life, it died a sudden death. He couldn't stay here. His vow wouldn't allow it. Eventually, his need to protect humans and guard the gate to Athanasia would overcome him and he would spend all his time desperately trying to find a way home.

For now he was content. Protecting Brenya and the women here was important. The children here were vital to winning the war. And protecting Grace, the only human he'd sensed here, was a true joy. But it wouldn't last.

Once he'd dealt with the threat, that contentedness would fade. He would become restless and, eventually, frantic to return home.

That wasn't the kind of thing he wanted Grace to witness.

So what were his choices? Take her home with him? Watch her age and die?

It would destroy him.

Even as he thought about it, he felt one of the leaves on his lifemark rip free and fall. The pain made him suck in a breath and dig his fingers into the damp ground.

It was a cruel fucking joke that a woman who touched him so deeply could never be the one he needed to survive.

Suddenly, a strange sense of calm came over him.

If anything ever happened to her, it would destroy him. He wouldn't have to suffer endless centuries without her. He would simply go with her when she left this life.

It was such an obvious solution, it was a wonder he hadn't thought of it before. He would have his life with Grace and then let go when she did. No more war, no more fighting, no more pain.

His brothers would be one warrior short, but they were having children of their own now—more fighters to fill the void he'd leave. They wouldn't miss him for long.

His decision made, Torr went foraging in the woods to feed the woman he would spend the rest of his life with.

All he had to do now was persuade her to have him.

•

Grace washed in a trickle of icy water seeping down the cave wall. There was no more light to guide her, so everything took twice as long. Still, it helped pass the time while Torr was gone.

Her body tingled with the memory of what he'd done to her as well as his dark promise for more. She didn't care about the food he'd bring back, only about the man who would bring it.

When she heard the slight swish of brush outside the cave entrance, she froze, stuck somewhere between fear and excitement.

"It's me," he whispered, and all fear drained away.

She couldn't see him, but she could sense him drawing nearer. The disk along her back vibrated slightly, but she couldn't tell if it was in response to the one he wore or if she was simply shaking with anticipation.

"I'm over here," she said.

"I can see you."

"Oh, right. I forget other people can see in the dark."

When he spoke again, he was much closer. She could smell the forest clinging to his clothes and skin, feel his body heat reaching for her. "If I could give you the power to see at night, I would. As it is, the best I can offer is a small fire at the back of the cave."

He was so sweet, always worrying about her needs. "Will the light give us away?"

"No. I'll cut some brush and create a screen. I need to cook the meat anyway."

"What can I do?"

"Rest," he said, his tone promising wicked delights. "You're going to need it."

Grace stifled a shiver and stayed where she was until he had the brush screen in place and a small fire going to light the space. It was little more than a single flame but seemed incredibly bright after so long in the dark.

He scrubbed a rock in the trickle of water, then set it by the fire and laid out several thin strips of raw meat.

"Good hunting?" she asked.

"Good enough. I found some berries, too. They look like the ones we ate earlier, but you should check them out, just to be sure."

She took the pouch he offered and saw that he'd found the sweet red ones that ripened this time of year. She popped one in her mouth. "They're safe."

He adjusted the strips of raw meat so they'd start cooking, and opened his mouth for one of the berries.

Grace moved closer to where he knelt. Giving in to the pull he had on her felt good. Right.

She took one of the berries and fed it to him. Before she could move away, his lips closed over her finger, sucking on it in a way that made her nipples harden.

He let her go, grinning as he chewed. His gaze was fixed on her chest, where the very obvious outline of her nipples was visible.

"I love it that I can do that to you," he told her. "Makes the playing field just a bit more level."

"What's that supposed to mean?"

He shifted his position so she could see the bulge of his erection. "Honey, I've been hard for you since I got here."

She felt her blush start at her cheeks, then work its way down beneath her tunic.

"If you keep looking at me like that, I'm going to let this meat burn."

"That idea should probably bother me more than it does."

He let out a low, rumbling growl that vibrated all the way to her core. "I could just feast on you."

Another intriguing idea, but not one that was going to keep them safe. "You need real food." She fed him another berry.

"Not as sweet as you, but close."

He finished cooking the meat. They ate around the little fire, watching it die down.

"Will it bother you if we let it go dark?" he asked.

"No." Not if he was here.

"We'll be safer that way."

"I understand. I'll be fine."

"You've had a long day. You're injured and tired. I should let you sleep now." He picked up the last berry and held it to her lips.

She took it and caught his finger in her teeth.

His amber eyes darkened to a deep, rich bronze. "But I'm not going to."

She swallowed her bite. "Good. Because I'm not tired."

He leaned closer, staring at her mouth. "When I'm done with you, you will be."

"Arrogant man."

"Honest man. I can't get enough of you, Grace. Not even close."

"Maybe not, but I think it's going to be fun for you to try."

Grace was naked under her tunic. That delightful discovery nearly shorted out Torr's brain. His hands slid up her bare legs as he kissed her, sure that he would encounter some kind of barrier, but all he felt was hot, smooth flesh.

His hands cupped her buttocks as he pulled her onto his lap. He wanted to lay her out and cover her with his body, driving deep, but his weight was too much for her on this hard ground. The disk on her back would cut into her delicate skin, taking away any pleasure he might give her.

Unacceptable.

It was better to let her ride him, let her set the pace so she could enjoy his body as much as possible.

Heaven knew he enjoyed hers.

He wanted to take things slow, give her time to warm up again. He wanted to prove he was a gentle man who would always set her needs above his own. But as soon as his fingers slid between her thighs and felt how slick she was for him, all thoughts of restraint vanished.

He had just enough functioning mental power left to remember how to open his jeans before he settled her on his erection and pulled her hips down.

Grace let out a sound somewhere between a sigh and a hiss. Her sex tightened around him, and he knew he'd been too rough, too fast.

He went still, sure he'd just broken whatever tenuous trust she'd extended him.

"Sorry." The word was thick, barely intelligible.

She didn't respond. Instead, she covered his mouth with hers and began to ride him.

His sweet Grace turned fierce. She nipped at his tongue and clawed at his back. She moved in a sinuous rhythm that had him speeding toward his climax way too fast.

He tried to tell her to slow down, but her mouth muted him. Her tongue demanded his attention, twirling and thrusting in a way that drove him mad.

He hadn't known she had this in her—this hot, insatiable need to claim and conquer—but he liked it. He liked everything she did. Too much.

Her soft sounds of pleasure filled his mouth. Her sex fluttered around him, just as it had before when she'd reached her peak.

She was close, perhaps even closer to completion than he was.

That she could burn this hot this fast ignited his blood. It made him crave her all the more, something he hadn't thought possible.

She sucked in a huge breath that pressed her breasts to his chest. If not for the need to hold her close, he would have ripped that leather from her body. He couldn't stand letting go of her long enough to do the job, so he slipped his hands inside the back opening and cupped her shoulders.

One hard pull down and he was seated within her fully. The move ground her clit against him and made her clench violently around his erection.

He caught her first cry of release with his mouth to muffle the sound. Some distant sliver of his mind was still aware of the possible danger outside. But then her sweet body rippled around him, and nothing else mattered.

His climax poured down on him like a waterfall, drowning him in pleasure. His seed jetted from his body to find its home within hers. Each wringing clench of her sex milked him harder, demanding more from him.

Finally, when he had nothing left to give, he carried her to the ground, cradling her trembling body.

It took him far too long to regain his senses, but by the time he did, Grace was asleep.

He felt bad for taking her battered body so roughly. The shallow cuts from the Warden's net had to sting. He hadn't exactly been gentle with her.

Still, she was resting now, and he doubted that would have been the case if he hadn't worn her out.

Slowly, so he wouldn't wake her, he disengaged their bodies and arranged her in what looked like a comfortable position, with a pack for a pillow and his discarded shirt for a blanket, It was the best he could do for now.

Soon he would have her in a real bed, take her in a real shower. But he knew better than to think he would wait until then. Grace was part of him now, and he would have her any way he could get her for as long as she'd let him.

Torr washed and knelt between her and the cave entrance. His sword was on the ground in front of him, and a deep sense of satisfaction settled in his chest.

This was what he'd been born to do. Theronai or not, Grace was his woman. All he had to do now was help her remember why she loved him so they could be together as they were meant to be.

Chapter 25

Grace dreamed of Torr naked and helpless, strapped to a bed while demons consumed his flesh. She dreamed of being forced to watch while he suffered, unable to do anything to save him.

She woke sweating and shaking, the darkness in the cave doing little to help her shed the sickening sense of dread the nightmare had given her.

Torr was at her side before she had time to even sit up. His fingers stroked her hair away from her face, and even though she could barely see him, she knew his touch, his scent.

"You're okay," he told her. "It was just a dream."

She forced herself to shake off the sickening sense of helplessness that clung to her. After several slow, even breaths, she was able to speak. "Can I have some water?"

He left for a minute, then returned and held a water skin to her mouth. She gulped down the cold liquid and the chill woke her up the rest of the way.

Outside, she could see a dim, foggy halo of gray light where the cave entrance stood. "It's almost morning."

"It is."

"We should get moving." She stretched and yawned. "Is there enough light for you to see to hike?"

"Not yet, but there will be by the time I get cleaned up."

She heard a whisper of movement, felt his heat fade. "I'll light the fire, then give you some privacy."

As soon as he had a small flame going, she made quick work of washing up. She put on fresh clothes she'd brought along and left the dirty ones behind.

There was a sense of foreboding in her gut, warning her to travel as light as possible. Between the supplies they'd lost or used and her discarded clothes, her pack was less than half full now.

She slid Tori's short sword in her belt, wondering if she should leave that behind, too. It wasn't like she knew how to use it.

Still, it gave her comfort to know it was there, and that was reason enough to hang on to it for now.

She found Torr waiting at the cave entrance, eating more berries that he'd found. He offered some to her.

Just the idea of putting anything in her stomach made it churn. "No, thanks. I'm good."

"What I wouldn't give for a steaming cup of coffee right now. Maybe some bacon."

Instantly, she knew what those things were and how they tasted, even though she couldn't remember ever having eaten them.

"Sorry. None of that here."

His face brightened with a grin. "It's okay. I have everything I need."

He was talking about her, and in that moment she knew she was falling for him.

Something deep inside her shifted, snapping into place. There was an almost audible click to it—a kind of absolute certainty that things were as they were supposed to be—the way they had been. Her whole body sagged with relief, and a void she hadn't even known she had filled with a soft, comforting warmth.

Grace swayed with shock. Torr's big hands gently gripped her arms, his touch careful of her injuries. "Are you okay?"

He eased her to the ground. She went, too stunned to even consider doing otherwise.

The things she was feelings for him weren't new. They were familiar. More than that. They were a part of her that had been missing for years.

She stared at him, unable to even think of what to ask. Finally, she settled for, "You're not a stranger."

His lips went flat and tight. He said nothing.

"I know you, don't I?"

Again he was silent.

"Why won't you answer me?"

"I want to, but I vowed not to. Please, Grace, just let it go. We'll talk to Brenya when we get back. She can explain everything."

"She won't. Explaining isn't one of her talents. She's more about issuing orders. You need to tell me."

He stroked her face, and even that was familiar. "I've said all I can. We have a job to do. We have to focus on that."

"You're asking me to just ignore the fact that you've been lying to me?"

"I haven't lied. Not once."

"But you've hidden the truth. It's the same thing. How can I trust you now?"

He pushed to his feet. Gone was the lover from last night. All that was here now was a hard, cold warrior. "I'll come back for you when I've found the Masons' building site. Stay here and stay quiet."

"If you think I'm letting you ditch me now just because I know your secret, you're crazy. I'm done sitting around, waiting on others. Waiting for the truth."

"Grace, I—"

"No. I'm done, Torr. We're going to finish this job and go back to Brenya. The sooner I have my answers from the two of you, the sooner I can move on with my life." She pushed to her feet and poked him hard in the chest. "But if you think I'm just going to forgive you for withholding information, you're wrong. I've always tried to be kind, but I'm not a doormat. You can't lie to me. Can't use me."

"Grace, no. I'd never use you."

"Then what do you call last night? Would I have done that with you if I'd known who you really were? If I'd known you were hiding details about my own life from me? I don't think so."

His jaw hardened. "It isn't what you think."

"Maybe it is, maybe it's not. All I know is that I can't be sure. I can't trust you."

His stomach clenched as if she'd just landed a hard blow. "I would never hurt you."

Her heart broke a little, and it was all she could do to keep her chin high and her eyes dry. "Too late. You already have."

With that, she turned and started hiking.

Torr wanted to kill Brenya for binding him to his word. He'd never meant for his promise of silence to hurt Grace, but it had.

Some things are better left forgotten, Brenya had said.

Apparently Torr was one of those things.

His stomach burned. His hands kept closing into fists.

This wasn't how it was supposed to be. Grace was supposed to love him again. He wasn't a pitiful invalid tied to a bed anymore. He was able to protect her, to make love to her. He was more of a man now than he'd been before, and yet she still couldn't love him.

What did that say about him?

Maybe she'd never loved him at all. Maybe her act of self-sacrifice had been one of pity, not love.

There was no way to know now. The woman who'd willingly sacrificed herself to save him couldn't remember why she'd done it.

But she'd remembered something.

He'd seen it in her eyes before she'd started asking questions. She'd looked at him with such warmth.

He'd been sure that what he'd seen glowing in those dark eyes had been love.

Maybe he'd been wrong. Or maybe he'd been right and his silence had killed whatever feelings she'd had for him.

She was too angry and hurt to talk to him, and he was too much of a coward to ask. He was afraid he might not want to know the answer. So instead of dealing with his feelings, he shoved them down and forced himself to concentrate on the job at hand.

That was something he'd had a lot of practice doing.

He picked up his pace, putting himself in front, just in case the Warden had left behind any more nasty surprises. As the ground sloped up again, he slowed down so Grace wouldn't have to struggle to keep up.

She hadn't eaten today, which grated on his sense of duty. And she hadn't slept nearly long enough, thanks to his need for more of her.

At least he hadn't given in to the urge to take her this morning. It would have been so easy to cover her body with his own, part her thighs and slide inside her. She would have been soft and relaxed, right up to the point where he made her burn.

Even the thought was enough to make his cock twitch and swell.

He checked over his shoulder to see that she'd fallen too far behind. Exhaustion bowed her body, and her skin was pale except where the stain of exertion painted her cheeks.

He stopped to give her time to catch up.

"You don't have to wait on me," she said. "I know where I'm going."

"I prefer to keep you close."

"And I prefer to get this job done and get back to where I'm not trapped with you. Just go. I'll be fine."

Her desire to get rid of him stung, but he ignored it. She had a right to be angry with him. She had even more of a right to be angry with Brenya.

So did he.

Torr kept his distance, trying to respect her need for privacy as much as he could. Letting her out of his sight wasn't an option—not with enemies so close by. At least he wasn't breathing down her neck.

When at last they neared the top of the final hill that shielded the lake where Brenya had found her own portal stone, he waited for Grace to catch up.

"It's just over this hill," she said as she caught her breath.

"We'll do it like before. Stay low and quiet. Only looking for now."

Grace nodded and followed him the last few yards. He found a vantage point inside a thicket and crawled through it until his view was clear.

Below was a small lake, just as she'd said. The water was a murky black color. Leading from one edge was a deep furrow in the ground, as if something large and heavy had been dragged away. It was dry, telling him that the mark wasn't fresh.

"They carried the stone off in the direction of the

southern village," said Grace. "Do you think that's a coincidence?"

Not likely. "We don't know anything for sure. We'll have to follow the trail to find out."

She started to stand.

Torr grabbed her arm and pulled her back down before she could break concealment. "Stay down. We've already run into one trap. I'd like to keep it that way."

"You think there's more?"

"I think that we'd be fools to assume this is going to be easy. Any creatures powerful enough to lift a heavy stone from the water and carve it into a portal would also be powerful enough to cover their tracks."

"What if they didn't go that way at all?" she asked.

"Anything is possible."

"So what do we do?" asked Grace. Before he even had time to answer, she did. "Wait. I know."

"You do? How?"

"That knowledge Brenya gave me? It's telling me that we need to go for a swim."

"How's that going to help?"

"We need another one of those rocks. One small enough to carry so it can lead us where we need to go."

"Okay, then. Stay here and be my lookout."

Before she could argue, he slipped away and skirted the ridge so if anyone saw him come down the hill, they wouldn't know where Grace was.

He stripped and dove into the lake. The water was murky and chilly against his heated skin. The pressure around him increased as he swam deeper. Only a faint glow from the twin suns made it all the way to the lake floor, but as he amplified his vision, he could tell the bottom was covered with rocks. All he needed to do was grab one.

The second his fingers closed around a small one, he felt the water shift violently around him. The pressure surged against his eardrums until he thought they'd burst. By the time he recovered from the sudden sense of vertigo, he realized he was pinned.

Touching the stone had triggered some kind of trap, and one of those monofilament nets had caged his body. He couldn't even move enough to reach his sword.

He was stuck, and if he didn't get free soon, he was going to drown down here and leave Grace to fend for herself against the Solarc's minions.

Serving as lookout for Torr was one of the better tasks Grace had been given.

Even if she was hurt by him keeping secrets from her, she still had to admit he had a fabulous body.

He'd stripped naked, then added only his sword belt to his body before he dove into the lake. The water rippled slightly before smoothing out once again.

She held her breath until her lungs burned. He still hadn't come up for air.

She took another deep breath and held it as long as she could. Still no Torr.

Anxiety crawled in her mind until she was queasy.

She couldn't lose him. He might have been lying to her, but he was a link to her past. She cared about him, perhaps even more than she was willing to admit.

Something wasn't right. Sure, he was superhuman and all, but even he had to breathe, didn't he?

She rushed down the slope, shedding the bags she carried as she went. She didn't even slow down, just dove into the water where she thought Torr had entered.

The water was thick, but she saw a flash of something from the corner of her eye. Torr.

He was trapped in one of those nets the Warden had left behind. He was still alive, but each movement was weaker than the last.

Grace swam to him, covered his mouth with hers, and gave him her air. She tried to pull him free, but the net confining him had been partially pinned under a huge stone. No way was she moving that.

She resurfaced just long enough to breathe again before she went back down, her short sword in hand.

She was only able to cut a few strands before her lungs started to ache. Another trip to the surface to breathe, and back down to feed that air to Torr.

The progress was slow, but she eventually freed one of his arms. Blood painted the water, making it even harder to see. She was going by feel now, alternating her trips for air and cutting away the bonds.

Finally, she sliced through one last strand and he shot like a rocket toward the surface.

She followed him, sucking in huge gulps of air to refill her lungs.

His lips were still blue, but the color was returning fast. His skin was shredded in places, but at least he was free.

"You okay?" she asked.

He nodded, not wasting his breath on words.

As soon as she could, she took another deep breath and dove to the bottom. She went by feel, grabbing a rock about the size of her fist before kicking back toward the sky.

She passed Torr on the way up.

"What the hell were you doing?" he demanded as soon as they surfaced. "I almost died doing that a minute ago."

"How many nets can there be down there?"

He took the stone from her hand. "Let's not find out. Back to shore."

He didn't need to tell her twice.

Her wet leather tunic weighed her down, but she was a strong enough swimmer to make it back safely. Once on land, she collapsed and just breathed.

Torr stood over her, naked, sword in hand, scanning the area as if expecting trouble.

"You don't think we're alone?"

Bloody water dripped down his body. "I've had enough surprises for one day."

She turned over and crawled to where she'd dropped her medical bag. "Sit down. Some of those cuts are bad enough you're going to need me to sew them up."

"They'll heal," he said, not even sparing her a glance. "If you don't want to do it here, we can go back into

the woods where we're out of sight, but you're bleeding pretty bad."

"I've bled worse. I'll live."

Okay. Clearly he had no intention of letting her do
her job.

She gathered her things, positioned them over her
wet clothes and picked up the rock from where he'd
tossed it.

She was sure she was supposed to feel something,
but all she felt was gravity. "I'm not sure this is the
right kind of rock."

"It is. I felt its pull a second ago."

"I don't feel anything."

"Maybe because you have no innate magic."

"Oh." Of course she didn't. The only thing she was
good at was healing, and he wouldn't even let her do
that. Despite what he thought, some of those gashes
were nasty, and who knew what kind of bacteria lived
in that water?

She examined his naked body from where she stood,
wishing he'd let her do something to help ease his pain.

A sharp sting sliced across her arm. She gasped a
little before she could control her surprised reaction.

She looked down and saw that she'd been cut, or
maybe had reopened one of the cuts from yesterday.

"Stop it," he nearly shouted.

She jumped at the force of his words and took several involuntary steps back. "What? I didn't do anything."

He swallowed a curse, and by the look of his face, it

had been a big one. "I'm sorry. I shouldn't have snapped. Let's get out of here and figure out our next move."

Water dripped into her eyes as she followed him. The view of his naked backside was a nice distraction from the general ache of her body and the sting of the cuts she'd gathered helping to free him.

By the time he stopped, she was more than ready. She pulled some bandages and salve from her bag and went to him. "Let me do this."

"You first."

He took the supplies from her and wrapped her cuts with a gentle touch. By the time he was done, she'd forgotten why she was supposed to be mad at him. All she could think about was how glad she was that he was alive and breathing.

"Thanks," he said, "for saving me back there. I thought for sure that was the end of the line."

She didn't even like to think about what could have happened. "You're welcome."

He lifted her chin so she was looking into his eyes. So pretty was the clear amber that she almost missed what he said. "You can't ever do it again."

"Do what?"

"Risk your life for me. If anything happened to you, it would destroy me."

"Nothing happened."

"But it could have. Far too easily." He stood and started pulling on his clothes.

His cuts had already scabbed over, leaving her little doubt that he would be fine and whole within a few hours. She, on the other hand, would take days to fully heal.

"Time to go?" she asked as she started packing away her things.

"Yes."

She picked up the stone and handed it to him. "Which way?"

He took it, but didn't seem to perform any magic that she could tell.

He pointed. "That way."

"So they did take the stone toward the southern village?"

He didn't answer her question. All he said was, "Let me know if you need a break. I plan to push hard and be there by nightfall."

"Don't worry. I'll keep up." And she would, even if it killed her.

Chapter 26

Torr had no intention of taking her to the Masons' building site. She was going right back to Brenya and the others, where there was absolutely no risk of her throwing herself into danger to save him. Again.

As grateful as he was to her for saving his life, he was also furious. How could she risk herself? Didn't she realize she was the center of his world?

Of course she didn't. And thanks to Brenya, he couldn't tell her.

Rage and frustration fueled his stride, giving him the feeling he could go on forever without stopping.

An hour into their trek, he felt a sudden shift in the direction the lake stone was pulling. The bag it was in lifted slightly from his hip, indicating that the other stone was to his left. He kept walking, and within a few minutes the stone was tugging his bag backward.

They'd just passed the site.

They were still a few miles from the southern village—too far for him to get there and back before nightfall.

It was stupid to be this close to his enemy and not at least take the opportunity to see what he was up against.

"Will you wait here for a minute?" he asked Grace. "I need a little privacy."

She slumped to the ground where she stood, her breathing heavy. "Sure."

He had set a hard pace, and as much as he hated pushing her, it was better than having her out here after dark.

"I won't be long."

He slipped into the trees, following the stone's pull. He didn't have to go far to find what he was looking for.

Inside a large clearing was what looked much like a Sentinel Stone. Two Masons hammered away at it, chipping tiny bits of rock from intricate runes. Even though he'd stolen a hammer, each of them still wielded one. With each strike of their tools, he could feel little sparks of energy shoot into the atmosphere—the same kind of sparks that fueled his power.

Each of those sparks seemed attracted to him and hit him like a minuscule stinging bite against his skin. He guessed that if he stayed here long, the power inside him would grow dangerously fast.

In addition to the two Masons, he saw a crystalline Warden standing guard over the site. Its clear sword was in its grip, catching fiery rays of sunshine. A cloud of rainbows covered the ground around it, each one cast from the Warden's prismatic body. It was so still it looked like a statue, but Torr knew better than to let that fool him.

Flanking it were two glittering black Hunters, sitting idle, ready to pounce.

He used some of the power bombarding him to amplify his vision. Glittering filaments crossed the area, indicating the presence of several traps. The entire perimeter was covered. In fact there was one only a few feet in front of him.

The runes carved into the stone appeared to be the same ones that had been Brenya's portal. They were progressing slowly, chip by chip. Even with both Masons working, he guessed he had at least a day to plan his attack.

With only him to wage the battle, he wasn't sure it would be enough time.

Torr backed up the way he'd come, being careful to retrace his steps so that he wouldn't accidentally run into any nasty surprises along the way. When he got back to Grace, she was sitting where he'd left her, hugging her knees with her head resting on them.

She didn't hear him coming until he was too close, which only served to highlight her human limitations and how vulnerable they made her.

He needed to get her back to the village. Now. And once he did, he was going to force Brenya to keep her safe.

Torr reached down and offered Grace his hand. "We need to keep moving."

She gave him a weary nod as she took his hand. He

pulled her up, the move putting her close enough to him that he could smell her scent.

He was instantly aroused. Every coherent thought he'd had only a moment ago had been knocked out by memories of having her naked in his arms, of being inside her, and wondering how he could get there again.

She stared up at him. Her lips parted, and all he could think about was kissing her, tasting her.

He saw her mouth move, but whatever she said was lost. It wasn't until he heard the sound of his name that he snapped out of the spell she wove around him.

"Are you okay?" she asked.

He closed his eyes to block out the sight of her sweet face. "Yes."

Her fingers settled on his brow, so gentle and warm. How many times had she touched him like this back at Dabyr? How many times had he wished he'd been a whole man, able to love her the way he wanted?

Now that he could, there was no time. She was angry at him for hiding the truth from her, and while he understood that anger, he couldn't change it.

"We should go," he said.

"You seem sick. If you need to rest—"

"No. That's not going to help." Not even close.

He pulled her into motion and let go of her hand to put some distance between them. He couldn't touch her and still keep his head where it needed to be. Danger was only a few minutes' walk away, and if she'd let him, he would have taken her right there on the forest floor.

It was better not to look at her or touch her, better to remember why he was here.

The rest of their trip was an exercise in self-discipline. Centuries of doing the hard things, of being responsible, gave him the mental fortitude he needed to get them where they were going.

As soon as she recognized where their path led, she stopped in her tracks. "You were bringing me here all along, weren't you?"

He turned to face her, and the look of betrayal on her face nearly brought him to his knees.

"Yes," he said, unwilling to lie to her. Misleading her had been bad enough. He wouldn't heap more sins on top of that.

Her voice wavered, but he couldn't tell if it was sadness or anger that caused it. "And that little pit stop you made? You found the Masons, didn't you? You found them and didn't even tell me."

"Yes. You'll be safe here while I go back and deal with the threat."

"I guess saving your life wasn't enough to prove I'm worthy of your trust, that I'm capable of not only taking care of myself, but also helping you."

"It's not like that."

She got right up in his face, close enough that he could see the wet sheen of pain glittering in her eyes. "I thought you were different from the others, that you didn't see me as a puny, weak human. I know now that I was wrong."

Grace turned and left, hurrying off into the village, where she disappeared inside one of the huts.

Brenya's voice came from behind him. "I see our Grace has kept you on your toes, young Theronai."

He'd been so absorbed in what Grace had been saying that he hadn't even realized the other woman was standing there. Now that he did, shock rocked him back on his heels.

She looked tired. Exhausted. Her skin hung on her frame, the smooth, ageless texture replaced with deep lines. Even her eyes, swirling with stormy waves, seemed duller, with a milky sheen of passing time.

He tried to hide his reaction so as not to insult her. "I guess that's one way to put it. Why the hell didn't you take her with you when you teleported everyone away?"

"You needed her. I trust the information I gave her was useful?"

"I found the Masons. They're not too far away, either. If they finish that stone and open a portal, this whole village will be overrun within hours."

"We can travel to the northern village, but the outcome would be the same. You must destroy the stone."

"Give me the crystals and tell me how to use them."

"Using them is simple. Surviving their use will take more skill."

"What's that supposed to mean?"

"There will be magical backlash when the crystals are activated."

"What kind of backlash?"

"The deadly kind. If you can see the crystals' blue fire, you are already too late. It will destroy all in its reach."

"You're telling me those crystals put off magical radiation?"

She frowned a second before nodding. "Yes."

"Okay. So what kind of skill is needed to avoid this unpleasantness?"

"Speed. Timing. You must be away from the area before the explosion occurs."

"I don't suppose you have some kind of long fuse, do you?"

"No. Any lengthy delays would give the Warden time to react. This would be a bad thing."

He instantly started thinking about the Masons' building site and the distance between the stone and the Warden. There were only a few yards—a distance the Warden could cross in a matter of seconds. That was assuming the Warden stayed at its current guard post. "I'm going to need a distraction."

A frown pulled at Brenya's wrinkles. "Indeed. I will provide this. Give me the night to do so."

"What do you have in mind?"

She ignored his question. "Get yourself food and rest. You will need it for what is to come."

Grace was neck-deep in a hot bath when Brenya walked in. She was stooped over, moving slowly, as if even a hard step would crush her brittle bones. She looked old, fragile.

Grace's heart gave a sharp squeeze as she realized that even Brenya wasn't invincible.

"You've pushed yourself too hard," said Grace.

"I do only what I must, child." Brenya eased onto the bench next to Grace's clothes. "Your warrior seemed upset. You scared him again." It wasn't a question.

"He lied to me. So did you."

"Hidden truths, not lies."

"Same thing."

"Do you think I would choose to hurt you? That my acts hold malice?"

"Just because you don't mean to hurt me doesn't mean it doesn't hurt."

"Convoluted logic. Very human."

"Well, I *am* human."

"Yes. And I should not hold you responsible for a mistake of your birth."

The unintentional jab hurt as much as the rest. Maybe all humans were as sensitive as Grace was, or maybe she was just a wimp. "Why are you here?"

"I sensed your injuries."

Grace knew better than to ask how. The woman wouldn't answer. "I'm fine. It's nothing serious. Save your strength."

"I also thought you might need to talk."

"About what?"

"You shared your body with a man you believe lied to you."

"I don't know how you know what we did, but I don't just *believe* he lied—I know it."

"Do you?"

"You should know, too. You forced him to lie."

"*Pretend* is a more accurate word, but I see how you could be confused."

Grace stifled a scream of frustration. "Look, I love you like a mother, but you don't get to decide how I should feel. You and Torr conspired to hide things from me. You even went so far as to force a vow from him. I'm not okay with any of that."

"Some things are better left forgotten, child."

Grace's voice dropped so close to a growl, it shocked her. "I'm not a child, and I'm sick of hearing you say that. It's *my* life. I have a right to know what was in it. I have a right to my memories."

"Forgive Torr. He had no choice. I knew his weak spot and used it against him in a way that ensured he could deny me nothing."

"That man doesn't have a weak spot."

"Yes, he does. You, child, are it."

She groaned and let her head fall back on the wooden rim of the tub. "Great. Now not only am I weak, but I make those around me the same way."

Brenya's tone was one of irritation and warning. "Cease your self-pity. You have what women all over the universe can only wish for."

"What's that?"

"A man who would do anything for you."

"You're wrong. I wanted to help him, but all he could think about was getting me back here, like some kind of naughty child sent to her room."

"Theronai males are protective creatures by nature—a trait on which I am depending."

Oh, no. Grace knew that tone. Devious, cunning, scheming. "What are you planning?"

"Victory."

Grace climbed out of the water, desperate to find out what she could so she could warn Torr. She grabbed Brenya's arm—something she never would have done two days ago. "Tell me what you're going to make him do."

Brenya covered her hand, and the hot tingle of healing raced over Grace's skin, erasing all the nicks and cuts she'd suffered.

The older woman bowed slightly for a second before straightening. "You have no need for concern, child. All will be as it is meant to be."

"What does that mean?"

"You will see," said Brenya. Then she walked away, leaving Grace dripping and cold.

Chapter 27

Grace burst through the door of the hut where Torr was changing. Her dark hair was dripping wet, her face pale and drawn with fear.

He dropped the loose pants that one of the village women had made for him, and drew his sword. "What's wrong?"

Grace came to a dead stop. "Wrong?" she asked, staring at his naked groin.

The door swung shut behind her, darkening the room. The little bit of orange light filtering through the rough thatch walls was enough for him to see her pupils flare. His animal brain took that as a sign that she liked what she saw, rather than that the room had suddenly gone dark.

A telltale tingle of arousal swept through him, but he choked it dead before it could take over.

"Yes, wrong. You stormed in here like demons were nipping at your heels. What happened?"

She was still staring, and it was getting harder by the second for him to remember his manners.

Grace cleared her throat and finally looked away. "Brenya."

"Something happened to Brenya?"

Grace's gaze strayed back to him, but only for a second before she squeezed her eyes shut. "No. She's happening to you."

"You're going to have to be more specific, honey."

At the sound of the endearment, she opened her eyes again, but this time she looked right at him. The pain he saw there nearly brought him to his knees. "She's going to hurt you, Torr. And she's going to use me to do it."

"Start at the beginning. What did she say?" He sheathed his sword, picked up the pants and used them to cover his growing erection.

The level of distraction in Grace's tone dropped significantly. "She said that I was your weak spot and that she was going to use that to get victory."

"Did she say how?" he asked, even as he knew the answer.

"No."

"Of course not." One deep breath. Two. Frustration trickled out, but only a little. "Let me get dressed and we'll go talk to her."

Grace grabbed his arm. "No. We can't. What if that's what she wants? What if it's part of her plan?"

"There's only one way to find out."

He started to put the pants on, but she ripped them

away and tossed them across the room. Fury and fear trembled out of her. "You're not listening to me. We can't play into her hands. We have to outsmart her."

Torr wanted to be the kind of man who could ease her worries, but all he could think about was how close she was, how sweet she smelled, how he was stark naked and wanted her that way, too. It didn't matter if she was mad at him or if she was more worried about something else. His body seemed to short-circuit his brain, narrowing his focus to a very small field.

He managed enough honor to ask, "What do you think we should do, honey?"

"Beat her at her own game."

"How are we going to do that? And why? We're on the same side."

"Because she's going to get you killed." She grabbed both of his shoulders and shook him—or at least she tried to. She swayed more than he did, but he understood the emphasis she was trying to achieve.

He wrapped his hands around her waist. He couldn't help it. She was too close, and her touch on him—whether for emphasis or not—was more than he could ignore.

He stepped closer until they were almost pressed together. He could feel the heat of her body against his naked skin and wished desperately for the power to make leather evaporate. "All Brenya wants is for this place to be safe. I'm going to see to it that it's done right. I've been fighting for a long, long time, and I know what I'm doing."

"I can't let her hurt you."

"Even though you think I lied?"

"You *did* lie, but Brenya forced you to."

"Does that mean you forgive me?"

"Are you going to tell me what you know about my old life?"

He shook his head. "You know I can't. I wish things were different, but we're playing by Brenya's rules."

"I don't trust her anymore, Torr. Neither should you."

"She saved your life. She kept you safe for years. For that, I owe her everything."

"I'm afraid that's what she's going to end up taking."

He brushed her damp hair behind her ear. "As long as she doesn't take you away from me, I can handle whatever she decides to dish out."

A pretty flush colored her cheeks. "I should leave and let you get dressed, go talk to her."

"Or you could stay."

That flush deepened, and she wet her lips. "I think it's better if I don't. If I stay, I'm going to want to touch you."

"Sounds like a good plan to me. I'm dying to kiss you again, Grace."

A delicate shiver raced through her. "I still want you, but I can't be with you like that again. You're not the man I thought you were. I can't trust you now, not after knowing you lied."

Something deep in his chest screamed in agony as it

died. The woman he loved didn't trust him. His sweet Grace, who willingly risked her life to heal him, no longer trusted him.

He'd lost something precious—something that, once shattered, could never be made whole again. Even if he proved himself worthy of her, the belief that he'd lied would always be in the back of her mind.

Torr stepped away and turned his back. His nudity was an embarrassment now. It hadn't bothered him before, but now she saw him as a liar, and that made shame fester in his soul. "You should go."

"Torr, I—"

"I have preparations to make and I need to secure the village perimeter before I go."

"We should talk."

He slid the loose pants on, glad to finally be covered. "There's nothing to talk about. You don't trust me and I can't change your mind about that, not when I'm bound by my vow. It's best if I just focus on keeping you and the others safe. It's what I do best."

"Promise me you'll be safe."

He didn't dare. That wasn't the kind of promise his kind ever made. Instead he said, "Don't worry about me."

"Of course I'll worry. I care about you."

"Don't," he snapped, his voice too loud and harsh. Then, more calmly, "It's better for both of us if you don't."

Grace had hurt Torr. She hadn't meant to, but his pain was both obvious and devastating.

All through dinner, she kept hoping for a glimpse of him. She wanted a chance to talk to him, to find a way to ease the sting she'd caused. She ached knowing that she'd hurt him, and no matter what she thought to say, nothing seemed right. She knew he had his reasons for lying to her, but until he was willing to tell her about them—about why he would give Brenya a vow that forced him to lie to Grace—she didn't see how she could forgive him.

Maybe that made her a bad person.

She questioned herself all night, searching for a chance to talk to him, but none came. As the women flowed through the center of the village, gathering their stew and bread, she never once caught sight of his head towering over the crowd. With each passing minute, her heart fell further, until she knew she had to fix it.

She couldn't live like this, her stomach twisting with anger and anxiety.

Grace gathered some food for him, using it as an excuse to speak to him, then went searching. He'd said he was going to check the perimeter, so she wove her way around the edge of the village, inching out more with each step.

Brenya usually had the humming protective barrier in place by this time of night, but Grace didn't feel it, didn't see its subtle shimmer.

By the time she realized that the barrier must not have been put up tonight, she was far enough into the woods that the flickering light of the central fire was barely visible.

"You shouldn't be out here," came Torr's voice from the darkness.

Grace jumped, jostling the food on the small tray she carried. He was next to her, steadying the cup of water before it had time to spill. "You scared me."

"At least it was me you ran into rather than one of the Hunters."

"I was paying attention to the temperature. If it had gotten cold, I would have bolted back to the others."

There wasn't much light to see by, but there was enough for her to make out his silhouette and a faint glitter of moonlight in his amber eyes. Even without those clues, she could smell the scents of heat and forest that clung to him. He'd used the same soap as everyone else, but on him, it smelled so much better. All she wanted to do was get closer.

"What are you doing out of the village?" The deep tone of his voice smoothed over her senses, making some deep part of her go still and quiet.

She was too drawn to this man. She'd thought it was bad before, but now that she knew what he felt like when sliding into her body—how he wrapped himself around her like he couldn't stand the thought of letting her go—she wanted even more of him.

Grace had to clear her throat to get the words to come out. "I didn't see you at dinner. You need to eat."

"I don't have much of an appetite. Give my share to one of the kids." His sword was propped up beside him, visible now that it wasn't attached to his body.

"There was more than enough to go around. Tori bagged several kills last night. And you need to eat."

"Fine. Leave the tray if it will make you feel better."

She found a smooth rock protruding from the ground and balanced the tray on it. "Are you going to eat?"

"Go back to the village, Grace."

Not "honey," just "Grace." The change shouldn't have hurt her, but it did. She was the one who'd pushed him away, so why was she so desperate to drag him close again?

"You're still angry with me," she guessed.

She felt him tense more than she saw it. She was so attuned to him that even his stillness was enough to warn her of a surge of emotion.

"Anger doesn't even begin to cover what I'm feeling. Not that it matters. Just go. I have work to do and you're far too much of a distraction to have around."

Again, the sting of his words hit her hard, but this time she actually flinched.

Torr let out a harsh curse as he ran his hand through his hair. "I hate it that you still react like that to me, after all we've been through together the last few days."

"I don't know what you mean."

"You jerked away like you thought I was going to hit you. I know you've had a rough life, but dammit, Grace, I'd never do something like that to you. I *love* you."

His words wrapped around her, squeezing the air from her lungs. The ground beneath her feet seemed to rock. The woods around her dissipated in a shower of glittery sparks, so bright that she was blinded.

In that instant, something in her head burst open, and she remembered everything. The night Torr rescued her and her baby brother—the night her mother was killed by demons. She remembered him lifting her away from her mom's brutalized body and cradling her close as he carried her out of the house, whispering words of comfort. She remembered the blast of fire behind them, and the scream of the demons consumed in the blaze. He hadn't even slowed down—not until that slimy, sluglike creature had shot out of the darkness and slammed into his back, poisoning him.

Even as he fell, he'd thought of protecting her first, spinning to land so he wouldn't crush her.

She could picture his room at Dabyr, the way he grew progressively sicker and more discouraged every day. She'd ached to help him, but there was so little she could do. He'd begged for death, and yet she hadn't been brave enough to give in to his wishes.

She remembered Dabyr and the safety it represented for her. She'd fallen in love with him there. Gilda, a powerful Theronai, had given her the means to save him there. And it was there that Grace had fastened the disks to their spines in a desperate effort to heal him.

Those disks had connected them for years. It had been his sorrow she'd felt, his anger. Even as far away as she was—worlds apart—she'd still felt his presence.

And now he was here—this man she loved so much and had somehow forgotten.

How could she have done that to him? How could she have forgotten a man she'd been willing to die for? How could she have been angry at him for withholding his past when he'd saved her life and Blake's?

It was such a miracle that he'd survived, that he was up and walking again. He was whole and strong, just as he'd been the night they'd met. How hard must it have been for him not to tell her what they'd shared?

Tears of joy filled her eyes. Torr—her Torr—was alive and well. She wanted to celebrate what a miracle he was.

Relief and love flowed through her. She surged upward, into his arms, kissing him as she'd been dying to do all those years ago.

He rocked back on his heels but recovered from his surprise fast. Within a heartbeat he was kissing her back, holding her tight. He cradled her as though he would never again let her go.

He loved her. She still couldn't wrap her head around that. He was such a good man—it was hard to believe he would choose her when he could have whoever he wanted.

Her feet left the ground. His tongue danced with hers. Her body heated in a mad rush, and all she could think about was getting as close to him as possible. She wanted to hold on forever and never let go.

Her brave, heroic warrior loved her—something she'd never thought possible.

"I need you," he said against her mouth.

Her body lit up like a torch, igniting with sudden arousal. She didn't know if the disk on her back was feeding her some of his desire, but she felt her skin heat and her nipples bead up against his chest.

She needed him, too. "There's something I need to tell you."

"I can't wait. I need you. Here. Now."

"Yes" was the only response to the fierce command ringing in his voice.

He stripped her tunic over her head, breaking their kiss just long enough to do the job. A second later, his nimble fingers unraveled the knots holding her underwear in place. She was naked from her knees up, wearing only the leather straps around her calves to hold her shoes in place.

His mouth moved down her body, hot against her neck. She felt the sweet sting of his teeth and strong suction bite at her skin. She knew he'd left a mark for everyone to see, and a small part of her reveled in it.

His big hands seemed to be everywhere, stroking her, cupping her breasts and bottom. Her whole body was alive, vibrating with a shimmering sense of completion.

This was the man she loved. And he loved her back. The sheer power of that was so overwhelming, so unbelievable, she wasn't sure she would ever get used to the idea. She wasn't big enough to hold so much emotion, so much sensation, and yet she couldn't shy away from even the tiniest scrap of it.

He left a trail of stinging love bites leading all the way to her nipple. His mouth covered her, the suction almost too much for her to take. She dug her fingernails into his scalp. The action made him moan, which vibrated her nipple in a way that had her careening toward climax.

He lifted his head and looked up at her. The heat in his gaze was enough to set her skin on fire. "Not yet. Not until I'm inside you."

Her fingers tugged at the drawstring holding his pants closed. She reached inside and let her fingers quest over him, gently, as if it were the first time she'd touched him.

In some ways it was. She'd been with him before, but never as herself. She'd been only a shadow then, only a part of the whole. Now that she knew who she was, who *he* was, she was going to enjoy him all the more.

Torr hissed in pleasure, going still as if to regain his self-control. His fingers clenched around her hips, and she could feel him tremble.

His loose pants slid down his legs. Grace fell to her knees, taking him in her mouth as she went.

The strangled sound he made was one that went to her head, making her feel powerful, feminine and completely desirable. His hands cupped her head, his fingers threading through her hair for a firm grip.

She couldn't take all of him, but he didn't seem to mind. Each shallow thrust made him pant with need. Each sucking pull made his fingers curl and tighten in her hair.

"Too much," he said on a sigh.

She pulled off of him and licked her lips as she looked up. "Not enough. Not even close."

Before she could go back for more, he lifted her body. She was forced to grip his hips with her thighs to keep her balance. The move spread her legs wide and gave her a clear view of his erection gleaming between them.

"Watch me take you." The low command made a shiver race across her skin. "I want you to know you're mine."

She didn't need to see him slide into her to be convinced of that. Her heart had been his for years. The fact that she knew it now only made their joining that much sweeter.

He shifted her weight, lining them up just right. She saw the wide head of his penis wedge just inside her body, felt the slow stretch as he eased into her. By the time he'd lowered her all the way, connecting them completely, she was barely able to pull in her next breath.

The memory of him breathing for her rose to the surface. She'd been so weak then, barely alive, and yet she'd felt his presence and knew she was safe. Whatever happened to her next she didn't fear because Torr had been there with her.

Grace kissed him, wordlessly thanking him for not giving up on her, for getting her to Brenya, and for saving her life. Twice. He hadn't sought any thanks or praise, but she swore she'd find a way to tell him properly how she felt. Later. Much later. For now, all she could manage was to cling to him while he moved inside her.

The pleasure he gave her was like a firestorm burning fast and hot. The angle of their bodies made him brush against her clit with each stroke. She barely even felt her orgasm building before it bore down on her and pushed the breath from her body.

"That's it, honey," whispered Torr against her cheek. "Just like that. So pretty."

He picked up speed, which made each rippling wave slam into the next. By the time she found the strength to pull in a breath, she felt his arms tighten around her. He pulled her down and covered her mouth with his as the first pulse of semen surged within her.

The last fading remnants of her orgasm fluttered around him as he came. He held her like she was the most precious thing in the universe, and in that moment, she believed it.

Torr sagged to the ground. He eased her back onto the damp leaves, and stared into her eyes while he caught his breath. The tender sweep of his fingers over her face melted her heart even more. He was so much a part of her now, both physically and emotionally, that she knew she'd be indelibly marked by his presence.

Just as he'd said, she knew she was now his, and the knowledge both exhilarated and terrified her.

"One of these days, I'll have you in a proper bed," he said.

"Back at Dabyr, maybe? They had the best mattresses there."

His finger stilled in the act of petting her. "You remember?"

She was almost afraid to say it for fear she'd forget again. "Everything. That's what I wanted to tell you."

"You remember us?" he asked, with such tenuous hope that it broke her heart.

How hard must it have been for him not to tell her who he was and what they'd meant to each other? And why had Brenya demanded that of him?

Some things are better left forgotten.

That had been her consistent answer, and yet Grace had no idea why the woman would say that. Sure, there had been some ugly times in Grace's life, but they were nothing compared to the beauty of the love she shared with Torr. How could Brenya—a woman who was never wrong—be so mistaken?

Grace kissed him again, long and slow, hoping to ease his worries. "I remember us clearest of all. I remember how you saved me, how you breathed for me, how you gave me up and let me go when coming here was my only hope for survival. That couldn't have been easy on you."

"I love you so much. Letting her take you away to a world I couldn't reach was the scariest thing I've ever done. But now here you are, safe. And mine."

"All yours."

He kissed her again but broke it off suddenly. "I hear something."

Grace didn't, but she trusted that he was right and she stayed silent.

"Go back to the village," he whispered. "I'm going to check it out."

She grabbed her clothes and slipped through the trees as fast and quietly as she could to warn the others of possible danger. The hiss of metal on metal sounded behind her as he drew his sword.

Chapter 28

Tori followed Grace to where she waited at the edge of the village, just inside the trees. The woman seemed to be okay, but then, what Tori had seen Torr do to Grace was nothing like what she was used to seeing back in the caves.

Grace seemed to *want* Torr to touch her. She seemed to enjoy it when he hurt her—although *hurt* wasn't the right word. Grace didn't seem to be suffering at all, except for one part where she cried out.

And even that didn't seem like pain to Tori.

She was confused, off balance. The calm she'd found earlier tonight vanished, leaving her fighting her rage once again.

She stepped out where Grace could see her and asked, "Why did you let him do that?"

Grace jumped and hugged her clothes to her chest. "Tori," she said on a relieved exhale. "What are you doing?"

"I saw you. I watched. You let him hurt you."

"He didn't hurt me. And you shouldn't have watched. It was private."

It was never private in the caves where Tori had grown up. But now that she thought about it, her sisters did the same thing—hiding their pain behind closed doors, letting their husbands touch them. "Then why did you do it in the open?"

"I didn't plan to. It just kind of happened." Grace's skin glowed. A small smile widened as she spoke. She wore a strange look on her face—one Tori couldn't quite figure out. It was almost like Grace was thinking about letting Torr near her again.

"You . . . liked it," said Tori, unable to believe what she saw. She was used to lies, but never from Grace.

Grace blushed and smoothed her hair. "Of course I did."

"Why?"

There was a slight pause, then a brief flash of sympathy on Grace's face. When she spoke, it was with the patience of someone speaking to a child. "Because I love him. Because it feels good." She pulled her tunic over her head to cover her nakedness. "You'll understand one of these days."

Nicholas's scarred face flashed in Tori's head for a second. He was one of the few men who'd dare to touch her. She'd plunged a knife into his chest, but it hadn't killed him. He was too strong for the puny girl she'd been then to kill. She was stronger now. More skilled with weapons. Maybe she could kill him now if she tried.

Strangely, she wasn't sure she wanted to try again.

"Torr will hurt you, Grace. He's being nice now so you'll let your guard down, but if you do—if you sleep—you'll wake up in pain."

Grace's eyes softened with sympathy, and it was all Tori could do not to plunge her sword into one of them.

Grace was kind. Gentle. Tori had to remember she wasn't the enemy. She was one of the people Tori needed to protect.

Don't kill Grace, kill for her.

Tori repeated the phrase in her mind, over and over, until her hands stopped shaking. She let go of her sword and took a deep breath.

"It's not like that," said Grace. "Not with me and Torr. I know you lived through something so horrible that few people would have survived, but what was done to you was abnormal. That was rape. What Torr and I did is love—that's the way it's supposed to be."

Love, rape, it was all the same. Grace's words were just pretty lies. Tori had heard enough of them to know. Zillah had held her captive for years. He was the worst liar of all, making her think the pain was over—leaving her alone just long enough for her to be lulled into thinking she was safe.

Tori knew better than to think she'd ever be safe again. But as long as she was still armed and breathing, she would fight.

Don't kill Grace, kill for her.

Next time someone tried to hurt Grace, Tori would

kill them. Maybe then, if she killed enough, Zillah would stop haunting her dreams.

For now, she would slip into the forest and hunt, to quiet her hungry rage.

The village would eat well tomorrow.

"I didn't see anything," said Torr as he came out of the woods.

"It was Tori," said Grace. "She saw us together. It upset her."

He winced. "Poor kid. I'll go talk to her."

"No, she won't trust you. Not that she really trusts anyone, but you being a man makes you a villain. Besides, it wouldn't matter what you said. She's so messed up."

"She was sent here because she tried to kill Nicholas. Has Brenya been able to help her control her violent outbursts?"

"She's less violent now than she was a few years ago, but she's still a long way from being a pacifist."

"She'll need to go home soon. We need all the female Theronai we can find."

"I understand, but she's not ready yet. If you'd seen her just now . . ."

Torr hugged Grace, unable to go another second without touching her. "We'll help her. Whatever she needs."

"Mostly, I think she just needs time. Every night that she goes to sleep warm, safe and fed is another victory.

Maybe after enough of them, she'll find some kind of life for herself."

"Time moves faster here than it does on Earth. That makes it a bit easier to be patient, but sooner or later, she'll need to step up."

"I'm sure she will. And when she does, there won't be a force in the universe powerful enough to stop her."

He grunted. "Yeah, well, let's just make sure she's nice and sane before we give her access to a giant pool of magical power."

Grace's body shifted. The languid feel of her leaning on him changed until she was standing firmly on her own feet. "Will you touch her before you go? Maybe see if you're compatible?"

Amazingly, the thought hadn't even crossed his mind. He had already touched her when she'd tried to unman him in the lake, but he hadn't considered that she might be his match. Now that he thought about it, though, there'd been no telltale tingle, no hum from his luceria. "We're not. The only woman I'm interested in being with is you."

She gave him a sad smile. "That's sweet, but we both know you have to find your mate."

"I've lived a long time without one. My lifemark is healthy." *Ish.* "I'll be fine."

Grace hid her face, but he felt her nod against his chest. "I'm going to get some sleep. Do you want to come?"

"I do, but I can't. The stakes are too high. I need to patrol the area, but I'll stop by before I leave. Brenya is supposed to have something ready for me by morning."

"I understand. If you change your mind, I'm in the third hut south of Brenya's. In a real bed."

He lifted her chin so he could see her pretty eyes. "You are pure temptation, honey."

She gave him a smile that didn't go very deep, but then again, she was probably worried about Tori and about him finding a compatible woman. What she didn't know was that he had no intention of looking for one—something he would tell her when things were a little more settled between them.

Right now he had a village to protect. Brenya's shield was nowhere in sight, and it was well past the time she usually put it up. It wasn't the kind of thing a person forgot, which made him wonder just how much power the woman had left in her.

He needed to find out, but there were also other things he needed to discuss with Brenya, and those were all things best left for after Grace was safely asleep.

Chapter 29

Torr rapped on the door to the hut where Brenya was staying. After a few seconds, she finally let out a faint "Come."

He ducked inside and shut the door behind him.

Brenya sat huddled in a pile of furs. Lines visibly marked her face, and her pale skin sagged along her jaw.

"You're not okay, are you?" he asked.

"I am as well as I must be."

"There's no barrier tonight to hide the village."

"I could choose only one task tonight, and this one was more important."

He looked at the small table in front of her. The box with the crystals sat there, along with a small pile of dull stones. They looked like all the others scattered across the ground in this area, but he could feel a subtle pulse of power radiating out from them.

"What are they?"

"The distraction I promised."

"How do they work?"

"You will drop them in bodies of water. Each one will create the energy of a Sanguinar stepping into direct sunlight."

"How is that going to help?"

"The Solarc hates their kind most of all. He watches for them constantly, peering through suns for signs of them so he can send his Wardens to destroy them. The presence of two suns here blinds him, but the closest Warden will be drawn to it—summoned."

"What if it doesn't want to go?"

"Wardens have no wishes, no will. They are empty instruments of destruction that live only to obey the Solarc's command."

"So I toss one of these in water, and *poof*, instant Warden?"

She nodded. "You must wait until the Masons' job is done before you attack. When they return home, you will then slay the Warden and any Hunters that remain."

"Will the Mason's hammer do the job?"

"It will when applied properly."

"And how is that?"

"With all the force you can muster." She gathered the stones and poured them into an oiled leather pouch. "Kill the Warden fast, young Theronai. I am too weak to be of much use to you if you fail."

"You should rest."

"Rest is not what I need to recover."

"What do you need?"

"I must return home. Here, I am cut off from the source of my power."

"And what source is that? Maybe I can bring it to you."

She gave him a weak smile. "I do not think even you can fetch an Athanasian moon for me."

"Sorry, no."

"I will go home soon, when my moon is at its most powerful and will restore me fastest. You will stay here and guard my people."

"I will, will I?"

"You will do this thing, for it is the only way to protect what your heart desires above all else."

Grace.

"I see you are interested, young Theronai."

"She remembered everything."

Brenya's shoulders bowed with sadness. "I know. And for that I am sorry."

"Why are you sorry? She remembers our time together. She remembers loving me."

"Her heart was always yours. She would have loved you again given enough time, even without her memories."

"But now I don't have to wait. What's so bad about that?"

"She remembers other things as well as her love for you."

"I know she had a hard life, but she's strong. She can handle it. Whatever bad memories she has, we'll work through them together."

"It is not her memories of abuse and loss that you should fear."

"What's that supposed to mean?"

Brenya shook her head. "All will be as it is meant to be. Like you, I can only watch."

"You're not making any sense."

"I am, but only time will prove that to you."

"How about we stop with the cryptic crap and you tell me how long you'll be gone. I want to take Grace back home as soon as possible."

"And then what?"

"I find a way to make her happy, keep her safe."

"Have you forgotten the disk you wear?"

"Of course not."

"Now that Grace remembers everything, she also remembers how to use the disks. What will happen to her the next time you are injured?"

His blood chilled as he realized what Brenya meant. "I'll make sure Grace knows she's not allowed to use them."

"If you believe that will stop her, then you are a fool."

He hated to admit it, but Brenya was right. "Okay, so we take them off."

"They were created by a bonded pair of Theronai whose son was dying. The woman had great skill with the creation of magical artifacts. Her husband had boundless strength, compassion and love for his child. The couple was willing to give their lives for their son. They did not waste time worrying about how they would survive the removal of the device. Neither expected to live—certainly not without the other."

"Surely the man wouldn't have willingly let his wife sacrifice her life."

"Such choices were not up to him. She created the device. She intended for it to stay on until her death, transferring every bit of health and power left in her."

"She had to have known that killing herself was also a death sentence for her husband."

"There were more female Theronai then, and one was compatible with his power. The wife had already seen to it that her family would survive, that her husband would live on."

"No way could she have hidden her intent from her husband like that. He would have known. The mental link the luceria creates . . ."

"And that was her mistake. She believed she had shielded her intent well, but her husband knew what she would do."

"He used the device himself," guessed Torr.

"Their child survived. He became Gilda's father."

Pieces clicked into place. Gilda was the one who gave Grace the device. She would have known what it could do.

And she'd let Grace use it anyway.

Fury lashed over his skin. Gilda had been willing to sacrifice Grace to save Torr.

"How could she have done that? Her vow to protect humans . . ."

"Sacrificing one human so that you could live and save countless more? It would be an easy thing to justify."

He didn't agree. Not when that one human was someone like Grace. Sacrificing her—choosing to do so—was so far beyond his comprehension it seemed . . . evil. He'd never before thought of Gilda that way, but maybe he'd been wrong.

"I won't let anyone hurt Grace like that again," he said. "You have to help me keep her safe. Isn't there some way to remove the disks?"

"Death is the only certain way. Removing them artificially would cause her years of torment. She would eventually recover, but she might never forgive you. That is why I commanded you to keep yours on."

"I won't hurt her. What else? There has to be something else we can do to keep her safe."

"You can vow to never see her again. I will send her back to Earth with no memories of you and you will vow to keep your distance, never speaking to her again."

His heart cracked open and bled at the mere thought. To never talk to her again? Never hold her again? Impossible. "No. I can't do that either."

"There is one other option."

"Name it."

The waves in Brenya's stormy eyes kicked up, seething with power as she held his gaze. "I knew it would come to this moment. I have always known."

"Just spit it out."

A truly frightening ripple of power seeped out of her, chilling Torr to the bone.

She lifted a bent finger toward him. "You, young Theronai, will become human."

Chapter 30

Grace was just about to walk into Brenya's hut when she heard the woman utter the statement. *You, young Theronai, will become human.*

Shock hit her hard, freezing her in place.

Torr's voice echoed that shock. "Is that even possible?"

"For me? Yes. You are Theronai. My design. I can unmake the parts of you that are mine, leaving behind the remnants of humanity within you."

"But if I was human, how would I protect Grace?"

"How do any human men protect their women?"

"But the Synestryn, my vows . . ."

"Your vows were made to my kind. Weakened as you would be, you would no longer be able to fulfill them. I would release the magic binding you to your will and rid you and Grace both of all traces of Athanasian blood. It would not be pleasant, but it would allow you to live out the rest of your short lives together."

Say no, say no, Grace silently chanted in her head.

"The Synestryn wouldn't be able to smell her blood?" he asked, his tone thoughtful, as though he was actually considering it.

"Or yours. You could live as you choose. Love each other. Have children."

"What about the war?"

"No longer your concern. You would no longer have any memories tying you to your old life. You and Grace would believe you were normal, simple humans, with small, insignificant lives."

"I'd lose my friends."

"But you would have Grace."

"Done," he said, far too fast. "I'll guard your people here until you come back, and then you'll make me human."

"But first you must destroy the portal. Once that is done and you have proven yourself worthy, only then will we discuss a deal."

"Give me the crystals and stones. I'll leave tonight."

"No. You will guard the village tonight. I will rest."

"Whatever you need, Brenya. I'll make sure it's yours."

"Then leave me to sleep."

Grace stepped behind the door just as it swung open. Torr hurried away, drawing his sword as he went. His step was lighter, his stride more buoyant.

He was happy. He'd just agreed to give up his powers for her—to become weak like her—and he was happy.

Suddenly the image of him lying in his bed at Dabyr

hit her. He'd been so helpless, so weak. He'd been angry, frustrated. Maybe he didn't remember how much pain his helplessness had caused him—how he ached to be out there with his brothers fighting, how he felt responsible for every one of them who fell because he'd been unable to be at their side—but she did. She remembered every second of it. She saw him die inside a little more each day.

Some things are better left forgotten.

She wouldn't let him do that to himself again. She couldn't stand watching him suffer like that. He had no idea what it meant to be a human—to be weak and fragile.

She would not let him sacrifice his life for her. He was too important—too vital to the survival of the people she loved. And even if he wasn't, she still wouldn't let him do this. She loved him too much.

There was only one sure way he would give up on her. She knew that now.

She took a few deep breaths to calm her nerves and still her shaking hands. When she was steady enough, she pasted a smile on her face and walked into Brenya's hut, armed with the excuse of checking on her before bed.

The woman was already asleep. She looked so old, so frail. Her head was tilted back against the chair, and her mouth hung open. There was no regal beauty in her now—only fatigue and age.

The box of crystals sat on the table in front of her. Next to it was a small leather bag. Grace tiptoed across the room and picked up the box. It was chilly in her fingers, and heavier than she remembered.

She opened the lid and saw that the crystals were still inside. All she had to do now was put them to good use—two birds with one stone. Or crystal, in this case.

She would take out the portal, and Torr's reason to destroy his life, all at once.

There would be no reason for him to become human if she was dead.

Brenya opened her eyes as Grace left. She had done all she could for the young woman. The rest was in Grace's hands.

And Torr's.

Brenya had seen the future play out in two ways, and even she could not tell which one was more likely. All she knew was that both futures ended in Grace's death.

Chapter 31

It took Grace most of the night to reach the place where Torr had seen the Masons building the portal.

A full moon hung heavy in the sky—so much closer and brighter than the one on Earth. It reminded her of just how far away from home she was, and how many lives were at stake if she failed here.

She was acutely aware of her humanity as she crept around to get a better view of the site. Each noise she made felt like a siren, and every time the moon hit her skin, she was sure the glow would alert the Hunters that stood guard over the giant stone portal.

A giant glass man—a Warden—stood in front of the place where the Masons hammered. Each clink of their chisels made her skin crawl, the way fingernails on a chalkboard did. The Warden was as still as a statue, but the knowledge that Brenya had shoved into her head warned her that if she was spotted, that creature would fly into action and kill her.

As soon as it was discovered that she'd left the village, Torr would come after her. She didn't doubt it for a second. Before he did, she needed this job to be done.

The markings in the stone were nearly complete. They looked just like the ones on the Sentinel Stone in the village, only with one single curving line incomplete.

Grace had spent hours running her finger over the mark, wondering what it meant and how it worked. All she knew was that when it started to glow, it was time for her to back away, because someone—or something—was coming through.

Once the last line was finished, the Masons would leave and she would make her move.

The progress seemed to creep along. Each hour that passed wore on her nerves, drawing them tighter.

Every few minutes, she would edge a few feet closer to where she needed to be. The box of crystals was a cold, heavy weight in her bag, and the knowledge of how to use them was burning in her mind.

Finally, after what seemed like half an eternity, the Masons' hammering stopped.

They lifted their hands in unison, and the markings began to glow. Grace could feel some kind of energy pouring out of the stone. It rippled over her skin, making the fine hairs rise and shudder.

A moment later, a line of light split the night. The Masons stepped through, disappearing. She saw a brief flash of sunlight and blue sky.

Earth. Home.

The light winked out.

She was blinded for a second while her eyes readjusted to the moonlight. By the time she was able to see again, the Warden had moved. It was at the stone, its giant clear hand pressed over the carved markings.

It did nothing for several minutes, as if waiting for something.

Grace had no idea what, but she was pretty sure it wasn't going to be good.

She moved into position, skirting through the woods as fast and silently as she could. She tried to stay out of sight but kept veering back close enough to make sure nothing at the portal had changed.

When she'd made it about halfway to her final destination, something had.

Through the Warden's body, she could see the rune light up again, only this time the glow was different. Darker.

Knowledge appeared in her head—thanks to Brenya's gift.

Grace couldn't wait any longer. If she was going to destroy the portal stone, it was now or never.

Brenya's knowledge had shown her how to use the crystals. They had to be heated. Grace had prepared for this moment, wrapping one of the pebbles she used to start a fire in kindling and rough fabric. As soon as she crushed the fire pebble, the whole thing would ignite. There was a little pocket in the cloth just the right size to hold the crystals. They would be right against the flame. She tucked them inside and raced into the clearing.

The Warden saw her immediately, but her momentum carried her forward before he had time to reach her. She slammed the bundle of kindling against the base of the portal stone, crushing the fire pebble. There was a crack, a pop, then the whole dry bundle erupted in fire.

The flaming ball fell to the ground, right where it needed to be, at the base of the stone. Yellow flames swiftly turned a vibrant cobalt blue as the fire spread to the crystals.

The Warden shifted. An enormous burst of pain landed against the side of her head. She flew through the air, and it was only after she landed that she realized the Warden had hit her.

Blood trickled down her cheek. She couldn't quite figure out what was going on, but she knew there was something important about the blue fire blazing next to that big rock. She couldn't let it go out.

The Warden looked at the blaze, then her, then back. It seemed to be trying to make up its mind about which was the bigger threat.

It must have decided she was weak, because it turned its back on her to put out the fire.

Grace shoved herself up and charged. A small sword appeared in her hand, though she couldn't remember how it got there.

She screamed as she ran. The blade slid off the hard, slick skin of the Warden, but at least she had its attention.

It turned. A ball of blue flame bloomed on the other

side of its body. There was some kind of explosion, but she didn't see it or hear it. Instead, it spread over her skin, through her body, vibrating her bones as it passed.

The light coming from the symbol carved into the stone went out. The rune turned black, and the rock began to crumble away.

The blue light from the crystals grew brighter until it was nearly blinding. The Warden's body seemed to catch that light and hold it for a split second too long.

The image of Christmas lights and dangling plastic icicles popped into her head.

A moment later, the blue blaze from the crystals winked out, its magic complete.

All around her, the leaves turned black and shriveled. Branches began to fall with dry, brittle crashes. Inside, the wood had turned to ash.

Her fingers burned like they'd been lit on fire, and they, too, started to blacken.

Whatever magic those crystals used to destroy the stone, it was killing everything else in the area, too. Including her.

The flames were gone, but the damage was already done.

The Warden saw that it was too late. It opened its mouth, letting out a scream that sounded like wind chimes in a blender. Its face twisted with rage. It turned to her, lifted a crystalline sword, gripped it in both hands, and swung it right at her head.

There was nothing she could do to avoid it. She was

too close, too dizzy, too weak. She couldn't dodge or run—not with the reach the Warden had on her. And even if she could get away, the magical radiation she'd been exposed to wouldn't let her get far.

An odd kind of surreal calm swept over her as she realized that this was how she died. This was how she set Torr free.

Chapter 32

Torr knew the second he saw that the box of crystals was missing. He knew what had happened. There wasn't a scrap of doubt in his mind.

Grace had decided to risk her life to save everyone else.

"You are too late, young Theronai," said Brenya from the doorway of her hut. "Grace is already gone, her choice—her willing sacrifice—complete."

Like hell it was.

He grabbed Brenya's rough clothes and dragged her to her feet with a hard shake. "Send me to her. Teleport me there."

"Why? Her choice has been made. She has freed you."

"I don't want to be free. Not from her."

"I will demand payment for this, young Theronai."

"Anything you want. I vow it."

She stared at him for too long, each second ticking by like an eternity. "I accept."

The weight of such an open-ended vow nearly crushed him. He could hardly breathe. His skin was so heavy he thought it might peel from his bones. A strangled scream erupted from his chest. He clamped his lips shut over the noise to save what little breath he had left.

"Gather yourself," ordered Brenya.

With that command came a sense of relief. The weight dissipated, and the pain started to fade.

Something small and heavy was shoved into his hands. He clutched it, willing to carry whatever she gave him. It took him a moment to realize it was the bag of stones she'd made him.

"Draw your hammer, warrior. I am certain you will have need of it."

He shoved the stones into his pocket and did as she ordered. After a few rapid blinks, his vision cleared enough for him to see the fine line of light forming in front of him.

Brenya gave him a hard shove, and when he stepped forward, his foot met soft ground. The air smelled different, colder. He could hear a terrified sob.

Grace.

He lifted his hammer as the light from Brenya's portal faded. Across the clearing, he could see a Warden pull back its sword. Through its body he saw a warped vision of Grace on her knees.

All around them, the forest rained down blackened leaves. Charred branches fell, spilling piles of ash.

He had no idea what had happened, but the whole place was falling down around them.

If you can see the crystals' blue fire, you are already too late. It will destroy all in its reach.

The portal stone was charred, black and crumbling. The magic of the crystals had already been activated. The blue fire had already gone out.

A sickening feeling bloomed in the pit of Torr's stomach. He prayed he was wrong—that Grace had taken cover and hadn't been in reach of the blast.

Across the clearing, the Warden screamed in rage. It lifted its blade, clearly intending to kill her.

Her hands flew up in front of her face, as if she could stop it.

A surge of angry denial filled Torr. No one was taking his Grace away. Not ever again.

He ripped a stone from his pocket. The rest of the stones spilled onto the ground, but there was no time to pick them up. He spit on the one in his hand.

The Warden appeared in front of him, summoned away from Grace. Its blade came down only inches from his head. He lifted his hammer to shield himself from the blow.

"Run, Grace!" he shouted.

From the corner of his eye, he saw her push to her feet. She wobbled heavily, as if she were drunk. She took only two steps before she stumbled and caught herself on the crumbling remains of the portal stone.

Something was definitely wrong with her. He prayed it was a blow to the head and not the magical radiation making her sway.

. . . already too late.

Torr used a series of powerful moves to disengage his hammer from the Warden's blade. When the brief opening to step back came, he took it and ran.

He could feel the ground shake with each heavy step of the crystalline warrior hard on his heels. He knew he wouldn't be able to stay ahead of it for long, but his intent was only to get it away from Grace—out of sight of her so she was no longer a target.

Finally, when the trees closed in around them, he turned and faced his opponent.

Chapter 33

Apair of sleek black Hunters stalked into the clearing.

Grace was sure that they would kill her on sight, but instead, they took one look at her, then dismissed her as unimportant.

Either that, or they knew she was already dead.

She could feel her insides dying, feel the rapid decay of her flesh. The charred appearance along her fingertips was creeping upward, burning hot for only a second before her nerves were consumed.

She didn't have long. Torr was already fighting the Warden—she could hear the battle being waged only a few yards inside the trees—and now two Hunters were closing in for the kill as well. She had to do something, but throwing herself in front of those Hunters was only going to slow them down for half a second.

Knowledge of the landscape came to her easily, as if she'd roamed every inch of the surrounding area for

years. There was a place not far from here—one that
might give Torr a fighting chance to survive.

She gathered a handful of the stones he'd dropped and
ran as fast as her burning body would carry her. She knew
exactly what the stones could do, even though she'd
never seen them before. The knowledge was familiar,
tinged with Brenya's regal dominance and wisdom.

Another mental gift, no doubt.

A tree branch slammed into Grace's arm. She heard
the bone crack, felt the pain of the break sear along her
spine.

She'd learned at the hands of her stepfather how to
ignore pain, how to keep moving with broken bones so
she could escape the next blow. She used every bit of
skill she had now to push forward and distance herself
from the agony crawling through her body.

The ground pitched up, the steep angle nearly slowing her to a stop. The sound of battle was softer now,
but the impact of steel on glass was an unmistakable
chime in the distance.

Each crawling step was harder than the last. Her left
arm was useless. Something in her foot cracked, giving
her a burst of pain she couldn't ignore.

Behind her, a Hunter let out a scream that cut off far
too soon. Torr had killed it with that huge hammer he
wielded.

Her breath sawed in and out of her lungs, misting
out in a thick fog.

That was when she realized she wasn't alone.

She looked around and saw that one of the Hunters

had followed her. Maybe it had decided to see if she was a threat, or maybe it thought she was easy prey. Either way, it was bad news.

She met its black gaze, let it know she saw it. She wasn't afraid of death. She knew she was going to die tonight. The only thing that scared her was letting Torr die with her.

Grace inched up the last few feet of the slope backward, keeping the Hunter in sight.

It dug its sharp, glassy claws into the ground, accelerating toward her.

She kept moving back, knowing the steep drop was right behind her. Just like last time, she would let the Hunter charge over the edge and shatter on the rocks below.

But it was smarter than that. It saw the trap and banked right, missing both her and the steep drop.

She used the time to regain her footing. Every inch of her body screamed in pain. Her foot could barely support her weight, and she didn't dare trust it with a full step. Instead, she limped to the place where an ancient tree had fallen. It formed a narrow bridge across the ravine, but was old and rotting with decay.

Fifty feet below, the river churned and frothed against a cluster of rocks as big as cars.

She took one of the stones and tossed it into the water. Instantly, the Warden appeared, standing in the middle of the river.

The strong current shoved at its body, but it still managed to make it to the shore.

It looked up. Saw her.

There was a flare of recognition in its transparent gaze—one that sent a primal chill of fear snaking through her.

Without a pause, it stalked to the wall of the ravine, sprouted thick, crystalline barbs from its arms and legs and began scaling the wall.

As fast as it was going, she didn't have much time. She had to finish what she'd come to do.

She looked back to the rocks below. Even though she knew she was dead, the idea of falling made bile rise in her throat.

No other choice.

She took a careful step onto the thick trunk. It held her weight but gave out a tired groan. She inched forward, blocking out the pain of her battered foot. Looking down would be her death, so she kept her head up and level.

The Hunter saw her. It slid back and forth nearby, cutting through the brush at the top of the hill. It looked almost like it was pacing, trying to decide how to reach her without falling to its death.

Grace was a few feet in now. The tree shifted slightly with each step, but held.

The Hunter veered close to the fallen tree. A frost formed along the surface, and a frigid crackling sound spread under her feet.

She couldn't feel the chill yet, but she knew it would come.

The Warden was nearly to the top of the ravine.

Once it reached solid ground, it could chop through the tree she stood on and end her.

It was now or never. This would have to be far enough.

Grace opened the water skin dangling from her body and shoved the last stone through the opening.

Everything happened at once.

The Warden appeared on the tree in front of her, barely keeping its balance. The Hunter charged onto the log. Torr's voice boomed nearby, screaming for her to stop.

She caught a glimpse of his face and felt love swell and fill her up. He would be the last thing she ever saw—the last, sweet image to take to her grave.

She closed her eyes, wrapped her arms around the Warden's waist and shoved herself sideways toward the rocks below.

Chapter 34

Torr stared over the edge of the cliff, praying for another ledge, hoping Grace would be staring up at him, reaching out her hand for help.

Instead, all he saw below was a trio of shattered bodies. The clear shards of the Warden and the black chips of the Hunter mixed in a glittering confetti across Grace's broken body. Blood frothed in the passing current for a moment before turning to pink ice. As the water flowed over her, new layers of ice formed, encasing her.

The disk on his back fell away.

Grace was dead.

The weight of his shock and grief drove him to his knees. This wasn't the way it was supposed to happen. She was supposed to be safe and warm in her bed right now, not dead and frozen in a block of bloody ice. She was supposed to love him forever, the way he loved her. They were supposed to have a life together, have children, grow old together.

Tears flooded his eyes and rained down his cheeks. A wrenching pain sliced across his lifemark, and he could feel the leaves begin to fall, one after another.

He welcomed the pain, welcomed the inevitable death it would bring. The sooner, the better.

"She could not let you become human," said Brenya.

He didn't know how she'd gotten here, but it hardly mattered. Nothing mattered without Grace.

He dug his fingers into the ground, fighting the need to jump in after her. Only his vow to Brenya held him back. He'd promised to repay her for teleporting him here, and he had no choice but to submit to that vow. "She didn't even know that I'd chosen that path."

"She knew. She also knew how torturous it was for you to be weak the way you had been, the way she saw herself."

"She wasn't weak. A weak woman would never give up her life to save others. She'd never throw herself off a cliff by choice."

"You and I know that. She did not. She did, however, remember every second of your paralysis, of your helplessness. Our gentle Grace would never have let you suffer like that again."

"I would have been happy. With her, I would have been happy."

Brenya bent down and picked up the disk. "Give me your hand, young Theronai. We will gather her body and take her home."

Torr did as she asked. A second later, he was back in the northern village, inside the hut where he'd first seen Grace after coming here. The ice covering her was mostly gone. Her broken body was facedown. The metal disk that she'd once worn was loose against her back, caught just inside the opening of her tunic.

He picked it up and set it aside.

Her skin was frozen. A thin layer of ice clung to her clothes and hair. Black, charred patches covered her hands. He could see now just how badly the fall had mangled her. Shards of bone had sliced through her skin. Her limbs lay at odd, sickening angles.

Torr's heart shattered. Shock and denial had gotten him this far, but they were wearing off fast, and once they did, he knew he'd collapse into a useless pile of grief.

"I want to bathe her," he said.

"As you wish." Brenya handed him a bowl of water and a cloth, and picked up a set of her own.

He gently rolled Grace onto her back. Her face had been spared the worst of the impact, leaving her as beautiful as ever. It seemed impossible that there was no life left in her—that she was only a shell. He kept staring, hoping to see some flicker of motion, some sign of life.

There was none. Grace was dead.

"Can I take her back to her family?" he asked.

"Perhaps when I return. The threat from the Solarc has passed. The portal destroyed. The Warden unable to report. I will leave tonight to recharge under the light of the Athanasian moon. You will stay here."

Torr nodded his understanding. Tears clogged his

throat. He held them off, knowing that if he let go, he would crack and become useless. His grief would have to wait until this task was done and he could find a private place to lick his wounds.

His sweet Grace. Dead.

It couldn't be real. No nightmare this horrible was ever real, and yet he didn't wake up.

He wet the cloth and started at her fingertips and worked his way up. Brenya did the same on the other side. They cut away her bloody, tattered clothes and covered her in a soft woven sheet of pale blue.

He brushed her hair until it was dry and braided it over one shoulder. By the time he was done, she looked perfect. The charred flesh was cleaned away, the blood was gone, her limbs were straight again with no sign of broken bones.

"There," said Brenya. "It is nearly done. I have given her as much of myself as I dare. Only one more thing and she will be ready." She held out her hands, and in each one was one of the metal disks.

"You want to bury her with them?" he asked.

"You will each wear them again. This one is yours now." She offered him the one he knew Grace had always worn. The markings on it were different—sparser than on his own.

"I don't understand."

"I know. But you will do this thing as repayment of your vow. Take off your shirt and kneel."

It didn't matter if Torr wanted to do it or not. His body was already moving, compelled by his open-ended promise. He felt to his knees, ripping his shirt away as he went.

She didn't give him time to brace himself; she merely slammed the metal prongs into his skin. He was still on his knees, panting through the pain when he felt something happen.

He looked up. Brenya had rolled Grace onto her side and had cast aside the sheet. Blood trickled from her skin where the disk had been embedded.

Rage detonated inside him, as fierce as it was inappropriate. No one could hurt Grace anymore. She was beyond pain. And still, the sight of her blood made him want to kill.

Brenya held up a hand. It trembled with fatigue, and for the first time, he saw just how frail she'd become—so much worse than even last night. Her skin hung on her bones, and she was stooped over much more than she'd been only a few minutes ago. She looked centuries old. Shriveled and frail. "Settle, young Theronai. I am nearly out of time."

Torr calmed down, though he couldn't tell whether it was because she'd ordered him to or because of his shock at seeing just how far and how fast she'd degraded.

And then it hit him.

All the cuts on Grace's body had healed. The broken bones realigned. The charred skin where radiation had damaged her was renewed. He'd been so overwhelmed with loss, he hadn't realized that Brenya must have been healing Grace's flesh all along. That was why she was so weakened.

But why would she heal the flesh of a dead woman?

Brenya caught his chin and held his gaze. The stormy waves in her eyes held far less power than before, but they still churned and swirled in a leaden display. "Do you love her?"

"Yes," he said.

"Will you vow to give your life for hers?"

Hope surged in his chest, and while he knew how dangerous it could be, he couldn't help but let it lift his soul.

"My life for hers," he vowed without hesitation.

"I have been preparing her body for this moment for years, hoping she would be worthy of the gift. Strong enough to receive it and survive. Still, even with all my efforts, she can never be what you have always sought. She will never truly be Theronai. If she lives again, healing will be her domain—only that and nothing else."

It didn't matter what she was or what she could do. Not if there was any hope his Grace could live. "She's all I need. All I've ever needed. I could never want more than her, however she comes back to me."

Brenya jerked his luceria from his throat, clenching it in her wizened fist. Her weight shifted suddenly, and she was leaning on him for support.

"Whoa. Hang on." Torr held her up and eased her into a nearby chair.

She held out her hand, offering him the luceria. "Take this. Claim her as your own. Will her to life."

A ripple of shock slipped through him, shaking him to his bones. "How did you take that off me?"

"Who do you think put it on you, young Theronai? You were my design. My creation. I put the luceria on you long before your birth. Now go and be worthy of what this cost me. I can do no more."

He took it. "Cost you? I don't understand."

It didn't matter. She was gone in a flash of light. Disappeared.

Torr stood there for a second, staring in shock at the band that had always graced his throat.

It was now Grace's.

He went to her side. His hands trembled as he slid the band around her neck. The blunt ends touched but did not lock in place as they were supposed to do.

She was still dead. How could they?

Will her to life.

The disks. They operated on will. He wore the one she had—the one that transferred health from one wearer to the other.

Will her to life.

Torr took her hand in his and let his love for her flow through him. He slid through every memory of them together, watching himself fall in love with her all over again. When he was angry, she made him smile. When he felt hopeless, she gave him joy and a glimpse of a brighter future. When he was afraid, she gave him a reason to fight through it. If there was even one spark of power in his body that he was able to give her, he would. Whatever she needed, for the rest of their lives—however long or short they might be.

A hot, tingling feeling passed over his spine and down his arms. He felt the disk on his back heat and vibrate. As the sensation grew, his strength seemed to fade.

He crawled onto the bed next to her, afraid that he would topple over if he didn't lie down. He wrapped his arms around her and felt the heat coming off of the disk she wore.

A huge rush of power gushed from his body. It burned as it passed, wrenching a scream from his chest. He'd never felt anything like it before—painful but right. Hot but sweet.

The longer the energy streamed out of him, the weaker he became. Still, he didn't try to stop it or slow it down. Whatever the disk wanted from him, it could take. Whatever Grace needed was hers.

He had no idea how long he lay there. All he knew was that he was now too weak to move. He could barely find the strength to breathe. Nearly all of his power was gone, but he used what little he had left to push more energy toward the disk, feeding it.

Finally, all that was left was a tiny trickle of his magic and the erratic beat of his own heart.

He heard a tiny click and opened his eyes. The luceria had locked closed around her throat.

Grace's eyes flew open. She sucked in a gasping breath.

She was alive. And she was his.

Chapter 35

It took Torr two days to wake up, and in that time Grace barely left his side.

She'd seen the luceria around her throat but still couldn't believe it was there. Had no clue what it meant. All she knew was that she felt . . . different.

Powerful.

She stifled all urges to use that newfound sense of power because she knew that the source was Torr and that draining anything from him right now was dangerous. So instead, she resorted to the herbs and roots that she knew to strengthen him.

His physical wounds healed fast. It was the condition of his lifemark that worried her the most. It was nearly bare now, when it had been much more full of leaves the last time she'd seen him.

The need to talk to Brenya churned inside Grace, but the village women said that she was gone—left to regain her strength.

There was no way to know how long she would be

gone, but the Athanasian women here guessed it would be weeks, possibly months.

"I need you to wake up, Torr. Come back to me." She stroked his brow, soaking in the feel of his skin under her hand.

She thought she saw his eyes flutter, but it was hard to tell if it had been real or wishful thinking.

"Can you hear me?" she asked. "I'm right here. Open your eyes."

This time there was no mistaking it. His eyelids moved. They seemed heavy and sluggish, but he definitely moved.

"Torr." She made her tone firm, trying to mimic Brenya. "Open your eyes."

He did, holding them wide. He tried to lurch from the bed, but she held him down.

The fact that it wasn't even hard to do spoke to just how weak he was.

"Everything's fine," she reassured him. "Just lie back."

He collapsed, panting.

When he'd regained his breath, she helped him drink some juice. The chill of it seemed to wake him up enough to realize where he was.

"You're okay?" he asked.

"Yes. I don't know how I survived, though."

"You didn't."

As soon as she heard the words she knew what had happened. Like all of the knowledge Brenya had planted in her head, it burst free, fully formed and easily understood.

She had died. There was no way she could have survived that fall.

"You brought me back to life," she whispered.

"Brenya did most of the work."

"That's why you're so weak. The disks . . ." She'd seen that he wore the wrong one when she'd washed him. It was all part of the mystery until now. "You could have died."

"Nah," he said with a little grin and a wink. "You're just a weak human. How hard could it be to restart your engine?"

She crawled on top of him, pinning him down. "Who's weak now?"

"Give me a few minutes. Maybe a few hours spent in contact with the ground. I'll be back in fighting shape in no time."

"It's not fighting I want to do."

"No?" he asked, looking more alert and much more interested.

"No. I want to spend about half a year showing you how much I love you."

"I like where this is going. Tell me more."

She got close and stared straight into his eyes. "I love you."

His whole body shuddered beneath her, making her wonder how she ever could have thought him weak. He rubbed his chest and said, "Look at what you've done."

She did, and saw his lifemark had begun to bud

again. In a little while, his tree would once again be covered with leaves. His soul was safe from decay now.

She traced the image with her finger, and this time the branches followed where she led, swaying toward her. "How is that possible?"

"I don't know. Brenya said you'll never be a Theronai—that you'll never be able to do more than heal—but you seem pretty damn close to me."

"I can feel your power. I haven't tried to use it, but I already know how. It's calling to me to heal you. It wants to be inside of me."

He gripped her hips and gave her a hot stare. "My power isn't the only thing that wants to be inside of you, but it'll have to wait until I can at least stand on my own two feet."

"So you're going to be okay? No lasting side effects from bringing me back to life?"

"None that will matter. As long as I have you, the rest is unimportant. Weakness, scars, pain—none of it matters. I love you, Grace. My life for yours, always and forever."

Warmth spread through her body, seeping into her soul. "And mine for yours."